State of Sweet Sorrow

ANDREW TURCINOVICH

Inspiring Publishers
P.O. Box 159, Calwell, ACT Australia 2905
Email: publishaspg@gmail.com
http://www.inspiringpublishers.com

 A catalogue record for this book is available from the National Library of Australia

National Library of Australia The Prepublication Data Service

Author: Andrew Turcinovich
Title: State of Sweet Sorrow
Genre: Fiction

Paperback ISBN: 978-1-923087-29-3
ePub ISBN: 978-1-923087-28-6

For Mia and Kiara

1

Cluj, 1978

Mihai Ionescu finished his coffee and reclined on the faded, walnut-toned sofa; his feet sprawled over the ripped armrest. The ripened-apricot-coloured carpet, littered with papers, files, and texts, bore stains from countless coffee spills that revealed themselves in the morning light.

Despite the thermostat hovering at zero, Mihai relished the solitude of working under the pale moonlight, before the world stirred, and the day beckoned. Through the yellow-tinted, bottle glass sliding door that led into the living room, Irina appeared.

"Another coffee?" she asked.

"Da."

She glanced at the mess on the floor but refrained from commenting. She had again spent another night alone while her husband toiled into the early hours before succumbing to a restless sleep on the couch.

In the kitchen, the percolator's gurgle and whistle mingled with the sound of Irina washing cups. Outside, a rooster heralded daybreak as the phone rang.

"Hospital?" Irina asked.

"Da. It was Adam. He wants to discuss a case."

"What case?"

"He didn't say."

"Couldn't it wait till you were at work? Isn't that a little odd?"

"A little." Mihai drank the dark brew in two swigs, scraping the coffee-infused sugar from the bottom of the cup.

Resigned to his brief response, Irina poured herself a cup of tea. "If you're working late tonight, please let me know. I don't want another dinner to go wasted."

Without responding, Mihai grabbed his coat and left. Despite the roiling sky and threatening clouds, he did not bother with the umbrella. The front gate, held together by chicken wire, squeaked open. The fence posts leaned like drunken sailors in a storm. A 1962 Renault Dauphine was parked on the gravel driveway, which led to the garage. The brick house was old, but its foundations strong, and had sheltered Mihai's family for generations. A children's swing hung from the backyard apple tree, which once brought so much joy.

He waved down the industrial green tram on Strada Gheorghe Marinescu, which bustled with people bracing against the encroaching winter. They wore oversized coats and sported woollen flat caps—standard attire for Romanian men. An old man meticulously filled his rolling paper with tobacco from a Tutun Regal tin box. The aroma of dry, sweet tobacco imbued the tram, as it screeched around a bend, rocking its passengers from side to side. A father in overalls dozed with the swaying tram, as his son, in similar attire, and barely fourteen years old, stared out the window. They were a testament to hard times, when an extra pair of hands meant the difference between survival and starvation.

As dawn battled against the night, the dim amber streetlights barely cut through the darkness. Thunder rumbled in the distance, beyond the Apuseni mountains. Cars and motorbikes puttered along, while others braved the biting frost on bicycles. The tram wound its way through the landscape, passing the hills of Calvaria and Cetățuia, heading south on Strada Plopilor, towards Hațieganu Park.

Despite the early hour, haphazard lines of men and women formed outside bakeries and grocery stores, waiting to buy rationed essentials—bread, bags of rice, toilet paper, cooking oil, sugar and watered-down milk. Women with black headscarves, cradling crying babies, prayed they'd reach the counter before supplies ran out. Some pushed shopping trolleys that rattled and careened on a shoddy wheel, hoping to stock up, while dozens of Pegas bicycles lay on the pavement while their owners waited in line. It was an increasingly common sight across the country. In the queues, men smoked, people huddled together, reading newspapers, or engaged in idle chatter—a collective attempt to pass the time and stave off the chilly, rimy morning. Those at the back of the lines would leave empty-handed, hoping for a better tomorrow, while those more fortunate paid exorbitant black-market prices.

A middle-aged woman riding her bike skidded on the ice, sending tomatoes, flour, and semi-rotten pears scattering across the muddy ground. Her cry was less for the gash on her thigh and more for the precious provisions lost.

On the tram, a man in his early twenties swore under his breath while reading the morning newspaper and dry spat at President Ceausescu's photo. "Ceausescu and his band of thieves are robbing the country blind!"

Passengers concurred in silent agreement, not daring to voice their opinions.

3

President Nicolae Ceausescu's smiling face adorned the front page. The headlines boasted of his summer trip to Buckingham Palace, claiming how he and his wife, Elena, the Deputy Prime Minister, had charmed the Queen and British Prime Minister, Harold Wilson, and secured economic windfalls for Romania.

"Da," Mihai declared, loud enough for all to hear. "I wouldn't piss on Ceausescu and his cronies if they were on fire."

A few passengers stifled giggles, while others cast fleeting, nervous glances. A woman clutched her bag, looking perturbed and uncomfortable. Nearby, a group of soldiers in khaki uniforms glanced at Mihai before resuming their conversation.

Throughout his life, Mihai had been cautioned: keep your opinions private, don't draw attention to yourself, and don't take risks. For Mihai Ionescu, this was impossible.

The tram's bell jingled, and with a screech of the brakes, it slowed beside a row of European larch trees lining Strada Republicii. Mihai dismounted before the tram stopped and hurried across the road, ahead of the oncoming traffic.

∽

Cluj University Hospital, one of Romania's oldest, began as a surgical unit specialising in gynaecology and neurology in the late nineteenth century. Over the years, the building had sprawled asymmetrically, a melange of sandstone and red brick that clashed with its original design. The initial structure, reminiscent of a nineteenth-century British mansion, featured a steep roof and white window frames. A low perimeter wall and a manned boom gate marked the entrance, while an overhead walkway connected the original building with the new one. Trees, benches, and patches of grass offered respite for staff and patients alike.

Yet, decay and despair had seeped into the hospital's very bones. Foundations had shifted, causing cracks and fissures. The leaking roof, betraying itself with buckets collecting dripping water during storms, cried out for repair.

Avoiding the perpetually out-of-order elevator, Mihai ascended the stairs to his second-floor office. The space was a chaotic archive of medical knowledge: texts, crammed cabinets, and a narrow table buried under papers and charts. Peeling walls and a window overlooking the street bore witness to years of neglect. A metal fan, more a relic than a relief, hung in the corner gathering dust, its clunking a tribute to summers past. Once, in a fit of frustration, Mihai had demolished a similarly noisy fan with a coat rack.

His desk, a panorama of paperwork, teetered under the weight of medical documents, X-rays, invoices, scribbled hand notes, patient histories, medical texts with cracked spines, and manilla folders piled up like the Tower of Pisa. It resembled a precarious game of chance, where one more addition could topple the entire assemblage. Amongst this chaos, faded cup stains blotted the surface of the desk like ancient cave paintings found in Western Australia.

The insignia on the door read:

Dr Mihai Ionescu
Neurosurgery
Neurology Department

A demanding day lay ahead: two spinal surgeries scheduled mid-morning, followed by rounds in the post-op ward, case reviews, and a ceaseless line of patients outside his office. But first, residents waited for him in the corridor.

"He's coming," whispered Sandu, her smile strained under the weight of apprehension. Beside her, Alin, her intermittent boyfriend, steeled himself for a stressful morning.

Teaching was not Mihai's forte; his impatience and lack of time rendered him a formidable, albeit skilled mentor. Despite his reputation, he was the hospital's finest surgeon, and the residents, eager to learn from the best, braced themselves for the coming storm.

They filed into a ward, divided by flimsy drapes hanging despondently from their hooks.

"Alin, you've been tending to this patient. What's the issue?" Mihai's voice cut through the tense air.

Alin, a young man with long flowing hair and infectious humour, faced a different reality today. As he fumbled through his notes, the usually jovial resident perspired and lost his train of thought. "The patient has a slight temperature, showing minor facial spasms and..." he hesitated, scanned the overnight report, "experienced a headache."

"A headache?" Mihai probed. "Could you be more specific?"

Alin, visibly flustered, rifled through his notes, seeking a reprieve from his sudden quandary. "I'm... not certain."

"The patient told you he had a headache?" asked Mihai.

While the other residents were relieved that it wasn't their neck on the chopping block, Alin shuffled his pages. "Not precisely," he admitted weakly.

"Then how did you come to know of it?" Mihai stepped closer, his tone growing more intense.

Alin met his gaze, momentarily distracted by the doctor's striking azure eyes and the distinct wave of his V-shaped hairline.

"Did you ask the patient about his headache?" Mihai's words were slow and deliberate.

"No," Alin confessed.

A dread filled the room. Sandu looked away, offering no support, despite last night's intimate promises of love and loyalty.

Mihai set his folder on the sleeping patient's bed. His patience wearing thin. "So, the patient mentioned a headache, and you didn't think to inquire further?"

"Just a slight headache," Alin tried to clarify.

Mihai slammed his hand on the bedside food tray, scattering utensils across the floor. Sandu let out a startled yelp as the butterflies in her belly circled the wagons. The nurses exchanged wary glances but kept their distance.

The patient stirred, disorientated by the commotion.

"Let me guess," said Mihai. "A nurse mentioned the headache, or you read it in his file?" The question was rhetorical, laced with irritation.

Alin grimaced. "The patient complained of a headache, according to the nurse. He was sleeping, so I let him rest."

Mihai slammed his hand again on the food tray, eliciting another yelp from Sandu. "You always wake the patient for such things. Understand?" He ran his hand through his toasted-wheat-coloured hair. "The nurse told you," he repeated to himself in a strained voice. "You need to ascertain the headache's intensity and exact location. That's your responsibility, not the nurse's!" His commanding voice reestablished. "Do you understand? Otherwise, give the nurse your residency badge and let her take over!"

Alin stood, mute and chastened, as Mihai's imposing figure loomed over him. The patient watched, bewildered, as the confrontation unfolded.

"If he dies," Mihai gestured towards the alarmed patient, "at least you'll have the comfort of knowing you didn't inconvenience him!"

The elderly patient sat up, attempting to interject, but Mihai's booming voice spoke over him.

"Now that we've inconvenienced the patient, Alin, I expect a detailed report on the patient's bodily functions since last night, his dietary intake, a thorough cognitive assessment, and for how bloody long he has had this headache!"

Alin nodded, absorbing the gravity of the instructions.

"And when you present me that report," Mihai continued, "we'll discuss the implications of a 'slight' headache and how it could spell the difference between life and death."

The old man, fear etched in his eyes, interjected. "Am I going to die?"

"Yes!" Mihai snapped. "You're going to die. We're all going to damn well die! You're just not going to die today!" With that, he stormed out, his entourage of residents in tow, leaving the patient clutching his bedsheet.

∽

In the sanctuary of the operating theatre, Mihai was transformed. After changing into scrubs and meticulously washing up to his elbows, he stepped into this haven where his decade-long, simmering anger found a brief respite.

Dumitra Sala, a twenty-five-year-old woman, lay on the operating table. Blurry vision had followed her complaints of a headache originating at the crown of her head. A CT scan had revealed a tumour in her pituitary gland, now haemorrhaging and pressing on her optic nerve, threatening her sight.

Mihai had invited Dr Victor Vladimirescu and three of his associates to observe this operation.

"Most standard procedures require drilling through the skull," he stated. "This is invasive, unnecessary and can host countless complications. Today, we will access the brain through the nasal cavity."

The gruesome procedure required the surgeon to slice beneath Dumitra's upper lip and peel the face up and away to expose the nasal passages. After cracking the nasal septum, Mihai navigated to the base of the skull, removing the sphenoid sinus, to reach the pituitary gland. A lack of state-of-the-art microscopes and optic lighting created a hurdle. Without these, surgeons felt blind in pinpointing delicate regions of the brain.

"I won't lie, gentlemen. Better quality microscopes would make things less daunting," he quipped, "but what we Romanians lack in equipment, we compensate with skill... and balls." His muffled laughter eased the tension in the room. A laser-like intensity surfaced as the surgeon sliced the skin, exposing tissue, muscle, blood, and nerves. The young woman's beauty juxtaposed against the visceral reality of the surgery. Navigating the nasal passage, Mihai located the tiny gland, believed by the ancient Greeks to be the soul's gateway. With precision, he excised the tumour, its mustard-yellow hue seeping from the gland.

Post-surgery, while planning for the next day, Mihai received a call from radiology: they couldn't perform the scans on his patients.

"We only have film for emergency cases. Sorry, Dr Ionescu."

Mihai slammed the phone receiver repeatedly. His vexation peaked as a secretary, with unfortunate timing, informed him of further delays in medical supplies.

"Lost or sent elsewhere," she explained timidly.

"Unbelievable! Anything else?" Mihai's voice was laced with irritation.

"No, Dr Ionescu, I just came to—"

"Then leave! Now!" swiping the papers from his desk, sending them parachuting to the floor.

The nurse hurried out, leaving Mihai to brood over the dysfunctionality that plagued a country where everything seemed broken.

∽

"Dr Ionescu, I have that report," said Alin, the first-year resident from the morning rounds, eager to go home after a long day.

"How is our patient with the 'slight headache' doing? Still alive, I trust?" Mihai joked.

Alin, cracking his knuckles, watched as his supervisor perused the report. "He's faring well, Doctor."

Mihai nodded in approval. "Good work, Alin." He gestured for the young man to sit, but the chair was buried under stacks of folders.

"That's okay, I'll stand."

"When do I see you next?"

"Thursday."

"Prepare a presentation for the residents based on your report."

The handsome young man inwardly groaned. "Yes, Dr Ionescu."

Mihai leaned back, eyeing the resident. "How are you finding your first year?"

"Challenging." Alin admitted, hesitating. "I... I apologise for this morning, I—"

"Don't fret over it. You will make mistakes. And I will rip you to shreds when you do." Mihai said it without a hint of animosity. "But you learn and become a better doctor because of it."

"But since starting neurology, I am struggling," confessed Alin.

"First year is always tough. Hang in there and keep working hard. It isn't easy. It's not meant to be."

"Thanks, Dr Ionescu." Alin left the office feeling buoyed. *Maybe he's not an asshole*, he thought, though that would change soon enough.

As the afternoon waned, a southerly breeze scattered the clouds. Leaving the hospital, and ready to play a game of tennis after work, Mihai ran into Radu Popescu.

"Dr Mihai!" Radu waved, in his stained blue overalls and tooth gapped smile.

"Radu?"

No one could remember a time when old man Radu didn't live in Cluj. His family had been farmers for generations. He lived in a modest farmhouse on the outskirts of town with his grandsons, Mircea and Igor, and his ailing wife.

"Oh, Doctor, I so happy I find you," Radu said, grinning. "Come. Odeta is very bad. I think she dying. You come now, no?"

Mihai had known the Popescu family since he had moved to Cluj as a young boy. His father and Radu had been friends, as they shared a love of mountain climbing and nature.

"Slow down, Radu. What's the problem? And who are you talking about?"

"My Odeta!" Radu said, as if stating the obvious. "She is my most loved goat, and she having baby. But baby not coming and mum in big pain. I try everything, but no good. You come now and save Odeta and baby, yes."

"Your goat!" Mihai barked. "Are you mad? I don't treat animals, for God's sakes!"

Undeterred, Radu persisted. "Yes, yes. But goat with baby is like woman with baby, no? Both come from same place, yes?" Radu's contagious smile made Mihai chuckle.

"I am not an obstetrician, either. And I certainly don't attend to pregnant goats, you old fool. Find a vet who can help you." Mihai's tone was a mix of exasperation and amusement.

Unfazed, Radu stood beside his donkey, his presence an anachronism amid the bustling city crowd. The old farmer continued to smile and tipped his cap to passing women.

Despite his initial resistance, Radu's earnest plea and the memory of their long-standing family friendship swayed Mihai.

"I swear, Radu, one of these days I'm going to wring your neck."

"Doctor!" Radu exclaimed, his optimism undimmed as he grabbed Mihai's bags. "I knew you would help. I just knew it!" The old man slapped his leg in confirmation and placed the bags in his cart, filled with a hodgepodge of potato sacks, leafage, carrots, and a shovel. "Wait till I tell Odeta that best doctor in Cluj going to take care of her!"

Mihai shook his head in mild disbelief. *How do I get myself into this?* But he relished the invigorating, crisp air as they headed south through Old Town, along Strada Potaissa. The rhythmic click-clack of Pip's hooves on cobblestones resonated against the ancient fortress walls that had protected Cluj since the thirteenth century.

As the countryside emerged, birds squabbled in the trees, and European goldfinches trumpeted the imminent end of the day.

Radu's calloused hands expertly guided the reins as he whispered to Pip, "The best doctor in Romania is here for Odeta."

The donkey twitched his ears and switched his tail; his old age and blotchy fur testimony to years of loyal service since rescued as a newborn.

"How old is Pip now?" asked Mihai.

"Ooh, he very old. Old like me," Radu grinned. "We meet in forest when he newborn. I tell you that story?"

"I only heard bits and pieces," answered Mihai.

"I chopping wood and I see baby donkey kicking and stuck in branches. He crying for mamma, but she gone. I tell him everything okay. And then noises coming from forest." Radu checked on Pip to gauge whether the story frightened his faithful companion. Pip snorted and moseyed along, unaffected.

"How'd a donkey end up in the woods, anyway?"

"I ask same question," the old farmer said, shrugging his shoulders. "Anyway, a black wolf come. He growling. Very mean. His sharp teeth showing. Saliva drooling. Little donkey more scared now."

"I bet," said Mihai.

"But no be scared, I told donkey. Radu is here!" The old man smiled again, as Pip's clonking steps provided a

13

comforting melody to the day's end. "But this wolf come closer. This is crazy wolf. I stand and grab my axe. Big bad wolf growling. His long legs spread, ready to fight. Baby donkey is kicking and screaming, hurting himself, and crying for mamma. I step closer and lift my axe. I look at wolf in eyes. He look at me in eyes. But is no love story, Doc!" Radu laughed again, slapping Mihai's leg. "I raise axe and wolf turn and disappear. I search for mamma donkey, but I no see her anywhere."

"Maybe the wolves got her," said Mihai.

"Doctor, no say that." Radu pointed to his head. "Mamma donkey know wolf is coming, so she run, so they no chase her baby. She is hero."

Mihai marvelled at Radu's perspective, a blend of simplicity and depth that seemed to transcend the complexities of life.

"Me and Pip together ever since that day."

The sun dipped, casting a golden hue over the landscape. Mihai found himself content in Radu's company, as he settled into the subtle rhythm of the cart along the dusty road.

In an era where horse-drawn wagons were giving way to modern machinery, Radu remained steadfast in his trusted donkey. Despite a decrepit flatbed truck parked under his makeshift carport and young horses at the helm, Radu's loyalty to his aged companion was unshakeable.

"How are things with the farm, Radu?" The question hung in the night air.

"No good. Everybody leaving. Go to big city or even Hungary."

Mihai wasn't surprised. The government's oppressive control destroyed farming, leaving poverty in its wake.

"Government idiots tell us how to run our farms. I have been farmer since I born. I know the land like the back of my bum."

Mihai laughed but didn't bother to correct the idiom.

"They say we work together to build better future." The reins lay across Radu's open palms. "Everything fair and everybody equal, they say."

Mihai murmured under his breath. "But some are more equal than others."

As they journeyed, the rolling green hills permeated the countryside, as picturesque mountain ridges formed the backdrop of this natural wonder. The beauty of Cluj left Mihai breathless as the sun slipped behind the mountain ranges in a blaze of theatrical wonderment. A purple as deep as bruised plums draped the valley, and a bedspread of russet covered the grounds, as autumn brushed her hues over the canvas. Stars twinkled in the evening sky as the chill set in.

Smoke billowed from Radu's pitched roof. The stone and timber home which stood for three generations looked tired, and the dilapidated wrap-around porch needed replacing. The property spanned over a thirty-five-acre valley surrounded by tall oaks. Rows of potatoes lined the land, as did corn stalks that rose above a man's head. Along the slope of the valley's edge, Tsurcana sheep and black goats grazed on the rich grass beside a small crop of soybeans and barley. Overgrown fig trees covered in white netting—to keep the pesky crows away—provided shade for the rabbits.

Radu's wife used to make fig jam, but that was long ago, before she took ill. On the south side, near the pond, two Carpathian Shepherds guarded a chicken coop on stilts. The dogs were siblings and kept foxes and wolves at bay. The huge red barn by the back of the property stored machinery, firewood, and grains. Pip slept in the stable but had the run of the place. Some nights, the donkey wound up in Radu's living room, enjoying the warm fireplace. In front of the barn, an A-framed windmill stood tall, whose sails, like those of an ancient vessel, creaked and squeaked when the breeze wafted down from the mountains. Nearing the farmhouse, an outline of a small wooden cross stood under the mound of an old oak tree: the burial site of Radu's eighteen-month-old daughter, born with a heart condition.

"You know, Irina won't be happy about this detour," Mihai said with a chuckle.

"Ahh, she will be happy when we arrive with vegetables and fresh eggs." Radu leaned in. "And wait till she try the pork," he said, miming a gesture of deliciousness.

As they approached the farmhouse, Radu leapt out the cart. "Come. Odeta expecting you."

∽

They reached Mihai's home at 10 p.m. As Radu unloaded boxes of fresh produce and tender cuts of pork, he offered Pip a carrot and filled his bucket with fresh water. Irina, silhouetted against the backdoor with hands on hips, awaited an explanation.

"Radu, always a pleasure," she said, though her stance betrayed her impatience.

Radu removed his cap. "Mrs Ionescu, so happy to see you. You look as beautiful as ever."

Irina smiled. A fingernail of moonlight illuminated her dark, luscious hair and mahogany eyes. "Mihai, why so late?" Her question carried a faint, accusatory tone.

Before Mihai could respond, Radu interceded. "We bring food! Fresh pork, straight from my farm."

She nodded in polite gratitude, still waiting for an answer.

"Don't be mad at husband. He saved mother Odeta today... and her newborn baby!"

"You saved a baby?" Irina asked in disbelief.

"Yes, yes," said Radu. "Your husband is big hero. He cut poor Odeta and stitched her up, but she be better in few days, yes?"

"Yes," said Mihai. "Make sure she gets some rest. And keep the baby away for at least a day."

Irina looked dumbfounded.

"So, you not mad?" asked Radu.

"How can I be mad at him for saving a newborn?"

Radu gave Mihai a triumphant look.

After Radu left, Mihai headed for the shower, smelling of gunk and slime.

"You want me to warm up some food?" asked Irina.

"I ate at Radu's."

"I can't believe you saved a mother and her child. What was her name... Odeta? You'll have to tell me all about it. That's amazing."

"Not really," he yelled, above the rumbling and rattling of the plumbing pipes, which sporadically spewed out bursts of hot and cold water. "Odeta is a goat and her baby, a kid. Quite cute."

Mihai swore when a hairbrush hit the back of his head. And when the bathroom door slammed, he roared with laughter while lather ran down his face.

17

2

Who's the Boy?

The next day, Mihai arrived at work before dawn. Besides being a renowned surgeon, his research into neurological diseases such as multiple sclerosis, Parkinson's disease, and epilepsy, had received acclaim in Europe and the U.S. Foreign friends and colleagues smuggled out Mihai's papers that criticized Romania's healthcare system. His analysis on the polio vaccine was scathing, and his findings into the under-reported abortion rates and the alarming increase in suicides had stirred controversy. Despite international invitations to medical conferences, Mihai remained confined within Romania's borders, as the bureaucracy always denied his passport requests because of a past indiscretion.

As he rechecked his schedule, the escapades of the previous night's foray into veterinary medicine gave way to the sobering reality of human suffering.

A knock at the door.

Professor Adam Bolan was the hospital director and a respected cardiac surgeon. Standing at five feet six inches, Adam's calm demeanour belied a shrewdness that had kept the hospital afloat and the wolves at bay for decades.

"Busy?" he queried, eyeing the queue of patients in the hallway.

Mihai gestured vaguely, his attention still on his paperwork. "What can I do for you?"

Adjusting his brown tie, Adam sat amidst the clutter. "About that epilepsy case. Have you had a chance to think it over?"

Mihai had suggested Adam try another colleague as he was far too busy. "As I said yesterday, I don't work with children."

Adam persisted. "Your expertise would be invaluable, Mihai. It would mean a lot to me."

Mihai sensed that Adam was under some pressure about this case but did not understand why. "Okay, Adam. Lunchtime, maybe," Mihai conceded, rummaging through the files on his desk.

"Great," Adam said, smiling at a passing nurse.

No sooner had Adam left when an emergency call jolted Mihai into action. He raced down the corridor, barking orders, bounding up the stairway, ordering the CT scanner ready for a head trauma. "Now!" he yelled at the nurse. His voice boomed through the stairwell. "Now!"

The thirty-year-old man walked into the emergency room with a three-inch-wide metal object protruding from his head: a road trauma involving a motorbike. No helmet. A crushed skull exposed brain tissue, and leakage of intracranial yellow fluid coagulated with his matted hair. His irises were sheathed in a ring of blood. When the nurse ran to his aid, she screamed as cerebral matter spilled out his nose.

Mihai prepped for emergency surgery, as he read the nurse's note: steel rod through head. Brain spillage from nasal cavity. "Shit," he grumbled, and scrubbed in as quickly as possible.

He went to work, calling for an intubation tray and checking vital signs, before pumping mannitol into the patient to reduce brain swelling. The CT scan revealed a shattered skull: heavy diffuse bleeding. "Tell me something I don't know," he uttered, while reaching for the drill to empty the build-up of blood.

The man's blood pressure dropped. His heart stopped beating. A cyclone of activity followed: catheters slipped into femoral arteries, drugs injected into the patient IV, and tubes pushed deep into his chest. Mihai pounded on his sternum, administering CPR. It was a futile endeavour.

∽

Bathed in the soft green glow of his office lamp, Mihai examined the file as evening descended. The mysterious boy had been seen by neurosurgeons in Bucharest and Paris. Yet, as Mihai scoured the documents, the child's identity had been blacked out. A sense of intrigue gripped him. *Who are you?* He arched back in his chair, pressing his finger against his temple. A nurse entered, asking if he wanted a dinner tray. He waved her off without lifting his gaze.

The case was a puzzle: severe, frequent seizures with no apparent cause and no family history. Experiencing over twenty seizures daily, varying from mild eyelid fluttering to full-body convulsions, the proposed solution for the child was radical—a corpus callosotomy. By severing the corpus callosum, a bundle of nerve fibres that connect the two hemispheres of the brain, surgeons aimed to contain the seizures to one hemisphere, thus reducing their severity and frequency. Mihai was asked to assess the prudence of this procedure.

Reports estimated that a third of the child's seizures affected the entire brain, meaning they were generalised. The rest were focalised and restricted to one hemisphere. Therefore, the surgery would help ease one-third, or somewhere between seven to ten seizures a day.

Mihai questioned the benefit of this procedure but believed surgeons felt pressured to come up with some solution to relieve the child's woes, despite it not being anywhere near a cure. He also questioned the estimations on the generalised seizures, believing that the numbers might be lower than the approximated one-third, which would raise further doubts about the benefits of performing a corpus callosotomy. He lowered the lamp on his desk, refilled his coffee cup, and settled in for a long night.

∽

The following day, Mihai raised his concerns. "There are inconsistencies and ambiguities, Adam. I'm wary of the conclusions drawn by the doctors."

"What are you suggesting?" asked Adam.

Mihai was firm. "Before contemplating such an invasive procedure, you need absolute certainty about the seizure patterns. Otherwise, the benefits, when weighed up against the potential risks, do not add up." Despite being a surgeon, Mihai regarded the scalpel as a last resort. "Who's the boy, Adam?"

Adam hesitated, as Dr Gheorghe Mitrea's interrupted their discussion.

Gheorghe was the head of neurology at Cluj University hospital. An experienced neurosurgeon who had worked at the hospital for four decades, he prided himself on being a stickler for procedure. With slicked-back silver-blue hair,

Gheorghe carried himself with an air of sophistication and snobbery. He was, if anything, a man with impeccable taste and punctilious rectitude.

Mihai thought him a querulous pain in the ass who should retire.

Adam welcomed Gheorghe. "We were discussing the epilepsy case, but first, there's an issue from last week that needs addressing."

"What's the problem, Gheorghe?" Mihai asked rather curtly.

"Well, you undermined me in front of the interns during a spinal surgery," Gheorghe said, clearing his throat and adjusting his silk tie.

Mihai, taken aback, replied with a hint of sarcasm, "Maybe I should steer clear of your surgeries then."

Adam, attempting to mediate, asked for specifics.

Gheorghe recounted the incident, his frustration palpable. "I was demonstrating a disc removal when Mihai intervened, claiming he had a faster method."

"Come on, Gheorghe, I stepped in to perform a better procedure." Mihai turned to Adam. "Using a Cobb instrument, a mallet, and a Kerrison rongeur, I had the disc removed in no time!" The superfluous tone added fuel to the fire.

"You showed off at my expense," Gheorghe retorted, turning his chair to face Mihai. "How are we to demand respect if you act with such arrogance?"

"First, I wasn't ridiculing you. I was showing a procedure our young surgeons better learn fast. And, I might add, you should too."

Adam rolled his eyes.

"Second, I wasn't showboating. That is your insecurity shining through." About to leave it at that, Mihai couldn't help himself. "Plus, I had to be somewhere. If I'd had let you continue, we'd have been there forever."

"You asshole!" shouted Gheorghe.

Adam had to intervene—not pleased with Mihai's riposte. There were many disagreements between the neurosurgeons. Gheorghe did not approve of Mihai's brash methods, especially from a relatively young, thirty-nine-year-old. Gheorghe confessed that Mihai's abilities were remarkable. However, he painted him as a dangerous maverick who disobeyed rules and struggled to conform—no one refuted the summation. According to Gheorghe, Mihai's hubris and volatile temperament were not befitting a surgeon.

"What you fail to realise, Dr Mihai, is that the method you demonstrated, though effective, can produce grave consequences if ill-delivered. Our residents don't have the expertise, experience, or confidence to perform such a technique. One wrong move and they could cause serious or permanent damage to the spinal cord."

"They'd better bloody well learn. And it's your damn job to equip them with the know-how and skills of modern neurosurgery."

Adam had to side with Mihai on this point, though he wished his star surgeon would use more tact.

"At some stage, Gheorghe, you need to abandon the surgeon's handbook of 1959," said Mihai. "We are approaching the eighties, my friend."

Adam could have throttled him.

Gheorghe, red-faced and indignant, stood his ground. "I am your superior at this hospital! Frankly, I am tired of your insolence. You view a more measured approach as substandard... boring. Well, let me tell you, it's not. It requires discipline and a rational mind." Gheorghe maintained a stiff back, his hands trembling while adjusting his silver cufflinks, his vexation apparent.

Screw it. Mihai had reached his threshold. "You know, I am tired of carrying this department and making excuses for your gutless practices. Grow some balls in the operating room, stop hand-selecting patients, stop taking bribes and maybe you'll earn a little respect."

Adam let them vent. There would be no truce today.

"Just last month," said Mihai, on a mini rant, "I performed a suboccipital craniectomy for a brain stem malformation on your former patient. You deemed it too risky and refused to operate. Well, because of me, he is doing just fine, thank you very much." Mihai leant forward, hands on the table, egging Gheorghe on.

"Are you aware if you had cut two millimetres deeper into the brain, you would have caused permanent paralysis?"

"Of course! I am no fool," said Mihai.

Gheorghe's composure was slipping. "Every expert I consulted advised against the surgery. You bypassed the ethics committee's recommendation. That's reckless."

Mihai scoffed at the mention of the ethics committee. "That is the difference between us. You have no spine."

Gheorghe abandoned his civility, waving his finger and taking umbrage at Mihai's remarks. "Going in guns blazing is not my idea of a surgeon I trust. For every breakthrough surgery of yours, there are two disasters."

Rumours of Mihai's questionable methods causing harm, even death, circulated among the staff.

Gheorghe continued, "In your short career, you've faced more misconduct charges than I have in forty years."

Adam, sensing the imminent explosion, leaned forward to intervene, but Gheorghe pressed on.

"Your approach is like Russian roulette, Mihai. I would not want my family, or anyone's children anywhere near you."

The acerbic remark was like vinegar on an open wound. In a flash of rage, Mihai hurled a coffee cup at the wall near Gheorghe's head.

"Mihai!" Adam yelled.

His eyes blazing with fury, Mihai towered over Gheorghe, before grabbing a chair and hurtling it against the wall. The clock on the wall crashed to the floor with its hands frozen at 09:47 a.m. Mihai slammed the door behind him, leaving his colleagues in stunned silence.

In the late afternoon, Adam passed the conga line that led to Mihai's office. Patients suffering from migraines, dementia, strokes, and a host of neurological diseases waited for hours, hoping to see the doctor. Some stood, as spinal nerve damage made it impossible for them to sit. A middle-aged nun sat thumbing her black rosary beads, mumbling to herself, while a restless young man moaned in agony. And next to him, a woman wearing hair netting, dressing gown and slippers, fought to keep her right hand from trembling. A pregnant woman with three toddlers in tow complained about her debilitating back pain and swollen breasts, as she rolled and yawed like a galleon in rough seas.

Adam hesitated outside Mihai's office, where another outburst was underway.

"Take your medication as prescribed!" Mihai yelled. "I'm the doctor, not you. If you won't listen, find someone else! Don't waste my bloody time!"

25

Adam sighed, reflecting on the paradox of Mihai's practice. Despite his brusque manner, patients kept returning, some out of admiration, others out of desperation.

Adam broached the earlier incident. "Gheorghe acknowledges your surgical prowess, for which he both admires and resents you."

Mihai, still fuming, dismissed the attempt at reconciliation. "Don't start, Adam. That son of a bitch deserved it."

Adam projected a stern yet supportive tone. "Gheorghe has lodged another complaint. I defended you but remember his political connections. You don't want to stir up trouble."

"I can handle Gheorghe, Adam," he said with a dismissive laugh. And you know I can make trouble too. I'm not afraid to stir the pot."

Adam, though supportive, was no stranger to the headaches Mihai caused. As a mentor and father figure, he had often shielded Mihai from the repercussions of his actions. The hospital, under Mihai's tenure, had become a hub of medical acclaim but also a ground for controversy. Accusations against the surgeon ranged from unprofessional conduct to serious allegations of surgical misconduct. There had been an enquiry eleven months ago regarding the death of a sixty-two-year-old man who developed blood poisoning after surgery and died. Dr Adam spoke on behalf of the hospital, supporting Mihai's procedures. Doctors and nurses gave mixed reviews on the case, though Mihai had allegedly disregarded administrative protocols, and may have tampered with, or post-dated paperwork, but inconsistent testimony and vague recollections obfuscated the evidence. Rumours of intimidation and Mihai chipping in favours owed, circulated like wildfire. After deliberation, the hearing returned a not-guilty verdict. Many had their doubts.

Adam's loyalties extended beyond personal affections. He was no quixotic fool. He saw in Mihai a brilliant surgeon, who, despite his flaws, had a drive and energy unsurpassed.

"It was my fault," said Adam. "I thought getting you together might mend fences."

Mihai scoffed. He believed in radical solutions, not in patching up what was irreparable.

"Gheorghe is still the head of neurology. His position demands a certain level of respect, regardless of your personal views."

Mihai bristled at the reminder of Gheorghe's seniority. "He's outdated, Adam. His approach, his thinking—it's all past its prime."

Adam tried to reason with Mihai, highlighting the need for departmental harmony. "Your absence at meetings doesn't help matters. Gheorghe feels undermined. He doesn't like being bypassed. Why, just yesterday, he said you skipped a departmental meeting… and," Adam added, "you missed the one before that."

"Give me a break," Mihai pleaded. "Who has time for these meetings? I don't need to hear people whine about the lack of facilities, resources, and money."

Adam sighed, careful not to touch any of the files on Mihai's desk that would send them tumbling.

"Plus," Mihai added, "when I attend, he asks me to leave."

"That's because you criticise everything he says! Come on," pleaded Adam, "what do you expect the guy to do?"

"He should retire, that's what. No offence, but he is past his use-by date."

"His age is not the issue. Despite his seniority in position and age, he feels you single him out and treat him like a subordinate."

"That's bullshit, Adam. I don't single him out." Mihai cracked a smile. "I treat everyone like a subordinate." The smile evaporated. "If I didn't push boundaries, we'd be stuck in mediocrity."

Adam understood. Miha's relentless drive set him apart, but it was also what made him a target for criticism.

"Why, last week, I pestered Victor Vladimirescu from the Medico-Pharmaceutical Institute to send us two boxes of X-ray film! After many phone calls, and even threatening to tear his liver out, Victor agreed. He even threw in a case of retractors and spreaders," Mihai said with a cheeky smirk. "And why does this happen?"

Adam understood the rhetorical nature of the question.

"It happens because I act, make calls, hustle, harass, and threaten when necessary. I do favours and broker deals. That's how things work here. My research alone has brought in vital funding, propping both our department and the hospital. You know this, Adam."

His words carried an underlying threat.

The government, eager for international recognition, funnelled funds into research. Mihai secured substantial grants, and his work earned accolades abroad. One notable project was a collaboration with Belgium's esteemed Born-Bunge Institute, exploring the basal ganglia's role in Parkinson's disease. This led to joint ventures with Bucharest and garnered interest from other international hospitals and facilities.

"Unlike our friend, who struts around like royalty, indulging in foie gras and sporting silk ties, I don't pocket a cent. I reinvest every damn dollar in the hospital or use it to further my knowledge. The way Gheorghe screens patients, judging by their capacity to pay, is downright despicable."

Corruption plagued the medical field. Doctors, earning less than factory workers, felt aggrieved. Accepting bribes from affluent, desperate patients had become a regrettable norm in Romania. For Mihai, this was a red line. Far from sanctimonious, he followed his own moral compass. His proverbial line in the sand stretched and swayed, but he refused to exploit the sick. He treated one and all, regardless. When patients offered extra money, he channelled those funds into buying equipment or furthering his skills. His vast collection of medical texts caused many a row in the Ionescu household.

"When did Gheorghe last contribute? Never, that's when. He claims to have filed funding requests. We all know how those requests pan out with this government— the most corrupt, incompetent buffoons on the planet. May they all burn in hell!"

"Not so loud," Adam cautioned, wary of eavesdroppers. "We'll talk after work, okay. You still giving me a lift?"

"Da," Mihai nodded, yelling for his next patient to enter.

∽

The Renault sputtered and groaned, starting on the third attempt. Mihai's head brushed against the sagging roof lining. Grinding the gears, he merged into traffic, clipping a cyclist's rear wheel, who yelled bloody murder.

Adam picked up the conversation. "I understand your point, but it's your temper that's the issue." He clutched his briefcase, eyeing the limp passenger side mirror. "You're a brilliant surgeon, undisputed. But you can't keep yelling at everyone, and I'm not just talking about Gheorghe. You shout at staff, interns, even patients!" he said with a bemused expression. "And yes, I heard about Dr Vali."

Dr Vali, an epidemiologist, had recently clashed with Mihai and filed a complaint, referencing Mihai's abusive language and aggressive posturing.

Mihai flung his hands up in exasperation. "He's an imbecile!"

"He's one of Transylvania's finest researchers, Mihai!"

"An imbecile, nonetheless."

They drove past the botanic gardens, spanning fourteen hectares in the city's south, Mihai's thoughts drifted to memories of strolling through the Japanese section of the gardens with his father, Ion. He remembered when ducks had chased him around the lake while his father followed, laughing to high heaven. Such moments of nostalgia were rare indulgences for Mihai.

Accelerating down Strada Napoca, farmers were setting up their stalls in Piaţa Unirii—Cluj's largest plaza. Once a bustling monthly event attracting thousands for its abundant produce, and carnival-like atmosphere, the market was now a remnant of its former glory.

St Michael's Gothic church, a fourteenth-century marvel dominated the plaza. Mihai admired its 76-metre bell tower that pierced the sky. In the square centre stood a bronze statue of Matthias Corvinus, the revered Hungarian King, mounted on a stallion. Corvinus, alongside his cousin, the legendary Count Dracula, had fended off Ottoman invasions, preserving their homeland.

"You have a big heart, Mihai, though not everyone sees it. You intimidate and polarise with your bellicose manner. And before you say anything, hear me out," Adam said, lecturing his protégé. "You achieve results, yes, but fear stifles questions and growth." The professor cracked a wry smile. "Try extending some patience to us mere mortals, okay?"

"I have the patience of a saint," Mihai quipped, honking at a car ahead.

Branded a bully, Mihai was no stranger to such admonitions. A perfectionist with an unyielding work ethic, he had scant tolerance for incompetence or laziness.

"Regarding Gheorghe," Adam continued in a more businesslike manner. "He was out of line, and I'm persuading him not to escalate matters. But I can't have my neurosurgeons at odds. Can you maintain a civil working relationship with him?"

They arrived at Adam's apartment complex.

Mihai grudgingly nodded. "For the record, I didn't yell at him," squeezing Adam in a playful bear hug, a gesture that belied their professional disagreements. Adam tried fending him off, uncomfortable with such displays. Despite their differences, Mihai found his boss as comfortable and reassuring as an old pair of slippers.

"So, how'd you get Victor Vladimirescu to hand over X-ray film and surgical equipment?"

"Ahh," Mihai grinned. "I invited Victor and his colleagues to observe my pituitary gland surgery."

Adam frowned, unsure why Victor would be so interested in such a procedure.

"I went in through the nasal cavity."

Adam's jaw dropped.

"See what I do for this hospital!" Mihai exclaimed, struggling with the gears before finding reverse. "So tell me, who's the boy?"

Adam removed his cap and brushed back strands of white hair. "His name is Alex Lupei."

31

"Do I know him?"

"No. But his father, Alexandru Lupei, might ring a bell." Adam's words were drowned out as rain hammered down, sending him scurrying for cover.

Mihai navigated the deluge with reckless haste, the name Alexandru Lupei crossing his mind. Accelerating hard around corners, the flooded roads challenged his control. As the rain subsided, he made a routine stop, his thoughts still swirling.

He entered the cemetery and paused. *Alexandru Lupei.* Under the silver glow of a gibbous moon, he murmured, "The Wolf."

3

The Wolf

Adam informed Mihai they were meeting Alexandru Lupei at dawn. Mr Lupei, with urgent business in Cluj, sought insights into his son's condition.

Major-General Alexandru Lupei was a commanding figure in the European bloc's most brutal and feared agency, the Departamentul Securității Statului. The Securitate evoked the fear of God into every Romanian citizen. Possessing unyielding powers, this organisation enforced the Communists' ubiquitous stranglehold, quashing any anti-government sentiment with the harshest and swiftest of Machiavellian reprisals. Nicknamed "The Wolf," Lupei operated in the shadows, a puppeteer orchestrating the regime's darkest deeds, and ill-reputed henchman of Lieutenant General Nicolae Pleşiţă, the Securitate's public face.

Entering the hospital, Lupei's formidable presence was palpable. Standing six-foot-four, his build reminiscent of a German Panzer, he moved with a deliberate, waddling gait, as his Herculean thighs rubbed against each other. His hair and eyes were as black as tar. The plump nose suited his enormous head, and his neck was as thick as a tree trunk. The cauliflower ears betrayed his past as a wrestler. Dressed in a navy suit that barely contained his frame, he exuded an air of controlled power as he shook hands with hospital officials. He came alone and sat in Adam's chair, adjusting his silk tie as staff poured him a black coffee with no sugar.

Mihai scrutinised this notorious figure sitting opposite him. His reputation, infamous, though one had to be wary of the propaganda surrounding the Securitate. Rumour had it that Lupei orchestrated the beatings and assassinations of some half-dozen prominent figures who opposed President Ceausescu. Mihai recalled recent headlines, where a former wrestler, believed to be Alexandru Lupei, had beaten Paul Goma, a writer and journalist, to within an inch of his life in response to a series of scathing letters criticising the government.

"Dr Ionescu has been reviewing Alex's case," Adam began, cautioning Mihai with a glance. "The floor is yours."

"Mr Lupei," Mihai started, his voice steady, "your son's condition is deteriorating. All conventional treatment has failed. Despite exhaustive efforts, the cause of the epilepsy remains elusive, and medications have been ineffective." He paused, collecting his thoughts. "Surgical intervention could mitigate the severity and frequency of his episodes by a third. It's a significant improvement, though not a complete solution."

The Major-General remained stoic. Mihai felt the weight of his stare as he rubbed his temple and pursed his lips.

"Why don't you speak your mind," Alexandru Lupei urged. "I'm here for answers, and I've been told you might provide them." It was a backhanded compliment of sorts.

"Assessing your son without direct observation hampers definitive conclusions, Mr Lupei." Mihai noted a fleeting change in the big man as he finished his black coffee.

"For the first time since this ordeal began, someone dares to use the word 'definitive,'" Lupei remarked, requesting a refill. "I appreciate your candour, Doctor. What do you suggest?"

Mihai hesitated. "I've found inconsistencies in the reports regarding your son's general seizures. Before removing your son's corpus callosum, I'd want to verify these details."

Adam interjected, "These are speculative points, Mr Lupei, and we must remember, we haven't yet seen your son."

Lupei reaffirmed he understood.

"The frequency of generalised seizures may be wrong," Mihai cautioned. "The EEG recordings and video monitoring methods used were suboptimal, leaving too much conjecture."

"What does this mean, if true?" asked Alexandru Lupei.

"It could mean the proposed surgery might have even less impact on reducing the severity of your son's episodes," Mihai said, noting Lupei's calculating expression.

Adam nervously tapped on the notepad.

Poor Adam will be doing cartwheels in a minute. "Again, I am speculating, Mr Lupei. I can only provide a definitive assessment after a twenty-four-hour observation of your son," Mihai clarified. "I won't make unfounded claims."

"You want my son to come in for more tests and observations? More plugs over his head and treated like some guinea pig?"

"I share your frustration," said Mihai, "but that is the only way. I cannot or will not make claims unless I see the patient. It's as simple as that."

Alexandru Lupei approved of the doctor's sentiment but did not approve of his tone. "And if your suspicions are correct? What if this surgery offers minimal improvement?"

"There is another option, though only as a last resort."

The man slammed his enormous fist on the table. Coffee spilt into the saucer, creating a moat around the cup. "My boy cannot go to school. He cannot play sport. He has no friends! I've wasted time and energy looking for answers that no one can give me. As you say, things are getting worse. He is my only son. My wife and I brace for the day a seizure will take his life. So, Doctor, I am searching for a last resort!" The Major-General took a breath, cracked his neck, and adjusted his collar.

Appreciating the man's desperation and turmoil, Mihai gave the man an option. "An anatomical hemispherectomy is an option if the seizures originate from the right hemisphere."

Adam choked on his coffee while Lupei waited for an explanation.

No point beating around the bush. "It involves removing the right hemisphere of your son's brain."

The air left the room.

"This will stop the seizures," Mihai explained, "as his seizures predominantly originate from his right hemisphere." It was a suggestion bordering on the fantastical, yet it was what Lupei sought—an alternative. "The Americans have had success with hemispherectomies. The conditions align well for your son: frequent episode, medication resistance, right-brain seizure origin, and his relative age."

"Let me get this straight," said Alexandru Lupei, shifting in his chair. "You're suggesting we remove half my boy's brain?"

"Yes," Mihai confirmed.

"Are you out of your fucking mind?"

"Not at all," said Mihai, unperturbed.

"How is that possible?" asked Alexandru Lupei, dumbfounded. "He can live with half a brain?"

"Yes. Johns Hopkins University is pioneering this procedure. Should you exhaust all other possibilities, they're worth consulting."

"Would you be willing to perform the surgery? Hypothetically speaking."

"No." Mihai's response was blunt. "You need a paediatric neurosurgeon, and one with experience in this procedure."

The Major-General caught a wounded flicker in the doctor's eyes and tucked it away for safe-keeping. "Why didn't anyone mention this earlier?" His question was laced with accusation.

"It's a radical, complex operation with little history. Doctors hesitate to suggest unfamiliar treatments. Only a few surgeons have expertise in this field. It comes with potential major complications."

After discussing the merits of such a radical procedure that sounded more like science fiction to Lupei, he thanked Mihai for his time and left.

"Are you out of your fucking mind!" cried Adam, shocked beyond belief.

Mihai chuckled. "He said the same thing!"

"Christ almighty, did you seriously suggest removing his son's brain? Do you know who you're talking to?"

37

Mihai embraced Adam in a playful hug, causing the old man discomfort. "You wanted a fresh perspective and that's what I offered. Risky, but not without merit."

Adam shook his head. "We all knew you were mad, but we never knew to what extent!"

Offering Adam a ride home, Mihai placed a supportive arm around his mentor, who deftly slipped away from the embrace.

The rain washed away the day as they drove towards Adam's apartment. Mihai used his jacket to clear the fogging windscreen. The statue of King Matthias Corvinus emerged as they navigated Piața Unirii's slippery roads. Adam gripped the dangling passenger sidearm door.

"What's your take on Lupei?" asked Mihai.

"He might just revoke your medical licence and commit you to an asylum."

Mihai's laughter filled the car, his attention wavering from the road.

"Careful!" Adam shouted, as they almost grazed a lorry. Horns blared in the chaos.

"Perhaps Ceausescu would hire me," Mihai joked. "I could perform lobotomies or hemispherectomies on his enemies. I'd be employed for life!"

The tyres scraped the curb outside Adam's residence. The professor's home was nestled in a cluster of unassuming grey concrete buildings. Watching the old man ascend the five flights of stairs, Mihai couldn't help but admire him. Despite his fifty years as a surgeon, Adam's modest two-bedroom flat, where a day of hot water and heating was a luxury, conflicted with Mihai's aspirations.

At home, Mihai recounted his meeting with The Wolf to Irina.

"He's a pig and belongs in prison," Irina affirmed in no uncertain terms. "The Securitate, under his command, silences any dissent against Ceausescu with ruthless efficiency."

As they prepared for dinner, noises emanated from the front gate.

"Dr Mihai!" a familiar voice called out. "The greatest man doctor and animal doctor in all of Europe! I have friend who comes bearing gifts."

Radu's unmistakable voice rang through the evening air.

"Radu. Good to see you, my friend!" Mihai greeted him with affection, amused by Radu's robust embrace. The strength of the wiry old man defied logic.

"What brings you here, Niko?" Mihai inquired, as he welcomed the newcomer.

"I told you," said Radu, "I have friend with gifts."

Niko Dalca, a past patient of Mihai's, had the weathered face of a man who'd known hard work, yet his robust physique spoke of strength and vitality. His thick black hair and moustache were as distinctive as the callouses on his broad hands and the blunt stub of his forefinger—a reminder of a long-ago farming mishap. Niko's life was a blend of tending to his small farm and gruelling shifts in the nearby steel mills.

Niko blushed, preferring to have left unnoticed.

"You're just in time," said Mihai, ushering them in. "Irina, we need more plates."

Niko brought fruits and vegetables, a stuffed chicken, fresh eggs, and a flask of home-made red wine: a heartfelt payment for medical assistance that the farmer could ill afford.

Radu held up the chicken by its feet. "Niko's finest," he beamed, planting a kiss on Irina's cheek. "Make wonderful soup as well."

"Oh Niko, you shouldn't have," Irina said. "Where will we put this food?"

"In your tummy," laughed Radu. "But we no stay for dinner."

"Don't be silly. Of course, you are," she declared.

"Thank goodness the chickens dead," said Irina. She tightened the bow at the back of her apron. "Years ago, someone brought us a live chicken." She glanced at her husband, who smiled. "After Mihai chopped its head off, it ran around the backyard flapping and smashing into everything, blood spraying from its neck. Maria was young and screamed as the headless chook ran laps." Irina laughed. "And Mihai chased the thing, cursing and yelling, as it kept slipping from his hands. It was a sight to behold."

Their laughter echoed memories of joyful times.

Irina set the oak kitchen table with a white lace tablecloth that hid a stubborn stain. Sunlight filtered through a yellow floral-patterned curtain, casting a warm glow over the pastel green cupboards, whose missing knobs were a testament to the passage of time. Above the laminate benchtop, a glass cabinet held their silverware: wedding gifts from a lifetime ago.

"Sit." Mihai motioned the men to the table. "We have polenta with sour cream. Irina, how about adding those fresh eggs for an omelette?"

"We have bacon too," Irina said, as yolks in the sizzling pan turned deep orange, filling the room with a tantalising aroma.

Mihai uncorked Niko's knotted rope flask of wine. "Noroc," he toasted, raising his glass.

"How are the children?" Mihai inquired, serving a generous portion of sour cream to his guests.

Niko told how his eldest son had migrated to Bucharest for work. "The farms are emptying. Everyone's drawn to the city."

Radu shook his head. "Everybody leaving," as he scooped up and mixed the omelette with the polenta. "I am glad we arrive in time," he said with a cheeky grin.

"And Annmarie?" asked Mihai.

"Ahh," Niko said, "she is in love. He is army boy. From Bucharest but stationed in Cluj. He is twenty-two."

"How old is Annmarie, now?"

"Seventeen. They want to get married," Niko said.

"That's lovely," interjected Irina. "You and your wife must be thrilled. It's difficult to find a good boy wanting to settle down these days."

"Da. Hard to find nice girls, too," said Niko.

"True," declared Mihai, as he scooped up the last remnants of polenta.

"Yes, but I worry. My daughter is finishing school and has a job in a butcher shop, but I cannot help them as they begin their new life together. They have nothing."

"Niko, we all have nothing!" said Mihai in high spirits. "I'm a brain surgeon, and I don't have a fridge that works." Mihai found it comical. Irina was not laughing.

"I'm glad you find it funny, Mihai, but I've thrown away good meat because of this fridge. That is the second time this month," she reminded him, as the fridge buzzed along, while the ventilation fan made a clanking sound.

Radu chuckled. "He best doctor in the world with no fridge!"

"But," she retorted, "ask your friend how many expensive medical books he has?"

41

The reluctant judges turned to the accused.

"I buy those books to help patients like you, Niko!"

The theatrics reached a crescendo as Mihai stood. "Don't you want your doctor to know a thing or two before he cuts your brain open, Niko?"

Irina scoffed in a half-mocking gesture, as Radu revelled in the banter.

"Besides," Mihai called out, raising his glass, "those books brought us the finest homemade wine in Cluj!"

Radu slapped his leg in hysterics. Their laughter filled the house, punctuated by the clinking of wine glasses and the occasional spill on the tablecloth.

While Irina checked the temperamental fridge for dessert, Radu stepped outside to check on his donkey.

"Here you go," handing his trusted friend a carrot. The beast chomped away while his master rubbed his furry neck and brushed off bits of bark and grass that were tangled in the animal's matted mane. "You no smell too good, Pip. Maybe we give you bath tomorrow, okay?" Radu took a sniff of his own underarm. "Maybe Radu join you," he said, cackling.

Pip's hind legs suffered from rheumatism and his eyes were not what they used to be. But, like his master, he was a tough nut. The most unlikely of friendships had formed between the pair ever since Radu rescued him from that frightful wolf in the woods. He covered Pip with a blanket as the donkey rubbed his enormous head against his human friend. Radu kissed Pip's muzzle and headed back, catching the tail-end of Mihai's story.

"... She is complaining of migraines, so I take her history, and without warning, she unbuttoned her blouse, insisting that massaging her breasts would relieve her migraines!"

"What did you do?" asked Niko, leaning forward in the chair.

"I swore an oath. I obliged, of course!" triggering roars of laughter. "And believe it or not," Mihai declared, "her migraines vanished!" His face flushed a deep red.

"I heard that!" Irina called out from the kitchen, doubling the merriment.

After dinner, Radu assisted with the dishes, but Irina shooed him back to join the others for coffee and dessert.

The conversation turned serious as Radu implored Niko to stay on the farm, countering his thoughts of full-time work at the steel mill.

"Change will come, Niko," said Radu, the eternal optimist. "Ceausescu can't rule forever."

"When?" Mihai pondered aloud. "The regime silences its critics, leaving poets, writers, and artists to bear the brunt, with many exiled or imprisoned. It's the masses that must rise to challenge the government."

"And the army," mumbled Niko, blowing on his coffee.

"Da," said Mihai and Radu in unison.

"Fear grips everyone," Niko lamented. "The Securitate sows distrust. Even children are indoctrinated." His large hands clenched. "One child denounced his father for cursing at Ceausescu on TV. They're turning children into informants."

Irina agreed, carrying the dessert into the living room. A primary school teacher for over a decade, she had witnessed the shift in education since the Communists' ascendance.

Private and religious schools had been abolished and the curriculum amended to instil allegiance to the regime. Teachers became the mouthpieces for promoting Communist ideology, glorifying Ceausescu as hero and

43

saviour. Irina's role had subtly transformed from educator to informant, with the Securitate's omnipresent eyes lurking in the background.

Perching on the sofa's edge, Irina carried a mix of concern and resentment. "They encourage children to monitor their parents. Last year, a couple were interrogated because their child reported them for praying and listening to Radio Free Europe."

Radio Free Europe, an American initiative, countered Communist propaganda, broadcasting to countries isolated from global discourse. Despite being forbidden in Romania, many defied the ban by rigging makeshift antennas in secrecy to tune into such broadcasts.

"What happened?" asked Niko.

"Thankfully, it was all a misunderstanding, but they put the parents on notice and the school commended the boy for upholding his national duty. In fact, they awarded him a red scarf and the boy was made a member of the Communist Pioneers, a privilege reserved for children of the ruling elite, and received invitations to summer retreats, where they were further brainwashed to Communist ideology."

"What are they teaching our children?" Niko asked in despair.

"Less about education, and more about propaganda," Irina lamented. "Our once vibrant education system is crumbling under austerity. Classrooms are icy cold, resources scarce, and fear of surveillance stifles any dissent."

Mihai knew too well the government's chokehold on resources.

"Our resources are depleting," she continued. "Most teachers are trying, as we love the kids. It breaks our heart to see students filling the soles of their shoes with cardboard, to prevent the rain and snow from soaking their feet." She offered her guests extra napkins while Mihai checked on the coffee. "How are students supposed to learn when the cement classrooms are freezing? The kids don't want to remove their hands from under their jumpers to write or draw. Not to mention the umpteen times the electricity shuts down. But what can we do? The bureaucracy is a nightmare, and everyone's wary of who is watching, making it difficult to speak out."

"They cut back on everything," said Radu. "Electricity they cut, hot water they cut, petrol they cut. Lucky my donkey no need petrol. Just a carrot and rub." His wrinkled face broke into a smile.

In the dimly lit living room, Mihai's voice carried a sombre tone. "During winter, the sick and elderly are freezing to death in their apartments, with no heating. It's tragic." He paused, recalling a harrowing incident where a father, returning from a night shift, found his entire family dead due to a gas leak. "And the food shortages are worsening. Malnutrition among children is rampant, and at the hospital, funds are stretched thin. It's infuriating to see Ceausescu indulging in palatial extravagances while his people suffer. They need to blow up these palaces with the Communists inside."

Radu smiled. "That is good start."

"They limit hot water to twice a week in many apartments," said Irina. "We're slightly better off, but it's not adequate."

"I wouldn't call it hot, Irina. And 'most days' is optimistic."

Radu lightened the mood, mimicking a rabbit hopping around the living room. "But Ceausescu no cutting back on babies! He wants us to breed like rabbits."

Irina playfully threw her apron at him.

The guests enjoyed Irina's homemade plăcintă (pancakes stuffed with jam), and while Mihai poured more coffee, the conversation turned to Niko's dilemma.

"I love the land, I do, but I can't stay here any longer."

"Farmers bear the brunt, but we're all struggling in our own way," said Mihai, finishing his coffee. I guess we are lucky that we don't queue for food."

Niko felt assuaged by Mihai's remarks, though it did not overshadow his shame at not being able to pay for medical services.

Mihai reflected on his own financial challenges. "After years of saving, all we have is a temperamental fridge and a vacuum cleaner."

Niko's head snapped back in dismay. "But you save lives. You're the best doctor we know. How is this possible?"

"He is best doctor," said Radu, matter of fact, as he polished off Irina's delicious plăcintă. A dollop of strawberry jam spilt onto the carpet. "Lucky, they have nice vacuum cleaner," Radu uttered to himself, as he licked the jam from his fingers.

Niko's thoughts turned nostalgic. "After the war, they promised us paradise. I was younger and believed in the oaths of a corruption-free, equal society. We celebrated in the streets. But look where we are now."

Mihai snickered. "Beware those promising the Garden of Eden."

The discussion shifted to the potential power of unity among farmers in maintaining freedom and independence on the production and sales of their produce, which had been overrun and desecrated by government intervention. In a country desperate to modernise, agriculture still constituted half the nation's workforce and economy.

Radu chimed in. "Yes, we must be together to save our farms, but young generation leaving."

Radu's eldest son, Toma, had fled the family farm to find a better life in Constanța, a major city near the coast, seven hundred kilometres from Cluj.

Mihai remembered the tragic night when Toma drove back to Constanța, after having visited the farm. Driving around a mountainous bend, a truck driver fell asleep and drifted into the opposite lane. Toma's Fiat and the truck tumbled over the edge, killing both drivers.

As the evening ended, Radu hugged Irina, offering her his culinary tips for the chicken.

Outside, by the front gate, Niko raised his concerns about Radu organising a late-night meeting on his farm. "It's risky. The Securitate has eyes and ears everywhere. If they learn of this gathering, the consequences could be dire."

Mihai tried to ease Niko's fears. "I wouldn't worry about it too much, Niko."

"Worry about what?" asked Radu as he approached.

"That your decrepit donkey won't make it home," said Mihai, as he grabbed old man Radu around the neck. "The streetlights are at half watts and only a third are working. Your blind old donkey might end up in Bulgaria!"

Radu covered Pip's ears and hugged his neck. The animal snorted.

"Goodnight, Doc, Goodnight Irina. Best pancakes in the world," yelled Radu as he waved goodbye, putting a smile on Irina's face.

The shrill ring of the phone shattered the moment. Adam's call from the hospital at this late hour was ominous.

Irina resumed washing dishes, anticipating trouble. Mihai's reaction was visceral. His jaw tightened. Despair

47

filled his face. He cursed as Irina stood with a dripping plate in her hands.

"God damn this cursed place!"

Irina braced herself.

"The bastards cut the power, and the back-up generator failed." He seethed as he ran his fingers through his hair. "The incubators in the neonatal intensive care unit... seven babies died."

The plate went crashing to the floor.

4

Young Alex Lupei

To the surprise of many, Alex Lupei arrived at Cluj University Hospital for a twenty-four-hour observation. The hospital's top floor, a jumble of offices, storage rooms, and a handful of intensive care units, housed a simple yet spacious private room. Known as the "honeymoon suite" due to its occasional use for discreet romances, this room, with views overlooking the terrace and gardens below, was to be Alex's temporary home.

Seven years old, Alex was polite, shy, and noticeably thin. His jet-black hair, falling in a long fringe, concealed a deep scar across his forehead—a stark reminder of a seizure-induced injury when he fell and smashed his head against a glass coffee table. Clad in navy-blue pyjamas and surrounded by a stack of comic books, he looked every bit the child he was.

"Ce mai faci, Alex?" asked Mihai.

The boy responded with a nonchalant "okay," avoiding eye contact.

Mihai lowered the bedside guard rail and sat on the edge, asking Alex if he liked the room. The boy shrugged. He had seen more than enough hospital rooms.

They talked about school, sports, and toys. Mihai avoided medical issues.

"I wish I could go back to school," Alex confessed, sipping apple juice. "I don't have many friends. Just Daniel and Laika, my dog. I named him after the first dog in space."

Laika, the Russian mongrel and the first dog to orbit Earth, had become a symbol of heroism, with monuments erected in his honour. However, Laika's voyage in space was a suicide mission: his food laced with poison, for the Sputnik 2 burned up and disintegrated on re-entry into the atmosphere.

"Is your Laika a space traveller, too?"

Alex smiled. "No, but he can shake hands, fetch the ball and roll over!"

"Wow. Did you teach him yourself?"

"Yep, all by myself. It took a long time because he is very, very stubborn. But lucky he likes treats." The boy grinned, as did Mihai. "I had a rat once. But Mum freaked, so I had to give him away."

"You like animals?" asked Mihai.

The boy nodded. "My favourite are lions. I love the zoo! And the circus! They are the best! But I haven't been since, you know."

Mihai took a liking to his young patient. "My daughter loved animals, too. She collected all kinds of little critters: nursing injured lizards that had fallen from trees. And she loved the circus."

Lost in memories, Mihai gazed out the window, recalling a summer day at the Transilvănean Aurit Circus on the Mic River: the blue and yellow tent, the aroma of popcorn mixed with the scent of sawdust—it all came rushing back.

∽

The elephants and horses mesmerised young Maria. She giggled with delight when her father arranged for her to sit atop a majestic grey mare, her laughter echoing as the horse playfully nipped at her hand.

She loved all God's creatures and spent hours playing with dogs in the park and mending injured birds she found in her backyard. Yet, it was a rare purple butterfly that stole Maria's heart, becoming her most treasured obsession.

The clowns caused a ruckus, stumbling about and being plain silly in their white gloves, green wigs, and oversized red shoes. Mihai and Maria giggled as popcorn and lemonade spilt over the ochre-coloured sawdust that smelt of dry earth.

While walking hand in hand across the grounds, Maria's chocolate ice-cream dripped over her teddy bear. No oil painting by any stretch, Babu the bear was a mismatch of faded colours with stitched-on bits that covered his many injuries.

Ice-cream also smeared over Maria's purple dress. "Oops, Mum won't be happy, Daddy," she said with a cheeky grin.

"Are you excited about school next year?" asked Mihai.

"Da!" Her dimples showed. "Mum got me a pencil case. I wanted the Mickey Mouse one, but the one she got was nice, too." Maria frowned. "But, Daddy, my shoes are too big."

Her response, full of anticipation yet tinged with a child's concern over oversized shoes, had warmed his heart. He placed his hands on his hips, mockingly appalled. "Well, that won't do, will it? We can't have the daughter of Dr Mihai Ionescu going to school with big shoes, can we? You're not a clown, right?"

Maria nodded in fierce agreement as he scooped her up and whirled her around in circles.

"Stop it, Dad!" She laughed.

"So, have you prepared your Christmas list?"

Her crystal blue eyes lit so bright that it seemed the sky radiated from them. "Well, I want a new pram for my doll and a trip to Disneyland!"

"Wow. You must have been a good girl."

Maria nodded exaggeratedly, her freckles dancing like tiny, perfect imperfections across her button-nose. She savoured her ice-cream with an innocence that only a child possesses.

"Well, let's start with a Mickey Mouse pencil case and a pair of school shoes that fit?"

She giggled, but only wished to spend more time with her daddy.

In the background, a rollercoaster whirred and whooshed, its elephant-painted carriages carrying shrieks of delight and terror. Maria, her heart aflutter with both excitement and fear, clung to her father as they boarded the ride.

"Don't be scared," he reassured her. "Daddy will protect you."

⌒

Alex's voice broke Mihai's reverie. "Are you okay, Doctor? You seem sad."

Mihai's mind returned from its sojourn to the past. "Yes, I'm fine, Alex. Nothing to worry about," he replied, masking his emotions.

Alex looked concerned. "I didn't mean to upset you."

"No, Alex, you did nothing of the sort." He ruffled the boy's growing hair. "I see you like superhero comics. Who is your favourite?"

"Superman!" His boyish grin reminded Mihai of his delicate age. "My dad got them for me. I like comics, though he doesn't always approve." Alex scrunched up his face, as if disapproving of his father's tastes. "My dad left a little while ago. The nurse asked him to leave, as it was past visiting hours, but my dad told her he wasn't going anywhere until he was good and ready."

"I'm sure he did."

Alex grabbed a Superman doll by the bed.

"And why is Superman your favourite?" Mihai asked.

"Because he's the strongest man in the world and nothing can hurt him."

Except kryptonite, Mihai mused.

"And he can fly," said Alex, making a swooshing noise as he lifted his figurine over his head—cape and all.

"Flying is cool. If I could choose one superpower, it would be flying," said Mihai.

"Laser beams are the coolest, though," Alex said, activating a feature on the toy that made its eyes flash red.

"That's an amazing Superman," Mihai exclaimed, sharing in Alex's excitement.

Suddenly, Alex's body convulsed, the seizure overtaking him. Mihai responded, ensuring the boy was safe within the padded confines of the bed. The seizure was brief, and Alex lay there, spent and unconscious.

"I'm sorry," Alex muttered when he regained consciousness.

"No need to apologise, Alex. That's why you're here."

Mihai extended Alex's hospital stay to thirty-six hours for comprehensive monitoring. The boy's brain activity was methodically recorded, capturing every detail of his epileptic episodes. The seizures varied in length and intensity—ranging from minutes, thrashing about like a shark on a fishing vessel, to mere seconds, with just an eye flutter.

Throughout this time, Mihai's professional observations were intertwined with a growing bond for Alex, fostering a connection beyond the doctor-patient relationship.

∽

Major-General Alexandru Lupei's arrival at the hospital was abrupt, demanding an immediate meeting with Dr Mihai Ionescu. Mihai, not one for being pushed around, made Lupei wait, attending to his existing commitments.

Twenty minutes later, under Adam's insistent direction, Mihai entered the office to find Lupei in a tense conversation with Dr Gheorghe.

"How can I assist you, Mr Lupei?" Mihai inquired.

"Your observation period has ended." The man's curt response showed his irritation.

Mihai noted the underlying anxiety beneath his stern demeanour. "I'll have the full report ready tomorrow," Mihai started, then realised that Lupei expected immediate answers. "Based on my observations, I estimate that the number of general seizures is significantly less than reported, and that about ninety percent of Alex's seizures originate from the right hemisphere."

"How certain are you, Doctor?"

"I'm confident that my estimations are closer to the mark. I stand by my judgement." Mihai never hid behind a veil of ambiguities and deflection. This was no time to start. He knew that a man like Alexandru Lupei appreciated straight talk and comprehended the world in black-and-white terms.

Lupei found Mihai's straightforwardness refreshing. *The man has balls*. He admired that. The others were cowards: they feared him. This man didn't. He wasn't sure why.

"Then, if your analysis holds, a corpus callosotomy would only marginally reduce the seizures?" Lupei questioned, grappling with the implications.

"Correct. Given the risks, I don't see a significant benefit in having the surgery."

"If you are correct," added Alexandru Lupei.

A knock at the door. An unfolding incident required that Alexandru Lupei return to the Cluj office. The giant of a man snatched his jacket off the chair. "If you hadn't kept me waiting, we could have finished our discussion here."

"Next time, make an appointment," said Mihai, unperturbed.

The big man stormed off.

∽

Alexandru Lupei opted for the corpus callosotomy in Bucharest, expressing his gratitude to the hospital and especially to Dr Ionescu for his diligence.

"Well, I guess that's that," noted Mihai.

"You're not disappointed?" inquired Adam. "I mean, the time and energy you spent this past week. Watching hours of videotape, consulting with surgeons, studying dozens of journal articles, and compiling extensive notes for your report. It was a superhuman feat."

Mihai brushed it off. "It's his decision to make," Mihai stated, though a sense of agitation lingered. The surgery, while offering some relief, might impair Alex's coordination and motor skills. Beyond the potential consequences for Alex, Mihai grappled with the rejection of his recommendations and the nagging feeling of a missed opportunity. Something within him stirred, unresolved and restless.

"The man was under immense pressure," Adam mused. "As a father, he's desperate for any measure that might ease his son's suffering, even if it reduces just a few seizures each day."

"It won't be as many as he hopes," Mihai countered with certainty. Despite his frustration, he had an inkling their paths would cross again. "Who's leading the surgery?"

"Someone mentioned Marcel Cristea," Adam replied.

"Marcel is an outstanding surgeon," said Mihai. "We went to medical school together."

5

Little Big Tower

Gaining admission to the Institute of Medicine and Pharmacy in Cluj was a formidable challenge, as the distinguished institution only accepted the brightest students, with limited placements offered. Known for his relentless work ethic and competitive spirit, Mihai ranked among the elite in his class.

His major rival was Marcel Cristea who came from a distinguished family—his father, an orthopaedic surgeon and his uncle, a former government minister. Despite his obvious advantages, Marcel's intelligence and skill were undeniable.

Studying six to seven hours a day, Mihai could not bridge the gap between himself and Marcel: placing a close second after the first exam. One more exam would determine who would claim the prestige of being named top of the graduating class. Marcel was a tormenting four percentage points ahead of Mihai. He had three weeks to devise a plan.

The university's main library provided inadequate and outdated medical texts. Mihai set his sights on the medical faculty's exclusive library, affectionately called "Mic turn mare"—little big tower. Resembling a stone tower wrapped in faded green ivy, it looked like something out of a Hans Christian Andersen fable. Access to this treasure trove was crucial for Mihai to outdo Marcel. However, this library had major restrictions on who gets access and for how long... and no books were allowed to leave the premises. And during the university break, the 'little big tower' was closed.

Under the cloak of darkness, Mihai climbed the willow tree that stood sentry by the unique library, its branches cascading over the tower like a frozen wave. As he ascended, a thunderous disturbance startled him—a swarm of fruit bats erupted from their roost, turning the sky into a black, pulsating canvas.

"Holy crap." His heart raced in tandem with the flapping wings, as he tumbled onto the grass below.

After several precarious climbs, interspersed with a cascade of profanities, Mihai reached the ajar window he had noticed earlier in the week. The climb had him whimsically wishing for Rapunzel's hair as an aid. Balancing on a creaking branch, he hurled his suitcase onto a higher fork in the tree. He steeled himself against the vertigo-inducing drop and lunged like a gibbon onto the upper branch. His initial efforts to pry open the window were futile. With a mix of desperation and determination, the stubborn window relented.

The moonlight seeped through the upper floor, casting a silver glow on the stacks of books that surrounded him, displacing the musky odour with the cool night breeze. This private sanctum housed invaluable medical texts and current research papers, accessible to a privileged few. He crouched low, avoiding the low-hanging wooden beams and cobwebs; the musty scent of aged paper filling the air.

Descending the staircase to the broader, more spacious middle floor, rows of bookshelves lined the room. The bottom floor was a tiny reception area with a couple of long tables and study areas, though it also housed many books and modern sketches and diagrams of the human body.

Settling into this clandestine library, Mihai prepared for a rigorous study marathon. He unpacked his provisions on the lower floor: food, a torch, batteries, and blankets that would serve as his makeshift bed.

His days turned into a fervent quest for learning. He delved into subjects ranging from neurosurgery to biochemistry, absorbing the wisdom of medical pioneers like Cushing and Sperry, whose experiments on split-brain epilepsy patients were renowned. He spent the evenings revising and re-reading until exhaustion overtook him, before a sudden insight propelled him up the creaky spiral staircase, as if on board an old galley on the high seas, in search of answers.

Meals were simple: bread, cheese, cured salami, fruit, and chocolate. The days melded together, marked only by his relentless pursuit of knowledge. Personal hygiene and grooming took a backseat; his long unkept hair and scruffy facial growth resembling some wild frontier man, alone and forsaken in the wilderness. Yet, the isolation never bothered him. Surrounded by the greatest medical works, Mihai found solace in their silent companionship.

On his fourth night, Mihai woke to unfamiliar sounds. His heart raced as a torchlight flickered outside the lower window. He feared discovery—either by security on a routine patrol or by chance. The muffled giggles and indistinct chatter of what sounded like teenagers. Hiding under the table, the recurrent laughter continued before it went quiet. *Moaning noise?* He couldn't be sure. The moans became consistent and rhythmic until it dawned on him. He chuckled, breathing a sigh of relief. *They're having a good time, and I'm stuck here with a bunch of dead scientists and doctors.* After what seemed forever, Mihai pulled the blanket over his head to muffle the romantic rendezvous and tried to sleep as the clock hands on the wall embraced like lovers.

By day six, Mihai slid down the banister, three books in check, and reading a fourth on descent. He came to terms with the library layout and knew where to find Sherrington's *The Integrative Action of the Nervous System*, or *Gray's Anatomy*, written by Englishman Henry Gray. Volumes of work by renowned Romanian doctors like Bagdasar and Moruzzi littered the ground floor. Mihai hopped, stepped, and jumped over a myriad of books. Finding a copy of the *Fabrica of Vesalius*, he sat on the staircase and read the rare text with great ardour before finding an interesting paper by Romanian Sofia Ionescu (no relation), the world's first female neurosurgeon.

Sofia Ionescu was a fifth-year medical intern during World War II and planned a career practising internal medicine. Surgeons were in short supply as hospitals struggled to keep up with the demands of wounded soldiers and civilians. Many required amputations as the indiscriminate bombings shattered the lives of one and all. Sofia did her best to assist the surgeons in every way possible. During a bombing raid in Bucharest, hospitals were inundated with the dead and dying. Surgeons frantically performed operations in every nook and cranny of the overfilled hospital. An eight-year-old comatose boy with an epidural hematoma was rushed through the crowded corridors of groaning bodies, needing emergency surgery. No surgeons were available. The boy was dying. Nurses pleaded for someone to operate on the child. Sofia Ionescu, exhausted and overwhelmed, raised her hand and said she could do it. The nurses balked, but neurosurgeon, Dr Bagdasar, performing a suppuration after completing three amputations, yelled to Sofia to scrub in. Thus, it came to be, that in 1944, in daring and dramatic circumstances, twenty-four-year-old Sofia Ionescu, using the drill procedure, was the first woman to perform a neurosurgical operation that saved a boy's life, and was awarded the Red Cross.

Fuelled by an insatiable thirst for knowledge and an unwavering determination to excel, Mihai devoured research papers, pharmacology, and biochemistry texts. He pondered his future in the field, aspiring to one day be mentioned alongside these medical giants.

After a week, drained but satisfied, Mihai prepared to leave the library. With his suitcase filled with 190 pages of compiled notes, he slipped out of the little big tower into the night, feeling more prepared and determined than ever to achieve his dream of becoming a surgeon: a great surgeon.

༄

By the third hour of the gruelling exam, the room had thinned out. A fifth of the students, their aspirations crumbling, had departed, defeated. The rest, including Mihai, were locked in a battle of wits with the clock. Mihai's pen flowed relentlessly across the page. A glance at Marcel Cristea revealed his rival, equally engrossed, as the final minutes ticked away.

As the examiner announced time, Mihai and Marcel simultaneously ceased writing. Their exchange of nods was a silent acknowledgment of mutual respect forged in the crucible of academic rivalry.

Two months later, the university foyer buzzed with post-summer chatter as students congregated to see their results. Mihai, a lone figure on the fringes, awaited in tense anticipation. His gaze found Marcel, ever the picture of composure. As the dean posted the results, a wave of students surged forward. Heart racing, Mihai navigated the crowd, elbowing his way to the pinboard. Above Marcel's name was his own—at the very top.

6

Borsa Castle

Dr Stela Albu, a colleague and paediatric neurologist, called Mihai with an unexpected offer. The government encouraged doctors to take a month's "residency" position in a field of medicine related to their specialty, to broaden their medical knowledge. Dr Stela had to withdraw from one of those positions when a family emergency arose.

"I know it's short notice, but I thought I'd try, knowing your interest in psychiatry. The hospital knows who you are and they're happy to have you. It's a four-week graveyard shift and not too long a drive. The extra money is handy," Dr Stela said, "and you can go home on Sundays."

The government-backed initiative allowed doctors to keep their regular salaries while earning additional income. Mihai had a few days to prepare, his desk already a testament to his busy schedule.

Borsa Psychiatric Hospital, housed in an erstwhile castle in Cluj County was his destination. The three-and-a-half-hour drive led to a structure steeped in history but marred by decay. Once a resplendent summer residence of the Hungarian Bánffy family, the nineteenth-century building had since lost its former glory. The once lush estate now lay barren, its statues and gardens succumbing to the ravages of time.

The castle's past was tumultuous. During World War II, it served as a sanctuary for wounded German soldiers, a decision that distressed Miklós Bánffy, who detested the Nazi war machine. In their hasty retreat, the German army left the estate in ruins.

The ensuing Communist takeover resulted in the exile of the Bánffy family, and according to legend, the Baroness, assisted by gypsies, cursed the estate, designating it as a madhouse for future occupants.

As Mihai approached the foreboding structure, he couldn't help but feel the weight of its history, the stories of its past imprinted in its crumbling walls.

Ward B, where Dr Mihai Ionescu was assigned, presented a picture of bleak functionality. Its arch doorway led into a narrow room lined with low-lying beds, each accompanied by a plain bedside table. High, narrow windows, tethered by short chains, offered meagre light and scant ventilation. The rusted underbellies of some of the beds revealed exposed springs and corroded hand cranks—remnants of World War II.

Next to the main building stood a low-ceiling sandstone lodge, refitted with guest rooms, and used for storage and administrative offices. Mihai's quarters were modest: a bunk bed, a simple table with chairs, and a two-seater sofa. His files crowded the table, while basic kitchen amenities occupied the rest of the space; the brown lino flooring added to the room's austere ambiance.

Sipping instant coffee mixed with long-life milk, Mihai delved into patient files in the communal office before one of the nurses escorted him around the ward. A security guard gave a faint nod as he walked the halls, a necessary precaution against violent inmates.

Romulus Veres, an infamous serial killer in Transylvania who killed his victims with a hammer, awaited transfer to the Stei psychiatric facility. "You!" he shouted at Mihai from a holding cell behind the main office. "You are rolling dice with Satan himself!" Romulus banged his shaved head against the bars until his protruding forehead drew blood. "He will die," the man hissed. "This game of yours will end in death! Death for him and death for you!" The crazed man howled like a wolf during a full harvest moon while he rattled the cell bars. Mihai approached the deranged madman, meeting his gaze, and whispered in his ear. Romulus listened as his eyes bulged, sending him retreating to the back of the cell.

While roaming the hospital floor, Mihai was surprised by the lack of visitors.

"Families rarely visit," the nurse explained. "This place is often used to abandon the elderly, alcoholics, and those who are uncontrollable, leaving them to wither away in neglect."

The hospital's state of disrepair reflected this grim reality. Peeling paint, cracked walls, and piles of crumbling plaster overshadowed impressive ceilings and ornaments. The large, draughty spaces were a challenge to keep warm and disrepair abundantly apparent. It was more akin to a psychiatric gulag than a hospital, with its overcrowded wards and outdated equipment.

Reviewing patient histories, Mihai noticed a disturbing pattern. Many patients were medicated before any psychiatric evaluation, thus, receiving treatment without a diagnosis. Among them were political dissidents, hospitalised by force and drugged into submission. The institution reeked of malpractice and misuse of power, a dark blight on the medical profession.

In the dead of night, Mihai made his rounds through the hospital's murky corridors. In the dining room, a towering figure in a blue hospital gown raged against invisible foes, his head thudding against the wall.

"Never mind him," said the nurse. "His name is Bogdan. He has been here forever. Trust me, it's best to let him be. He'll calm down soon enough."

The nurse's nonchalant reaction to the man struck Mihai as a sign of the ward's desensitisation to such scenes.

A closer inspection of Ward B revealed a disturbing discovery: lice infested the beds and danced from patient to patient in a made-to-order cesspool of lice idyll. Mihai felt an overwhelming urge to scratch himself.

Three nurses sipped tea and chatted in the kitchen.

"Don't you have anything to do?" Mihai asked in an accusatory tone. "The place is filthy, and you stand around doing nothing! You will strip the beds and wash every sheet in this ward. Do you understand?"

No reply.

"Do you understand?!"

"But patients are sleeping and…"

"Wake them!" he yelled.

They jumped, as did several sleeping patients.

"Anything else?" he said, daring them to retort. "Is there anything else?"

Mihai ordered everyone out of bed, roaming the aisles like a bloodhound on a trail. Nurses piled sheets, blankets, and pillowcases into the hallway, creating a mountain of stifling stench that only worsened. Patients complained and protested at being awakened by this strange man. The doctor left the nurses dumbstruck, though some knew of his reputation. They herded twenty-six patients into the dining area and provided them with hot tea, while another group of nurses, led by Mihai, went down to the laundry.

Halfway down the hallway, with one foot propped up against the wall, a young woman, sucking a lollipop, watched the night's activities with mild amusement. Wearing a thin pyjama that extended below her knee, and an oversized pea-green jumper that fell off her shoulders, the young patient rolled the lollipop in her mouth with passive indifference. She had a mousy face, with sharp, elegant features, and stood five feet two inches tall. Her short, jagged black hair exposed a string of earrings that ran the length of one ear, while her nose sometimes sparkled when the light struck her tiny nose-ring. The slender frame and size gave her an almost boyish, childlike appearance, yet her demeanour belied her looks. As Mihai crossed her path, he gave the aloof young woman an intense, deathly stare before winking. Her lollipop drooped, almost falling out of her mouth as she stared until he reached the end of the hallway.

Six rusted washing machines stood in the dank basement of the hospital, though they were the biggest damn things Mihai had ever seen—dinosaurs from a bygone era. However, only three were in working order. He stormed back upstairs.

"Tomas!" he yelled. While scanning files that morning, Mihai recalled that Tomas Bencic had been a mechanic. "I need you to fix a washing machine. Can you do it?"

Tomas just stared. In his late fifties and having bipolar disorder, the man was hard to read. Mihai wasn't sure whether Tomas understood a word he said, as the one-time mechanic stood there, wearing a stained white singlet beneath his open robe and wafer-thin slippers. Frustrated and pressed for time, Mihai was about to move on when Tomas spoke.

"During the war, a Russian tank rolled by our village," he said. "I was a young apprentice mechanic at the time."

Mihai had no time to reminisce and listen to old war stories.

"The tank broke down and sat for hours. The Russians were running about, trying to fix it. We gathered round and watched the spectacle. The army captain asked if anyone could help. I stepped forward. I'd never seen a tank, but it had an engine, belt, sparks, and plugs, and these things I knew. In an hour, the Russians were on their merry way." A faint smile crossed his lips. "They gave me a bottle of vodka. Those damn Russians gave me a bottle of vodka." The reminiscence brought a fleeting smile to his face. "So yes, I can fix your damn washing machine."

With Tomas's affirmation, Mihai ordered a thorough cleansing of Ward B. Linens were laundered, bedsheets and blankets disinfected, and lice checks scheduled. Discovering blankets and soap in a locked cabinet, Mihai kicked the cabinet door open, determined to improve the patients' living conditions.

꒰꒱

The following night, most patients slept soundly, except for a few who roamed in their undergarments, lost in their own world. An old lady, wrapped in a blanket, approached Mihai and rubbed his arm affectionately.

"Cristian," she said as her little sausage hands reached for Mihai's cheek. "You must visit your mama more often. I sit by the window waiting for you, but you never come, and I eat alone. But I am glad you're here now." She placed her head against Mihai's arm. "Will you stay for dinner? I made your favourite pumpkin soup."

"Of course, I'll stay," replied Mihai, as she smiled before wandering off.

In the common room, the patients stared vacantly at a flickering black-and-white television. President Ceausescu's portrait hung on the wall, overlooking his "beloved" citizens. One wiry young man named Pavel sat on a sofa chair, cross-legged like a Turk, puffing on a hand-rolled cigarette, while an unlit cigarette rested in his other hand. Pavel became a chain smoker after being admitted to Borsa Hospital with alcohol poisoning. When alcohol was no longer available, or affordable, Pavel resorted to drinking methylated spirits, which not only affected his physical health but caused mild brain damage. He now smoked thirty cigarettes a day and spent his time re-reading outdated issues of *Magazin Istoric*. The smoke-filled rooms added another layer of depression that suffocated its inhabitants.

Amidst his duties of reviewing files and reports, Mihai found his thoughts drifting back to Alexandru Lupei and Alex, wondering about the outcome of the surgery.

While discussing medications with a nurse, Mihai noticed the young female patient with the short black hair staring at him in the dining hall.

"Can't sleep?" he asked.

No reply. Casually biting her nails, she shrugged and turned away.

"I can't sleep either when a full moon's out," he said.

She glanced out the window.

"It brings out the werewolf in me," Mihai said.

She gave a faint smile. "I better get my silver bullet out."

Mihai smiled back. "Best to save that silver bullet for when you need it."

As he continued his rounds, he came across a patient doubled over in an armchair in front of the television, his body tilted so far over that his head touched the ground and his right arm pointed to the ceiling. The man suffered from catatonic schizophrenia. Some patients with this condition often experienced periods of rigidity and stupor, which could last days, as their bodies locked into extraordinary positions while in a comatose state, while others had mobility and made loud, repetitive noises. Mihai recalled a man who paced up and down the hospital corridor, making cock-a-doodle-doo sounds for hours on end.

At dawn, before ending his shift, Mihai checked on his ward, and heard a whimper emanating from a bed against the far wall.

"Hey," he whispered. "Ces-a intamplat?"

The young woman did not react.

"What's wrong?" he asked again. He recognised the mousy face and short black hair. "My name is Mihai Ionescu."

Still no response.

"We've already met, but I don't know your name."

He waited. "Anyway, I…"

"Olga. My name is Olga Zamfir."

"Nice to meet you, Olga. Can't sleep?"

She looked out the window. "Full moon, remember?"

He grinned. "My grandmother's name was Olga. She used to give me all kinds of sweets when I was a child."

Olga raised her knees to her chest and wrapped her arms around her legs.

"Are you from here?" Mihai asked.

Olga gave the doctor an absurd look. She told him that she had never been outside her hometown. "I almost went to Bucharest." A distant smile crossed her face. "But when they took my father away, we had no money to go anywhere."

A disgruntled patient in the neighbouring bed didn't appreciate the disruptive chatter. Mihai and Olga looked at each other and giggled like schoolchildren.

The splotchy, pale skin, emaciated frame, sunken eyes and cracked lips hid Olga's beauty. Her unusual, heterochronic eyes caught Mihai's attention: one hazel, the other a hyacinth blue.

"How old are you, Olga?"

"Nineteen. Are you really a doctor?"

"Da," he answered. "Why do you ask?"

"Well," she said, shifting in her bed, "you don't act like a doctor."

"What does that mean?" His puzzled expression invited her to continue.

"You cuss and boss everyone around, but you give a crap."

He was better looking than most doctors. Handsome enough, but something captivating: a presence, an assuredness, a strength. A confident gait that few carried. And his clean-shaven face and baby skin added a touch of softness that juxtaposed the intensity in his China-blue eyes. His short hair did not do his curls justice, and his sharp receding hairline somehow suited him.

Mihai chuckled.

"What's funny?" she asked.

"I'm not sure everyone would agree with your appraisal."

"I saw you bitch out the nurses. That was pretty cool."

"I don't think cool was the effect I was going for."

Her confidence grew as the wall around her dissolved. "So, people think you're an asshole?" The question held no malice.

He liked Olga. "Some would say worse than that."

She liked him back. "Is that how you see yourself?" Had she crossed a line in asking such a question?

"When I need to be."

She looked at him longer than she should have. "Like the other night, when you tore the house down?"

"Just like that."

"That was awesome, by the way."

"I'm glad you approve."

"But you were justified. I mean, they never wash the sheets. And the smell. Well, don't get me started."

Mihai couldn't disagree. *What are you doing here, Olga? Is there a history of mental illness? Had some trauma set you off? Alcohol or drug addiction?* He didn't notice any obvious signs. But these questions could wait while he got to know Olga Zamfir. There is a person behind every disease and illness, he recalled his associate professor telling him during his medical school days.

Olga's gaze was inquisitive, trying to decipher Mihai. No easy task. "I don't know who you are, mister, to come here and rip into everybody, but you don't fool me for a minute." She placed her pillow on her lap, smacking the middle to form a comfortable groove.

"Call me Mihai."

"You stalk the ward like a crazed werewolf, but deep inside, I think you're a teddy bear."

Mihai smiled at her perception. "Get some rest now, Olga," he said, tucking her in, feeling an unexpected paternal instinct.

"Thanks for not asking why I'm here," Olga called out as he turned to leave.

"What's your favourite lollipop flavour?"

Her face lit up. "The green ones."

∽

Back in his room, Mihai prepared a cup of tea, slicing a lemon into the dark brew. As dawn broke, he settled at his cluttered table, his thoughts on Olga. He found her file. "So, Olga Zamfir, let's see what brought you to Borsa Hospital."

He pursed his lips and shook his head. Olga did not receive the care and treatment required. Administered with high doses of anti-psychotic drugs, therapy twice a week, and a psychiatric evaluation after six months, Mihai found sporadic traces of her therapy sessions and nothing on her six-month evaluation. Nor could he find the doctor assigned to her case. Her file showed several medical staff signing off documents—not too unusual. But no one oversaw her case, which raised alarm bells. Olga had fallen through large cracks. He then checked her visitor's record and noticed that an aunt had visited twice. It also appeared that her mother tried to visit, but Olga refused to see her.

The next night, after discussions with the hospital psychiatrist, Mihai sought Olga again. "How long have you been here?" he asked, knowing the answer.

"Thirteen months," she replied, her tone bitter.

"Are you getting better?"

"Better? You're joking, right? This place is filthy and cold. The food is disgusting, and they pump us with drugs. I can't remember the last time I had a fucking shower with soap until you showed up!"

Mihai did not expect the vitriol. He felt a pang of sympathy for her plight.

He cautiously broached the subject of her arrival at the hospital. Olga hesitated, wary of his intentions. To ease her apprehension, he offered her a mug of hot chocolate and waited patiently until she spoke.

"When I was fourteen, after Father's arrest, we lived with my uncle in his two-bedroom apartment. My mother and little sis slept in one room, while I had the other. My widowed uncle slept in the lounge. Without him, we would've been on the streets."

Olga bit on her worn-down thumbnail, bracing for something difficult. "About a year later, Father died in a labour camp on the Black Sea Canal." She choked up. "I miss him." She looked away. "Six months later, my uncle started coming to my room at night." She blinked, sending tears trickling down her pale face. "Mother told me we should be grateful." She scoffed.

"Six months later, my uncle started coming to my room at night."

"She knew?" Mihai asked.

"She knew. I ran away but came back to protect my sister. So, he raped me about once a month, sometimes more. After a while, it became part and parcel of everyday life," she said, shrugging her shoulders.

Mihai pressed his lips and shook his head.

"I got pregnant." She wiped her sleeve across her face. "There was no way in hell I was having that baby—his baby." A strong conviction resounded in her voice. "Abortions were illegal, though a doctor hinted that we could make certain arrangements."

"Did you tell your uncle?"

"No!" She kicked off her blanket. "I had a fucking official question me about my pregnancy. Can you believe that?"

Mihai believed it. The government devised a plan to yield more workers—make abortions illegal. They required doctors to report pregnant women to the authorities and assigned officials to watch over them. In fact, they subjected women under forty to mandatory medical exams, and suspicious miscarriages were investigated, with criminal charges pending.

"Did you inform the authorities?" The law made allowances for rape, especially in cases of incest.

"I tried, but they didn't believe me. The Securitate officer said it was a ploy by women to abort." Olga hesitated, judging whether to reveal her secrets to this stranger. "One night, I take a steel coat hanger, straighten the hook and flatten the other side as best I can. I turn the cold water on, sit on the shower floor, stuff a washcloth in my mouth and insert the hanger, stabbing it deep inside me over and over again." Olga is crying but does not flinch.

Mihai admired her courage in telling her traumatic story.

"The pain was excruciating, and the washcloth muffled my screams. Thick dark clots oozed out of me and mixed with the running water, forming crimson spirals like a messed up Van Gogh painting." Despite her anguish, she felt compelled to share her story. "My body shivered while my insides burned. I stabbed with both hands, thrusting the makeshift weapon deep: a brutal act of butchery, mutilation, and termination. I wanted to expel this violation from me. My womanhood was ripped and torn, yet it seemed to welcome the pain. It was a tragic yet poetic end. I was on the brink of passing out, but I couldn't stop. My insides felt raw. Finally, I dropped the hanger onto the cold, hard floor and sat motionless, feeling close to death, a relief of sorts. I closed my eyes, hoping it would all end soon. I remember hearing screams." Olga's face, marred by sorrow, revealed her pain as snot trickled over her thin lips. "I killed my baby," she whimpered, her stoicism replaced by soul-crushing guilt and angst. She sobbed into her pillow. "I killed my baby."

Mihai embraced her, comforting her through the subsiding sobs and staggered breaths.

Olga recounted waking in the hospital, her mother and uncle by her side. Her mother knitted a jumper, grateful for the distraction. "Mum made some tea. My uncle, the pig, hid behind his newspaper, sighing as if burdened by my presence. When my mother stepped out, I got out of bed, grabbed her knitting needles, and thrust them through the newspaper into his chest."

This did not surprise Mihai. The girl had spirit.

"I stabbed him repeatedly. His fingers clawed at my face, drawing blood, but I didn't relent. The horror of the shower returned in a wave of déjà vu. He toppled over, and I fell atop him. The bastard restrained one arm, but I continued to stab his corpulent body with my free arm. Hospital staff rushed in. I kicked and screamed, my head spinning until I passed out."

He enfolded Olga's delicate hands in his large, bear-like palms—hands that could protect or destroy.

"I've told no one the details of what happened." The abrasive young woman disappeared, replaced by a sad, frightened girl in need of love and reassurance.

Mihai wiped his face, his tears mingling with the stubble of his two-day growth.

"I tried to escape this place," she confessed. "The second time, a patient ratted on me. They put me in a straitjacket."

Appalled and enraged, Mihai had absorbed the details of Olga's escape attempts and her confrontation with her uncle. Her file painted her as psychotic, suicidal, and a threat to herself and society. To the judge's credit, he had opted for a psychiatric facility over prison for her attempted murder charge. The report hinted at promiscuity and suggested her delusional state had misdirected blame on her uncle. Mihai, however, questioned the validity of these claims. Reviewing Olga's medication, he was struck by the dosage being prescribed. With such quantities, she should have been almost catatonic. And then it dawned on him. She wasn't taking them.

∽

Nights were tranquil, affording Mihai the opportunity to delve into psychiatric case studies and seeking insights from resident psychiatrists.

After visiting Olga, Mihai retreated to his office, intending to research the genetic and infectious factors in paediatric epilepsy. His thoughts were interrupted by a gentleman in his eighties, lost in the melodies of Edith Piaf's "La Vie En Rose." The man swayed back and forth, his right arm outstretched, his left encircling an unseen partner. Transported to a bygone era, he moved with a charm and rhythm that belied his age, swaying in sync with Piaf's melodious voice. Mihai watched, captivated by this poignant scene, wondering what memories it evoked in the old man's heart.

"Hurry, Doctor!" A nurse's urgent voice shattered the tranquillity. "It's Bogdan. He's attacked another patient, and we can't find him."

So much for the serene interlude.

"How is the patient?" Mihai inquired.

"Badly shaken. Bogdan bit his ear off."

A search was organised. The guard scoured the north wing while Mihai descended into the basement.

"Be careful," yelled the nurse.

Mihai navigated the narrow hallway, checking each room. He heard scratching noises from one of the rooms as his hand gripped the door handle. He entered. Plaster boards, paint cans, and neglected shelves cluttered the room, emitting a musty scent of mildew. Disturbing the plastic sheets, he was besieged by a horde of rats. One leaped onto his shoulder. He screamed and flung it against the wall. His eyes wide with panic, he fought off the rodents scrambling over his feet, ran out and slammed the door behind him.

Regaining his composure, he proceeded to the last room in the basement. The door creaked open. He braced himself for another rat onslaught.

"Jesus!"

Bogdan hung from the ceiling; his lifeless legs swaying above a toppled chair. Mihai lunged forward, grasping Bogdan's legs, his shouts unheard in the basement depths. Bogdan's face had swelled, a grotesque shade of red, his tongue protruding, purplish and swollen. The belt around his neck constricted his jugular veins and carotid arteries, starving his brain of oxygen and blood, while simultaneously crushing his windpipe. Contrary to popular belief, death by hanging was seldom swift; it was often a prolonged, torturous ordeal.

Mihai needed all his strength to keep the pressure off Bogdan's neck. He awkwardly shuffled the chair towards him with his foot, all the while clutching Bogdan's legs to his chest; the stench of urine from Bogdan's soiled pyjamas filled his nostrils. After several exhausting attempts, he clambered onto the chair. Straining to reach the belt, his hands flailed, desperately trying to unhook the belt from the beam.

Bogdan's body slipped, tightening the noose. "Damn it!" His shoulder throbbed, his fingers trembled, and his calves burned as he fumbled for the hook. With one final effort, he unhooked the belt, sending both men crashing to the floor. Mihai screamed as Bogdan landed on top of him, sending searing pain through his shoulder. Full of adrenaline, the doctor began compressions, inadvertently breaking ribs, before administering life-saving breaths. Collapsing onto his back, Mihai lay there, spent, waiting for staff to arrive.

∽

"You did what!" Olga exclaimed, incredulous, as she lounged in the dining hall.

"You heard me," Mihai replied, his left arm in a sling.

Olga uncrossed her legs, straightening up. "You saved him. Bogdan, of all people. Are you out of your mind?"

Mihai gestured exasperatedly with his good arm. "That's all I've been hearing! 'Why save him?' 'You could've waited a little longer.'"

The staff were less than thrilled at Bogdan's resuscitation. His rap sheet was extensive: assaulting patients, harassing staff, property destruction, and cruelty to animals. He once found kittens under the building and crushed their heads against the wall. Yet, despite being sedated and often restrained, he remained a menacing presence.

"You know, I expected a medal, or at least some recognition. Instead, I'm met with condemnation and reprimand for saving that bastard!" Mihai's laughter boomed, his face turning beet red.

"Yeah," Olga chimed in, her tone laced with sarcasm. "What was the doctor thinking, trying to save someone? God, couldn't you let a man achieve his goal?"

Their laughter rang out, childlike and unrestrained. A nurse, prepared to scold the disruptive patients, halted upon spotting Dr Mihai Ionescu. She shot him a stern look, wagged her finger, then retreated. The pair exchanged glances and erupted into even louder laughter.

When their laughter subsided, Olga inquired about his arm.

"The shoulder's dislocated, but should heal in a week or two," he replied.

As a male nurse passed by, Olga cursed him under her breath.

"What was that about?" Mihai asked.

"Not long after I got here, that weasel groped me. I grabbed him by the balls and squeezed hard. He is hollering and squealing like a bitch in heat, but I won't let go. Staff came running, causing quite the scene." Olga shook her head in bemusement. "But he makes a complaint, saying how I attacked him unprovoked. The hospital took his side, of course. It's bullshit. But I told him if he ever came near me again, I would slit his balls off."

"He hasn't bothered you since?"

"Hell, no."

Those who underestimated Olga Zamfir did so at their peril.

Changing the subject, Mihai asked, "How are the nurses treating you?"

She shrugged. "They do their job. But," she prodded, "I've heard they're not too fond of you."

"And how did you stumble upon this important piece of information?" His patronising tone did not stop her from continuing.

"Well, I hear them talking and they tell me stuff."

"They tell you stuff?"

"When I ask."

"Well, I'd say that nurses should refrain from divulging their personal opinions about doctors to patients."

Olga waited for him to take the bait, but he didn't bite. She relented. "You want to know what they say?"

"Not particularly."

She did not let his lack of enthusiasm get in her way. "Well," she said, sounding childlike, "they say you're rude, obnoxious, and arrogant."

"You forgot crude, vociferous, belligerent, churlish, stubborn, and a pain in the ass," Mihai added, handing her a bag of green lollipops.

"Why are you nice to me?" Her tone softened.

"Because I am nice," he whispered conspiratorially. "But keep it between us."

"Do you want to fuck me?"

Though shocked, Mihai had heard it before. Patients sometimes offered their bodies for preferential treatment or for payments they could not afford. Some doctors could not resist the temptation.

Olga's expression turned to fear. "I'm so sorry," she blurted out, rueful at what she said.

Mihai, unfazed, looked at her earnestly. "Olga, you have potential that shouldn't be wasted. This system has failed you, but I intend to make things right. You deserve better." His sincerity and compassion filled her with pride and hope; something she gave up on years ago.

~

Mihai's advocacy for Olga took the form of a vehement report to the hospital director and the Ministry of Health. Frustrated by the lack of action, he also reached out to Judge Dan Grigorescu, the one who had sentenced Olga to the hospital. He highlighted the negligence in her case. The judge, appalled by the oversight, engaged in a lengthy discussion with Mihai about duty and caring for the less fortunate.

Mihai confronted the hospital director with a barrage of accusations: "negligence," "incompetence." As the director retorted, Mihai escalated his critique to include staff misconduct, demanding a legal investigation. "How can you justify chaining patients to their beds, abandoning them in their own waste? Is this a Soviet-era gulag? And let's not overlook the sexual assault and misconduct allegations. I intend to inform the Politburo members about these transgressions in their state-funded institution. Perhaps even Major-General Alexandru Lupei from the Securitate should know, given he's both a patient and friend of mine."

The director, despite his political connections, was visibly shaken, unable to counter Mihai's relentless onslaught. But Mihai didn't stop there. He reached out to Minister Razvan Funar, an old tennis companion from Bucharest. The Minister's inquiries sent ripples through the hospital administration. If that wasn't enough, Judge Grigorescu sent the hospital director a scathing letter, threatening legal action.

The result was immediate. Borsa Hospital discharged Olga Zamfir, declaring her "cured" and no longer a threat to herself or society. The court documentation specified that a psychiatrist, recommended by Dr Mihai Ionescu, would oversee Olga's outpatient care.

❧

"You ready to go?" Mihai asked.

Dressed in jeans, sneakers, and a black t-shirt, Olga nodded emphatically. Her aunt waited downstairs.

"I'll stay with my aunt for a bit until I sort things out. She's offered to have me, but I don't want to impose."

"Have you spoken to your mum?"

"She wants to talk, but I'm not there yet."

Mihai nodded, understanding her need for space.

"You sure shook things up around here," she said.

"That's what werewolves do, right?"

"Just remember," she said with a playful smirk, "I've still got that silver bullet."

"Keep it safe. You might need it someday." Mihai smiled, then gestured towards the exit. "Let's get you out of here."

Olga dropped her bag and hugged him tight. Mihai winced at the pain in his shoulder.

"How can I ever thank you?" she whispered, not wanting to let go.

Mihai knelt, placing his hands on her arms. "Don't look back. Pursue your dreams and live a life that's yours. That's all the thanks I need." His voice trembled. "You were let down by a system riddled with corruption, and I regret being a part of that. I'm sorry we failed you."

Olga Zamfir looked into his eyes, now seeing a friend, not a figure of authority. "You didn't fail me. You're my fucking hero." She kissed his cheek, wiped her tears unashamedly, picked up her bag and never looked back.

7

Indecent Proposal

While swaying on the backyard swing, Mihai noticed the tree sap leaking golden blood, while the ground beneath the apple tree was dappled with its blossom. His thoughts turned to Olga. Despite the world's unkindness, he believed in her fortitude to find meaning in life. Before departing Borsa Hospital, he had arranged for a psychiatrist to aid Olga in confronting her traumatic past. He hoped she would find closure and wondered if he could too.

～

A summons from Alexandru Lupei beckoned Mihai to downtown Cluj. Despite a backlog of patients, he had little choice but to leave work by mid-afternoon and accept the man's invitation.

The building was nondescript, nestled between a family-run tobacconist and a linen store. It was an unassuming three-storey structure, with a modest gold-plated plaque by the door. Just two streets from the police station, this building served as the Securitate's hub for routine administrative tasks, enquiries, and background checks, functioning much like any other government department.

Inside, the ground floor was sparse and utilitarian, furnished with white plastic tables and chairs, a small front counter manned by a solitary employee. A carpeted staircase, partially hidden, led to the upper floors. The bare walls and minimal furnishings exuded an air of artificiality. Footsteps reverberated from above.

Mihai had braced himself for this meeting during his tenure at Borsa Hospital. Though a sense of dread gnawed at him, he was clear about his purpose. He rolled his left shoulder and moaned.

Major-General Alexandru Lupei, clad in a short-sleeved white shirt, appeared with no preamble. "You were right, and they were wrong," he declared.

Lupei detailed how the corpus callosotomy on his son had failed to produce significant results, as Mihai predicted. The procedure, which involved severing nerve fibres connecting the brain's hemispheres, had only minimally reduced the frequency of Alex's seizures.

"I trusted them, though my gut told me otherwise. They split my son's skull open—for next to nothing. My decision-making process became hindered due to my emotional involvement in the case," he said, as if stating a notice or declaration to self.

"We were all working with the best information we had," Mihai responded diplomatically.

"You're being modest, Doctor. It does not suit you." The Major-General unbuttoned his shirt. "Most of the surgeons I spoke to said that your proposal of removing half my son's brain is madness. They say the surgery is dangerous and in its infancy as a medical procedure.

The evidence of success is scant, and best performed on children under five."

Mihai acknowledged the dangers but maintained his stance on the surgery's potential. "Every surgery carries risks. Regarding the age, I believe five years is a conservative threshold."

Alexandru Lupei continued to read his notes. "From the case studies available, its success is questionable." The Major-General raised his finger as Mihai tried to intercede. "Yes, there are successes. But there are many failures, with death rates above twenty percent."

"Yes, the surgery is fraught with risk," Mihai conceded. "Many of the deaths stem from surgical errors, rather than the procedure itself."

Alexandru Lupei raised an eyebrow.

"Bleeding, especially in children with limited blood volumes, is a significant concern. We're talking about a fifteen-hour operation. The longer they're on the table, the more they bleed. It requires a surgeon with velvet hands and nerves of steel, particularly when navigating near the hippocampus and hypothalamus." Mihai paused, letting the gravity of his words sink in as he rubbed his aching shoulder. "Mr Lupei, Alex's current situation is untenable. The question is, does the potential benefit outweigh the risk?" He saw the confusion in Lupei's eyes. "Undergoing the procedure means Alex will lose function in his left arm and vision in his left field. Rehabilitation will be arduous. Despite the need to relearn basic skills, his left brain will adapt to perform right brain functions. He might walk, run, and play again, albeit at a moderate level."

Those words were like a piercing light that penetrated Alexandru Lupei's black soul. The big man had plenty to digest.

"Of course, there's always a chance of failure, even death. I'd be remiss to suggest otherwise. You need to consider these factors. Have you discussed this with Alex?"

Lupei's expression revealed the fear inherent in any father's heart and told of his wife's struggle to conceive. When she miraculously fell pregnant, Alex became their miracle and beacon of hope.

"Alex is young, Doctor. How can I pose such questions to a child?"

"Alex understands more than you might think. We've discussed many profound topics, including mortality. He's aware of his condition. If you talk to him, I believe he will express his wishes."

Lupei excused himself, returning with a folder and bottle of wine. "It's the end of the working day. Let's drink, shall we?" He poured the wine into plastic cups. "I've reviewed your file." Such scrutiny was standard for the Secret Police. "We share similar beginnings, both born on farms, both losing our mothers at a young age. Do you remember her?"

Suddenly, they were kinsmen.

Mihai found the question unexpected. His mother was a kind soul with a voice like an angel. "I remember her vividly. She passed during childbirth, and the baby didn't survive either." He sipped the wine, welcoming its numbing effect. "We couldn't afford a doctor. By the time one arrived, it was too late."

"Is that why you became a doctor?"

Mihai shrugged. "It's a common assumption, but not the reason." He recalled kneeling by his mother's bedside, her laboured breathing filling the room alongside the crackle of the fireplace.

"So, when did you move to Cluj, Doctor?"

"Two months after my mother's death. My younger sister had died eating poisonous mushrooms two years before that. My father had had enough. He sold the farm and took us to our ancestral home in Cluj. I reside there still."

Alexandru Lupei read over Mihai's file. "Graduated top of your class in medical school and a top junior tennis player in Transylvania. A man adept with both scalpel and tennis racket," he remarked, attempting light-heartedness.

Mihai, however, remained stoic, feeling a sense of violation at having his life so casually scrutinised.

"Did you always receive top grades in school?" Lupei asked.

"Da."

"Are you sure? It seems you did not have an aptitude for languages."

Mihai detected a hint of sarcasm. He spoke French, English, Hungarian, German, and, of course, Romanian.

"The report showed you had difficulties with the Russian language."

Mihai felt a sting at the mention. His defiance, a protest against the Soviet influence over his country.

"Yes," he affirmed, his stance unchanged.

The big man leaned forward; his tone laced with insinuation. "Any reason for your aversion to our Soviet allies?"

Mihai shifted, uncomfortable with this probing. "Mr Lupei, I doubt my language skills are pertinent, considering your son's situation."

Lupei's expression hardened. "I don't need reminding of my son's situation."

Mihai regretted his words but felt his patience waning.

"What is it about our Soviet brothers you begrudge?" Lupei pressed.

Mihai was not one to be intimidated, but Lupei's presence was unsettling. "It's their politics, not the people, that I find distasteful."

"And our system? Does it evoke the same sentiment?" Lupei inquired, his gaze sharp.

Mihai had no allegiance to this man, nor did he fear him, though he understood the power he held. It was not in his nature to be intimidated, though the man across the table disturbed that equipoise. Unflinching, he met Lupei's stare. "They are the same to me."

Lupei's smile was cold, almost predatory. "Your candour is... intriguing. But tell me, what leaves such a bitter taste?"

Mihai took a sip of his wine, weighing his words. Opting for honesty, he met Lupei's eyes. "I abhor everything about this Communist regime. Their actions have ravaged our country, devastated countless lives. I blame them for the loss of my daughter. My disdain is boundless." His raw honesty took Lupei aback.

The tragedy he referenced harked back to the late 1950s and early 60s, during the rollout of the polio vaccine. Polio, a devastating illness that had tormented humanity for millennia, preyed on children with weakened immune systems, leading to paralysis, breathing difficulties, and often death.

The bureaucratic mismanagement of the polio vaccine was a scandal of tragic proportions. Vital supplies trickled in, often diverted to the privileged or lost in forgotten storage facilities. Unrefrigerated and sun-exposed shipments from the Soviet Union compromised the vaccine's efficacy. The haphazard scheduling and mishandling of patient records meant many never completed their vaccination series, with doses administered well beyond recommended intervals. This gross negligence led to the deaths of thousands.

Among the victims was Mihai's four-year-old daughter, Maria Ionescu. Her symptoms began with stomach pain, vomiting, and fever, before escalating to respiratory infection. Diagnosed with polio, Maria had received only the initial vaccine dose, missing the critical follow-up because of administrative delays. Paralysis crept up her right leg, leading to meningitis and complete immobilisation as the virus ravaged her spinal neurons. Dependent on an iron lung, her ability to breathe and swallow waned.

Mihai's recollections of those last weeks were agonising. Maria held on until Christmas, a bittersweet miracle. While the world celebrated, the Ionescu family held a vigil in a quarantined hospital room. Mihai, a junior surgeon, spent every moment beside her, sleeping fitfully on a makeshift bed. Irina arrived each morning, barred from overnight stays by hospital regulations. She prayed, sang, and comforted Maria, bringing a cassette player that filled the room with Christmas carols. Mihai and Irina clung to their daughter, their smiles a façade to mask their pain, cherishing every moment with her. Mihai often stepped outside to collapse in the hospital corridors, overwhelmed by grief. Despite the infectious nature of polio, neither parent contracted it. But this was not the miracle they desired. On Christmas night, as "I Heard the Bells on Christmas Day" played and snowflakes fell over Cluj, Maria's struggle ended. Her dreams of circuses and outgrowing her school shoes remained unfulfilled. She took her last breath and died.

Alexandru Lupei listened to Mihai's impassioned words, familiar with the criticisms.

"I've imprisoned men for less than you've just said."

"Are you planning to arrest me?" Mihai's voice carried a defiant edge. Any reservations he had about confronting the Major-General vanished, fuelled by the resurgence of his daughter's memory.

Lupei's smirk was chilling. "I am aware of your loss. It was unfortunate."

"No, not unfortunate—it was avoidable!" Mihai's stare hardened into shards of ice. "Amidst the crucial need for vaccinations, this regime—through its sheer ineptitude—decided bureaucrats should manage medical programs. The resulting fiasco was not just deplorable, it was criminal. Those bastards should have hung for crimes against humanity. Every single last one of them!" His voice thundered through the room, prompting agents to hurtle down the stairs. A dismissive gesture from Alexandru Lupei sent them retreating.

"And when my daughter—" Mihai's voice cracked as he battled his sorrow. "When she needed an iron lung, there were none, despite stockpiles rotting in storage!"

Mihai and a group of audacious doctors had once 'liberated' several machines from a government warehouse, an act of defiance born of desperation.

He had pleaded with every official within reach, including the Minister of Health, clamouring for the vital distribution of the vaccine, only to be met with silence. When tainted vaccines in the United States led to catastrophe, it only exacerbated the inertia, fuelling pointless debates over vaccine efficacy.

In a last, frantic bid, Mihai had performed an unauthorised blood transfusion from a polio survivor, hoping against hope to save his daughter's life.

"I watched my little girl take her final breath," he confessed, towering over Lupei, his condemnation unmistakable.

Lupei's expression softened. "I share your indignation. With my son's life in peril, empathy is not a luxury, but a necessity. Our government's missteps with the polio program will forever tarnish our history. May we never repeat such mistakes."

Draining his wine, Mihai felt a release, having laid bare his grievances. He harboured no regrets for his candid outburst.

Coffee and biscuits diffused the charged atmosphere, granting both men an interlude from their contentious dialogue.

As Lupei poured another coffee, the night's celestial canvas twinkled above. Stirring his cup, he seemed lost in contemplation. Mihai braced himself, anticipating the next move.

Is he going to arrest me?

Lupei ceased his stirring. "Doctor, I want you to operate on my son. Proceed with the hemispherectomy."

Though not entirely surprised, Mihai found himself paralysed by doubt. He thought his outburst had sabotaged such a request. Yet here it was, the opportunity he yearned for. This was the moment of truth, and with it the proviso that needed to be put on the table. A demand that could have him thrown in prison.

Lupei's gaze was unyielding.

"I will do the surgery," Mihai stated, "on one condition."

The room was thick with anticipation.

"I require passports and visas for my wife and me—to a destination of our choosing."

93

"And where might that be, Doctor?"

"The United States," Mihai declared, his resolve as firm as the ground beneath him.

Lupei's reaction was unreadable as he assessed the proposition, his neck cracking under the tension. A passport from the Securitate was a bargaining chip of immense value, and Mihai had just placed his bet.

Mihai's legs jittered like pistons in overdrive. He held his breath, his future hanging in the balance, dependent on Alexandru Lupei's response.

"I can arrange your passport and visa," Lupei began, his voice measured. "But I can't make the same promise for your wife. Save my son, and I'll save you. That's the deal."

"I understand," Mihai said, concealing his disappointment, but not daring to push further.

Lupei leaned in, his imposing frame casting a shadow over Mihai. "Understand this: my son is not a lab rat or a bargaining chip. If he doesn't recover, you'll regret our meeting. Don't mess this up."

The tension lifted as they sipped coffee laced with grappa.

"Why me?" Mihai ventured.

"You've shown dedication to my son's case and predicted the outcome of his last surgery. Alex likes you, Doctor, but more than that, you're a skilled surgeon and a father who knows loss. You understand the stakes."

Lupei's words struck Mihai to the core.

"And now, you have a purpose," Lupei added, his understanding of human nature clear. "We have a deal." Their handshake sealed the agreement.

Despite the Major-General's notoriety for manipulation and ruthlessness, Mihai sensed he would honour their agreement. His skewed ethics wouldn't allow otherwise, but Mihai also knew the dire consequences should he fail.

Stepping onto the quiet street, Mihai shivered, but not from the cold. The night's events swirled in his mind, a maelstrom of excitement and apprehension merging into an indistinguishable whirlwind. The vision of a life abroad beckoned tantalisingly close, as the image of young Alex, playing with his Superman doll, fluttered across his mind.

As Lupei's cigarette ash fell like snowflakes in the dim light, his long, black astrakhan coat emphasised his sheer size. They conversed in the desolate street, the wind whisking debris along the gutters. Mihai pondered the ramifications of his bold proposal yet felt an unspoken assurance from Lupei.

"You know, we've crossed paths before," Lupei said, as if sharing a private joke.

Mihai, puzzled, couldn't recall any such meeting. He felt hard pressed not to remember someone of Lupei's stature.

"Bucharest, 1972," Lupei reminded him, exhaling a plume of smoke into the frosty air. "The biggest sporting event of the year."

Mihai's mind raced. There could only be one event Lupei referred to—the Davis Cup tennis final between Romania and the United States.

8

Davis Cup, 1972

Three days prior to the 1972 Davis Cup tennis final between Romania and the United States, Mihai received an unexpected phone call from Nicu Rizea, an official working with the Romanian national team. The assistant team doctor for the Davis Cup final had taken ill and a replacement was urgently required. The sudden offer brought a much-needed sense of excitement and anticipation in Mihai's life. His prominence as a formidable junior player, coupled with the need for an immediate replacement, tipped the scales in Mihai's favour, despite being a neurologist. His lifelong affinity for tennis, an ember that refused to die, found joy in the spectacle of the sport.

As the train conductor's voice reverberated through the carriage, announcing their arrival at Bucharest's Gara de Nord, Mihai closed the reports sent from the Federatia Româna de Tenis, which outlined regulations and protocols pertaining to the Davis Cup. The overnight train whistle's sharp blast and billowing steam heralded their entry into Romania's capital.

The heart of Bucharest, perched along the Dâmboviţa River, bore the enchanting moniker "Little Paris of the East." Its maze of cobbled streets and vine-draped villas birthed a vibrant cultural hub. The city's soul sang through the grandeur of the Atheneum, where music and theatre flourished, and through the quaint charm of ancient edifices like the Biserica Alba.

From his taxi window, Mihai traced the baroque spirit of Bucharest, its regal boulevards lined with groomed trees and monuments. Memories of past visits flickered in his mind— children's laughter in parks, old men engrossed in chess, and the allure of Magheru Boulevard's fashion boutiques. He recalled Irina's mixed emotions over an extravagant Yves St Laurent scarf—a rare luxury she wore with pride.

As the taxi wove through downtown, a stark contrast unfolded before Mihai. The once-thriving city now bore the scars of President Ceausescu's unchecked ambition. Buildings crumbled under the weight of rapid transformation.

"We must detour, mister. Ceausescu is erecting a grand palace for his wife," quipped Ivan, as he fumbled for a bag of peanuts. His appearance, an embodiment of weariness and neglect, was as striking as his humour. "My name is Ivantie. Call me Ivan."

The unkempt hair, scruffy beard, and missing shirt buttons, Ivan could have been anywhere between thirty-five and fifty. He turned to Mihai, a faint smile playing on his lips. "Emperor Ceausescu's palace will have seven thousand rooms in the heart of our city. What the emperor desires, the emperor receives."

Mihai could only nod in agreement.

Ivan lamented the city's fate, his words dripping with disdain. "Ceausescu's recklessness knows no bounds.

Churches, synagogues, monuments that have stood for centuries—mere obstacles to him. He even razed a hospital. To a tyrant like Ceausescu, ravenous for power, such destruction is trivial. He's a true fiend, eclipsing even Dracula in his soul-crushing tyranny."

As the vocal taxi driver played a new cassette, "Bird on a Wire" filled the car with melancholic strains that crackled through old speakers. "The cost is astronomical!" he bellowed over the music. "Thirty percent of our national budget, while we scrape by to survive!" His casual defiance, in a country teetering on the brink of chaos, was as unkempt as his appearance.

The Bucharest skyline was a forest of cranes, reminiscent of alien tripods from War of the Worlds, reshaping the city, and terraforming the landscape. The devastation resembled meteor strikes, with vast quarries and swathes of forest razed for marble and timber to construct this vision of Caligula. Ceausescu's Centrul Civic, a twelve-storey behemoth, would dwarf even Versailles in size, and the boulevard leading to the palace would extend further than the Champs-Élysées in Paris: its grandeur a grotesque testament to his megalomania. Over ten kilometres of the city's rich history was being effaced, its people displaced or herded into cramped government housing.

"It's incomprehensible," Mihai murmured, watching the relentless construction devour the cityscape.

"It gets worse," said Ivan. "Over forty thousand residents had one day's notice to evacuate their homes before moving to government housing blocks the size of a shoebox."

"It's madness," cried Mihai.

"The shoemaker," a reference to the President's prior occupation, "has become drunk on his increasing thirst for power. There are rumours he is building a nuclear bunker ninety metres under the palace for him and his lovely wife." Ivan checked the glovebox again, as he emptied half the content onto the floor. Still no luck. "Anyway, enough talk about politics. What brings you to Bucharest?"

"The tennis."

"Ah, yes. For the past few weeks, they have been cleaning up the city, making it nice for our American guests." Ivan laughed. "They are clearing out the garbage and throwing out the homeless and the gipsies." On cue, as they stopped at a traffic light, a barefoot, gipsy boy, no older than eight, tapped on Mihai's window.

Their arrival at the InterContinental Hotel marked a stark contrast. This towering edifice, crowned with a fountain soaring skyward and flags fluttering, stood as a beacon amidst the city's decay. Mihai checked in and then strolled down Strada Ion Câmpineanu, where the signs of dilapidation were clear, save for the bustling Origo café, a familiar haven amidst the turmoil.

Bucharest, though altered, clung to its former splendour, now ignited by Davis Cup fervour. Images of the suave Nastase and valiant Tiriac adorned the city's thoroughfares. Bakeries, brimming with creativity, churned out thousands of Davis Cup trophy cakes and tennis-racket-shaped cookies. Commemorative merchandise—plaques, towels, postcards—proliferated and were snatched up by the swelling tide of tourists. A sea of jingoistic yellow and red—the national colours—washed over the city centre, with posters and banners heralding an event steeped in political, social, and emotional significance.

The local taverns and bars buzzed with tennis debates, where men in nondescript coats sipped espressos and spirits, their conversations brimming with passion. Mihai, settling into a quaint, tucked-away tavern, overheard confident predictions from his fellow patrons.

"Nastase will wipe the floor with the Yankees," one man claimed.

"The Americans will be in big shock," boasted another. "Tiriac scares them. They're shaking in their cowboy boots."

Nastase, a whirlwind of talent and charisma, represented the vanguard of modern tennis. An international sensation, his artistry and flair were undisputed. Fresh from winning the U.S. Open in New York, Nastase was a national icon, poised to dismantle the American opposition.

Tiriac, the seasoned captain, lacked Nastase's finesse but compensated with a formidable blend of brute strength and cunning. His tenacity on the court was a testament to his streetwise approach to the game.

In Romania, sports discussions were akin to a national pastime, charged with fervour and conviction. Questioning Romania's victory was unthinkable, almost blasphemous. The clash against the United States was more than a sporting event; it was a narrative rich in drama. Historians and romantics alike framed it as a David versus Goliath showdown, capturing the world's attention and embodying the East-West geopolitical divide.

As Mihai wandered through Via Pasajul Nicolae Balcescu towards University Square, he observed students congregating near the marble effigy of George Lazar, the founder of the Romanian language. Others perused makeshift second-hand bookstalls, their hands brushing over the spines of Dostoevsky and Dickens.

The University of Bucharest, a beacon of neoclassical architecture, withstood the ravages of war and time.

As Mihai strolled through its grounds, he absorbed the atmosphere of promise and intellectual pursuit, the surrounding students a reflection of hope for a brighter future.

"Mihai Ionescu! Welcome to Bucharest!"

Dr Dorin Gobej was an orthopaedic surgeon who worked at the nearby Colkea Hospital, the oldest in the city and built in 1701. Dorin, a decade older than Mihai, was renowned for his expertise and dedication.

"What can I get you, Mihai?"

They ordered coffees and settled outside, moving their chairs to bask in the unexpected sunlight. Their conversation veered towards the much-anticipated Davis Cup.

"Nastase and Tiriac are getting more media coverage than Ceausescu!" Dorin laughed, a note of irony in his voice. "Do you think we stand a chance against the Americans?"

"Da," said Mihai. "Playing on home ground gives us an edge. Nastase will be the key. If he can display his brilliance at the U.S. Open, we can win."

As they sipped their coffees, the sun dipped behind the clouds. Mihai's thoughts turned to the state of healthcare. "How are things at the hospital?"

Dorin's expression darkened. "Dire," he confessed. "We're turning away patients, suffering from a dearth of staff and resources. Essential surgeries are being postponed, putting patient lives in jeopardy. And the ministry remains indifferent."

"Sorry to hear that," said Mihai, not surprised by the revelation.

"It's the same story right across Bucharest," Dorin lamented. "Doctors plead with administration,

administration with the government. Yet the government's response is always a dismissive demand to cut costs. It's a tangled web, Mihai. You, with your youth and talent, should consider a future beyond Romania's borders."

Despite Dorin's exceptional skills as a surgeon, his career stalled, permanently marked by past transgressions against the state.

∽

The university uprising of 1956 still echoed in Dorin's memory. Being a doctoral student at the time, he led many of the protests.

"We sought dialogue with the government on critical political and economic issues. Our unanswered pleas escalated into a forceful stand," Dorin recalled, his voice tinged with reminiscence. He remembered rallying his fellow students, his voice booming through a makeshift megaphone, as their discontent resonated beyond the university walls. "That was the new regime's first real challenge. Their reaction was immediate and brutal: soldiers swarmed the square, tanks rolled in, their barrels pointing ominously at us."

Skewed state media portrayals, depicting the protesters as anarchists, limited Mihai's understanding of these events. He had heard whispers of Dorin's involvement, but never broached the subject.

"We naively believed their show of force was just a bluff," Dorin continued, pausing as university administrators passed by. "But then, the gunfire shattered our illusion of a peaceful protest. Chaos ensued, students fleeing in terror. The brutality was relentless." Dorin's voice hardened as he recounted the baton blows and the crushing weight of military boots. "I never imagined our calls for justice would be met with such ferocity."

"I didn't know," said Mihai. "The media branded the protestors as foreign troublemakers and lauded the government's swift action. It's textbook Orwellian distortion."

"And Marxian manipulation," Dorin added with a dry chuckle, finishing his coffee.

The aftermath of the "university siege" was grim: mass arrests, imprisonments, and Dorin's four-year sentence of hard labour.

Mihai, looking at Dorin with admiration, jested, "I never knew you were a revolutionary! You're the Ion Gavrilă Ogoranu of surgeons!"

Ion Gavrilă Ogoranu, an anti-Communist guerrilla, had eluded capture for decades, becoming a symbol of resistance.

"He's still out there," Dorin laughed, a spark of defiance in his eyes. "Hiding in the Făgăraş Mountains, outsmarting the Securitate."

Both men shared a moment of pride in Ogoranu's resilience. Dorin's past, however, had rendered him a pariah, his aspirations curtailed. Despite his determination to leave Romania, his dreams remained out of reach.

Dorin's voice dropped to a murmur, recounting his stifled escape attempt. "A colleague tried to flee first, but the authorities were on him in an instant, concocting embezzlement charges to discredit him. They succeeded; everyone either believed the lie or feigned belief. His family is still under house arrest, shadowed by the Securitate's unrelenting watch." Dorin's eyes narrowed. "I visited the family once, only to be reminded by the Securitate of my sordid history and that it was best not to visit."

As they conversed, a group of friendly students waved in Dorin's direction, heading towards the library, as the men changed topics.

"It's been three years since that neuroscience conference," Dorin mused. "Sofia Ionescu's keynote speech was unforgettable. We lined the aisles, hanging on her every word."

Mihai's jaw tightened. "Yes, I remember."

Dorin eyed his friend, cautious of what he was about to say. "I also remember how devastated you were, understandably. We were all worried about you. How are things now, Mihai?"

"A little better. There are still many bad days. Scar tissue takes time to heal." Mihai scratched a scab on his finger.

"I can't imagine. Any thoughts of having another child?"

Mihai shook his head and left it at that. He thanked Dorin for the phone calls over the years before the conversation circled back to the tennis. As bells chimed somewhere in the city, it was time to leave.

"Next time, tell Camelia I want to taste her delicious borş soup!" said Mihai.

"It's the only dish she knows how to make!"

They laughed and hugged goodbye.

"I'll leave you two tickets at the hotel lobby. Forza Romania!"

✑

That afternoon, Mihai delved into a comprehensive briefing with Dr Leonard Istrate, a renowned figure in cardiovascular health and sports psychology. They discussed the players' medical histories, injuries, and psychological profiles, painting a detailed picture of the team's condition.

Later, Mihai ventured to the Club Sportiv Progresul, which now resembled a fortified compound with soldiers adding seating to accommodate an expected crowd of over ten thousand. The scene was surreal: rows of soldiers stamping their boots, mimicking the roar of a passionate crowd, testing the stadium's resilience.

Meeting Tiriac and Nastase, Mihai noted their contrasting demeanours. Nastase exuded a light-hearted charm, always ready with a joke, while Tiriac appeared brooding and aloof. Their attire was as flamboyant as their personalities—Nastase was dressed in vivid bellbottoms and a paisley shirt, while Tiriac was clad in heavy gold chains and wore clunky clogs. Amidst the media frenzy, Mihai felt out of place in his saggy jeans and faded jean jacket.

"Welcome to the biggest circus in town," joked Nastase as they shook hands.

"Congratulations on your U.S. Open victory, Ilie. That was incredible," said Mihai.

"Da. It was something. The New York crowd is almost as crazy as the Romanians." Nastase laughed as he grabbed several rackets from his bag. "Have you been to New York, Doctor?"

"I have not had the good fortune. Maybe one day."

The upcoming Davis Cup was structured as a gruelling five-match tie: two singles matched played on Friday, one doubles match on Saturday, and two reverse singles matches on Sunday. The first team to clinch three wins would raise the cup. For the Romanians, Nastase and Tiriac would play singles and doubles: an immense physical and mental challenge with the weight of national expectation on their shoulders.

"The Americans are weak," said Tiriac. "They don't understand what it's like to play here. They will crumble when they enter the stadium."

"Do not underestimate Smith," warned Mihai. "It will take a lot to break the Californian."

"This is true. Smith is a military man. He is stoic and rigid. But his strength is also his weakness. Once he realises this is no ordinary tennis match, he will fall apart," as Tiriac puffed on a Montecristo Cuban cigar.

"I hope you are right," said Mihai. "I believe Smith will struggle on the clay courts."

The team captain smiled. "They won't be clay courts. They'll be sand pits. We are laying ten bags of extra clay and flooding the courts daily. The courts will be so slow, I will return Smith's powerful serve with my left hand." Tiriac laughed before stubbing out his half-finished cigar.

∽

In Bucharest, Mihai's life was a blend of luxury and networking, mingling with high-profile individuals and enjoying the city's finest offerings. The influx of international visitors for the Davis Cup stirred in him a sense of wanderlust; he envied their freedom to traverse the globe.

Razvan Funar, a senior Defence Ministry official and tennis enthusiast, was a notable figure in the crowd. Having witnessed the Soviet withdrawal and Ceausescu's rise, Razvan had navigated the treacherous waters of politics with a rare joviality. His friendly demeanour set him apart in the cut-throat political arena.

Mihai and Razvan engaged in a friendly tennis match on a private court belonging to a Ceausescu relative. Razvan, though overweight, played with enthusiasm, joking about his fitness.

"Are you trying to give me a heart attack?" the short, tubby man jested as his cheeks turned bright red. "That's one way to eliminate the government."

Mihai's laugh would have woken the neighbours as the housemaid brought cold drinks for the early morning guests.

"I have to lose twenty kilos," Razvan stated, as he squeezed the fat around his belly. "It's this sedentary life and restaurant meals. My daughter is always chastising me about my eating habits. She means well, but sometimes she can be a pain in the backside! I tell her I don't need another woman telling me what to do. Her mother does a good job of that!"

Mihai enjoyed his company. The minister had not lost touch with the person on the street, though he swam in a sea of sharks.

Their tennis sessions became a routine, followed by breakfast on the estate's terrace, where discussions meandered from politics to tennis. The recent tragedy at the Munich Olympics cast a sombre shadow over their conversation, as they reflected on the event with a sense of disbelief and sorrow.

Minister Razvan's appreciation for Mihai's companionship was genuine, and he offered his assistance should Mihai ever need it. This offer would come to light in the years to come.

The Davis Cup final, set against the backdrop of the Munich Olympic Games tragedy, became a political cauldron. The brutal killing of eleven Israeli athletes by

Palestinian terrorists had cast a pall over international sports, heightening tensions to an unprecedented level. Tensions increased when rumours spread that Arab terrorists were planning to assassinate Brian Gottfried and Harold Solomon, two Jewish players on the U.S. team. The Americans considered pulling the plug.

Ceausescu and President Nixon spoke over the phone, with the Romanian leader assuring the Americans' safety. Ceausescu would not miss the opportunity to showcase his nation, and the Americans did not want to alienate an Eastern Bloc leader who denounced the Soviets.

In the dead of night, the arrival of the U.S. team at Aurel Vlaicu International Airport was a scene straight out of a thriller. A contingent of armed Special Forces escorted the team under the highest security to the Intercontinental Hotel. The level of protection was extraordinary, with every movement monitored and every hotel floor guarded as if harbouring a head of state.

Whispers that Carlos the Jackal, the infamous assassin, might be en route to Bucharest only intensified the drama. The narrative was taking on the hues of a spy novel, with every twist and turn adding to the tension.

On October 15th, the atmosphere at Club Sportiv Progresul Stadium was electric. The security measures were rigorous, with thorough checks for weapons and communication devices. Securitate agents, disguised as fans, mingled with the crowd, their eyes alert and watchful.

The match between Nastase and Smith was more than a sporting event; it was a display of national pride and geopolitical tension. The crowd was partisan to the extreme, jeering Smith at every opportunity, and the line calls were blatantly biased, leading to numerous disputes and delays.

Mihai, seated in the VIP section next to Minister Razvan, found himself caught up in the fervour. Despite his medical objectivity, the patriotic surge was overwhelming. He cheered and jeered along with the crowd, living each point as if it were a matter of life and death. Swept up in the atmosphere, he joined the chorus of thousands, as his heart raced with each excruciating point. Yet, with each falter, he slumped and squirmed in his seat, his whispered curses a testament to his internal turmoil.

The outcome was a blow to the Romanian spirit. Despite Nastase's valiant efforts, Smith secured a decisive victory. The silence in the stadium was palpable, their disbelief thick in the air. Mihai felt a profound respect for Smith's resilience, yet the weight of the loss bore heavily on him.

Ion Tiriac's match against Tom Gorman was theatrical in contrast. Trailing in sets, the Romanian resorted to tactics that turned the tennis court into a stage. His confrontations with the referee and provocations towards the opposition whipped the crowd into a frenzy when he snapped his racket over his knee in a display of gladiatorial defiance and challenged the Americans with a fierce glare. Officials paused the match as the crowd's chants overpowered the umpire's attempts to restore order. Against all odds, Tiriac's comeback and subsequent victory was a spectacle, reigniting the country's hopes.

Mihai bathed in the carnival atmosphere. The bars overflowed with drink, song, and laughter, as the revolutionary anthem… "with weapons in their arms, with your fire in their veins," reverberated from an overcrowded bar. Despite Mihai's hatred of the Communist regime, his heart filled with pride as he rejoiced in the celebration, laughing and drinking with hundreds of his new best friends.

The following day, the pivotal doubles match would take the stage. Another sell-out crowd expected a Romanian victory as compatriots squeezed into the overfilled stadium. National flags of blue, yellow, and red swirled in the Balkan breeze.

However, the Romanians were in for a rude awakening as the Americans outplayed the dynamic duo of Nastase and Tiriac. This gave the U.S. a crucial 2-1 lead. One more win and it was over. They could smell victory.

The decisive reverse singles were upon them. Mihai, greeting Minister Razvan, took his seat amidst the charged atmosphere. "My legs are still feeling that tennis lesson," Razvan joked, his smile belying the tension of the day.

Ion Tiriac took on the undefeated Stan Smith. For Romania, this was a must win match tin order o give Nastase the opportunity of winning the tie against Gorman. It proved to be an epic contest.

Tiriac played the match of his life, despite Smith being the superior player. The cagey Romanian employed every tactic in the book to unravel the ardent American. At one point, Tiriac sat in a linesman's chair and refused to play. He tested the American's resolve by engaging in rhetoric and banter while the crowd laughed and jeered. The wily Romanian had turned the match into a circus—his plan all along, as he knew it would be his only chance of defeating the classy Californian.

To everyone's surprise, the match went into a fifth and final set. The delirious crowd endeavoured to lift their exhausted hero, but Smith romped home in the final set, giving the Americans victory.

Amid their shock, the sound of gunfire sparked panic, sending the crowd into a frenzied dash for the exits. Mihai, caught in the turmoil, collided with a burly man with a tree trunk neck, issuing orders to several military personnel.

"Pardon me," the big man said, helping Mihai to his feet, while checking and dusting off the doctor's official pass.

The chaos subsided as quickly as it erupted when children were discovered setting off firecrackers behind the stadium.

⤳

The fairytale had ended. On the train ride home, Mihai reflected on the incredible week he had experienced, and how amazed he was by Nastase's talent and Tiriac's tenacity, while admiring the discipline of Smith.

He deliberated on his conversations with Tiriac. Despite a lukewarm beginning, the two struck a chord. Tiriac talked of the opportunities abroad, especially in the United States. If one had the drive, he said, one could achieve whatever one wanted in America. Dorin's words, too, crossed his mind, advising him to leave Romania while still young enough. Since Maria's passing, the future painted a bleak landscape. He twirled the ruby necklace he had bought Irina as the train chugged along, dreaming of a better tomorrow.

9

All I Want for Christmas

"Are you joining me for dinner, or should I eat alone again?" Irina's voice carried from the kitchen.

"I'm coming," Mihai called from the living room.

"You said that twenty minutes ago!" She slammed a cupboard door.

Fifteen minutes later, Mihai sat at the kitchen table. "The chicken is cold, for Christ's sake."

Irina turned on her heel.

"I'm joking," he said, hands in the air, signalling surrender.

She tapped her fingers on the table as her husband dipped the bread, soaking up the excess juices.

"You've been distant since meeting the boy's father. Is something on your mind?" she probed.

Mihai hesitated. Sharing his thoughts about the surgery and the potential move abroad seemed daunting. Irina wouldn't share his enthusiasm for a new beginning. "I've agreed to operate on the child," he finally said, avoiding her gaze.

Irina's heart sank. "Let someone else do it, Mihai. You're not the only neurosurgeon here. Why are you doing this?" she asked.

"It's a once-in-a-lifetime case. But more than that. If successful, the boy can lead a relatively normal life." He refrained from divulging the full extent of the story, as she would question him in ways that would cut to the core. He was not armed for such an encounter.

"You are swimming in dangerous waters," she said. "This Lupei fellow isn't someone to associate with. This does not worry you?" She sensed nothing good would come of it. "What am I missing here, Mihai? Why the intrigue with this child?"

"He's a nice kid." It sounded trite.

"You swore you would never work with children again. What's changed?"

He could not decipher whether the tone was conciliatory or accusatory.

"Is this about Maria? Will saving this boy remedy your misplaced guilt?"

They had avoided discussing their daughter for so long. It had become taboo.

"Please, Irina," he pleaded, "let's not delve into that."

Irina's frustration spilled over, her voice trembling with emotion. "I'm in the dark, Mihai. I don't understand what you're going through, but I'm hurting too." Her hand caressed his face, a gesture of shared sorrow as she softened. "You don't talk about it, and you won't even consider another child. And here I am, at thirty-five, feeling like it's too late for us. Night after night, you're there, holding that bear, lost in your grief, while I grieve in solitude."

After their daughter's passing, a deep chasm had formed between them. They struggled with their grief, barely getting by from one day to the next. Irina could not stop crying and broke down incessantly. She needed consoling and reassurance. When she would crumble on the kitchen floor, Mihai watched with a detached, taciturn apathy, as he retreated to the backyard. He had not the strength nor courage to be sucked up into Irina's struggle, and when he looked into his wife's eyes, his own pain stared back at him. And any form of consolation made matters worse. Hollow expressions such as, "grateful for the time given," or "Maria looked down on them from heaven," made Mihai sick to the core. Fake. Forced. Untrue. Bullshit. A bitter numbness had crept over him. His feelings calcified: a means of survival. Every man for himself.

In the ensuing months after their daughter's passing, Irina was bedridden, her world reduced to the confines of their home. Her days were a blur of medication and aimless hours on the couch. As days turned into weeks, months and years, their home became a living necropolis in a void of unspoken pain.

Irina sought her husband's strength, the same strength she had always leaned on, but Mihai was adrift in his own sea of sorrow, withdrawing further into his solitude.

Mihai should have done more for his wife. He failed as a husband in being a pillar of strength. When she turned to him in her most despairing moments, he chose solace and distance. And when she yelled at the top of her lungs, he sat on the backyard swing, or withdrew into the garage—his fortress of solitude—building walls within the mausoleum of their marriage, and keeping the world out, or entrapping him in. The Ionescu home became the house of the living dead for five years.

"I asked you to see Dr Gorin," said Irina, "and you refused. She helped me with my depression. She was the one who got me on my feet."

"I don't need a shrink."

"Of course, you don't. You're doing so well on your own." Her words had bite.

A police siren in the distance broke the spell.

"Why are you doing this, Mihai?"

"Not now, Irina."

"Why this change of heart? And why this case?"

"Please. Not now."

She wouldn't let it go. "What are you hiding?"

Frustration boiling over, Mihai tossed his napkin down in defeat. "I'm doing this to give us a chance to escape this place. To start anew." His admission hung heavy in the air.

Irina's eyes widened in disbelief. "What have you done, Mihai? How?"

"I made a deal with Alexandru Lupei."

Irina's eyes, a tempest of emotions, bore into Mihai as she processed this revelation. The unspoken accusations hung in the air: the risks he had taken, the decisions made without her input, and the potential danger for them both. "You son of a bitch," she whispered, her voice a mix of hurt and disbelief.

∽

Alex Lupei, propped up in his hospital bed, surveyed the familiar room. The nurses flitted around, taking blood samples for safekeeping, their productivity a contrast to the stillness in Alex's eyes. The room buzzed with preparations, from stocking additional blood supplies to installing new generators, all measures to ensure the upcoming surgery's success.

Mihai stepped into the room, greeting Alex with a warm smile. Mrs Lupei, sensing the need for a private conversation, excused herself despite Mihai's reassurances.

"So, Alex, are you ready for the big day?"

The child nodded, his eyes brimming with fear.

"You'll be asleep for the surgery, and when you wake up, the seizures will be a thing of the past. I promise," Mihai explained, trying to reassure his patient.

Alex's eyes shimmered with a hint of disbelief and hope. "Will the seizures really stop? Can I play soccer again?"

"Da. Why not?" Mihai said with a dollop of optimism. "Perhaps not straight away. But in time, you could dribble past a few defenders and score that winning goal. Who is your favourite player?"

"Johan Cruyff!" the boy replied with a flicker of excitement.

"The Dutchman. Yes, he is one of the best, though I also like Nicolae Dobrin." Mihai paused. "Now, Alex, I am not saying you will play like Cruyff. You will have difficulties with your coordination—but not enough to prevent you from playing soccer."

"Getting on the pitch would be a dream come true. When I started having seizures, I sat on the bench. I hoped my teammates would call me up. They never did. For Christmas," he said, quietly, "I wished Santa would make my seizures go away. I didn't ask for toys or anything, I promise. That's all I wanted. On Christmas Day, I woke up so excited. I thought Santa heard my wish. And then it would happen. I cried all day."

Mihai pressed his lips together. Christmas brought back the demons.

Alex's eyes, tinged with a mix of sadness and acceptance, met Mihai's. "I don't have friends," he confided. "They're scared of me, thinking I'm contagious or something. Last year, Mum threw me a birthday party. I didn't expect anyone to come, but deep down, I hoped. Two classmates showed up, probably out of obligation." A bittersweet smile flickered across his face. "But then, I had a seizure and hit my head on the coffee table." He pointed to a faint scar on his forehead. "I never even got to blow out my candles."

Alex's voice faltered as he recounted the isolation following his seizures. "I used to get so angry. It felt so unfair. But then, at the hospital, I met Calin. He had leukaemia. We bonded over our shaved heads and shared toys." Alex's smile vanished as he remembered rushing to Calin's room one day, only to find it empty, his friend gone without a goodbye. The boy wiped his sleeve across his face. "It made me realise others have it worse. I try not to get mad anymore. Bad stuff happens to people. It's just the way it is."

Yes, bad stuff happens to lots of people. Mihai nodded, acknowledging the boy's resilience.

"But I'm sick of these shitty seizures." Shocked at his language, Alex covered his gaping mouth with his hand.

"Don't worry," said Mihai. "It's fair to say that the seizures are shitty."

Alex gaped again. He had the biggest grin on his face. He spoke about his homeschooling and his dwindling interactions with his best friend, Daniel. "My mum is so protective. She fusses over every little thing." He rolled his eyes in mock frustration. "And Dad... he always encourages me to push my limits, but I can tell he gets upset when my seizures interrupt."

117

Mihai saw his own family's struggles in Alex's story. "You're facing your challenges like a superhero, Alex."

The boy beamed, as curiosity lit up his face. "What happened to your arm?"

A lengthy scar ran along Mihai's forearm. "It was an accident when I was young. Not much older than you, I'd say. I tried jumping a barbed wire fence, and my arm got caught."

"Ouch. Barbed wire. That must have hurt?"

"It did."

"Will I have scars after the operation?"

Mihai ruffled the boy's growing hair. "Once it grows back, no one will be the wiser." He gave a child-friendly rundown of the surgery and what would follow. Despite the practice of minimising trauma or stress on children, he tried to be as upfront as possible. The adults were often the fragile ones.

10

Theatre of the Mind

Meticulous preparations for the surgery consumed the day. Mihai's morning began with a detailed meeting with the radiologist, reviewing the critical areas in Alex's brain. They double-checked the imaging to map out the essential nerve fibres and arteries and to reaffirm the approximation of dangerous blood vessels.

In the conference room, the surgical team gathered. Mihai led the discussion, outlining each step of the procedure, from the incision and the split of the Sylvian fissure to the intricate disconnection processes. He planned to perform the bulk of the surgery himself, with the assistant surgeon stepping in during less complex stages.

They inspected the theatre equipment, ensuring everything was primed for the operation. State-of-the-art Zeiss microscopes, courtesy of Alexandru Lupei, stood ready, and Adam confirmed the reliability of the newly installed generators.

Blood loss estimations for the lengthy procedure were discussed, and Mihai made sure a sufficient supply of Alex's blood type was on hand. Marta Hesz and Mirela

Net, senior nurses, joined Mihai to finalise the surgical plan, ensuring every instrument was accounted for and the blood supply matched.

The team left no stone unturned in their preparations, aware that their greatest adversary was not a surgical error but the unseen threat of bacteria and infection. Mirela led the charge in sterilising the operating theatre, following a rigorous cleaning protocol that left the space immaculate and as germ-free as humanly possible.

Later, Mihai met with Alexandru Lupei and his wife, reassuring them of the comprehensive measures in place for a successful surgery. The medical staff made the final checks, confirming that the parents had signed all necessary consent forms.

As the day ended, Mihai reviewed the plan once more, his mind focused on the delicate task ahead. With the team ready and the theatre secure, a brave young boy stood at the heart of it all.

In the muted light of Mihai's office, Alex's mother sat silently, her hair tucked into a netted bun. Her hands, clasped in her lap, betrayed a silent prayer, while her red swollen eyes spoke volumes of her inner turmoil. Alexandru Lupei, restless with anxiety, paced the room, his forehead glistening with sweat. Before leaving, he clasped Mihai's arm. "My son's life rests in your hands. Remember, I'll be watching from the viewing area." The pressure on Mihai's arm lingered long after Alexandru Lupei departed.

In the patient's room, Alex was absorbed in his comics when Mihai stepped in for one final visit.

"How are you feeling?" Mihai asked, sounding upbeat.

Alex's response was a mix of anxiety and acceptance. "I'm a bit scared. People say I might die or never be the same again." His voice was a whisper, revealing his understanding of the surgery's gravity.

"It's okay to feel scared, Alex. This is a big step, but you're in safe hands." He offered a reassuring wink, though a knot of apprehension tightened in his stomach.

Alex put on a brave face. "Mum and Dad were here, and they looked scared, even though they tried to hide it. Mum cried and hugged me, which was normal, and Dad hugged me—he squished me so hard I couldn't breathe. He told me he loved me more than anything in the world."

"Your parents love you very much, Alex. And they are worried. But you needn't worry. Before you know it, you'll be back in this bed reading your comics!"

Alex's head snapped back, his eyes rolled upward, and he shook uncontrollably. As Mihai lunged, the boy's flailing arm struck him in the face. Alex's body flung from side to side before turning stiff as a board, his hands stretched out by his side, and fingers extended; his stiff legs pushed against the blankets at the end of the bed. The tendons in his neck bulged and his head snapped back, exposing his Adam's apple. Within a minute, it was over, as the electrical storm in his brain subsided. His eyes glazed over before consciousness returned.

After tucking Alex in and ensuring he drank some water, Mihai instructed the nurse to monitor the patient every twenty minutes. "Get some rest, and I'll see you first thing in the morning."

Alex's voice was faint but determined. "Dr Mihai, this is the last one, right? No more surgeries after this?

Mihai nodded, a solemn promise in his eyes. "Yes, Alex, no more surgeries after this."

∽

Mihai couldn't sleep.

Staring at the cracked ceiling, he gave up the charade and wandered out back, sitting on the swing, waiting for dawn to arrive.

He had reviewed Alex's scans, read over his surgical notes, and reviewed the checklists hundreds of times. Doubt, like an uninvited guest, crept into his mind. Irina's words echoed, questioning whether his ambition clouded his judgement. In the stillness, he grappled with these thoughts, aware, that as a surgeon, his decision-making must be precise, unclouded by emotion. Yet he recognised the importance of humility to guard against overconfidence. The line between bravery and recklessness, wisdom and cowardice, blurred, and often became discernible only in retrospect.

Lost in quiet reflection, he remained on the swing, the night's chill seeping through his robe. It was a rare moment of tranquillity before the day's storm.

∽

In the scrub room, Mihai's mind sharpened to a singular focus. The impending fifteen-hour surgery demanded his utmost concentration. A child's life was at stake, with no room for error. He remembered his days in the little big tower library, admiring the eminent surgeons of the past, where he dreamed of becoming a great surgeon.

Medical students, doctors, and notable figures from the neurosurgical community filled the viewing area above the operating theatre. Alexandru Lupei, seated front and centre presided over the room like a silent judge.

Entering the theatre, Mihai was enveloped in the familiar sterility. Alex, the focal point of this intricate dance, lay still, his head shaved and secured by a clamping device. Mihai hoped he would not become the antagonist in this unfolding drama.

It began.

The frenzy of the drill perforating the skull shattered the silence. The smell of bone dust mingled with the sterile scent of the room. Mihai carefully cracked opened the hard dura, revealing the pulsating, shimmering brain beneath—a structure he considered the most magnificent in existence.

As he checked the monitors, a surreal vision confronted him. His daughter, Maria, sat on the surgical bed in her unicorn pyjamas.

"Hi, Daddy." Her innocent smile and cheerful voice struck Mihai with a sense of shock and sweet sorrow.

Disorientation gripped Mihai. His eyes darted around, seeking validation for what he saw. He took a step back, his heart racing.

"Why didn't you save me, Daddy? We trusted him, didn't we, Babu?" Maria's teddy bear sat by her side, nodding in agreement, though his colours were all wrong.

The anaesthetist's voice snapped Mihai back to reality. "Mihai, are we good to go?"

The staff exchanged confused glances.

Battling the hallucination, Mihai took deep breaths. "Da." He wiped his brow and glanced at the table. Alex lay undisturbed.

Upstairs, Alexandru Lupei tapped his fingers on the armrest, shifting in his seat. Mihai gave everyone a reassuring nod. He reached for the scalpel, his hand trembling.

Maria's apparition reappeared and transformed: maggots wriggled from her nose, her breath foul and suffocating. She accused him again in her childlike tone, "Why did you let them kill me, Daddy?"

The nurse's concerned voice reached him from afar. "Are you alright, Doctor?"

Everyone looked like cardboard cut-outs, stiff and fake, and spoke in muffled, slow-motion voices.

"Why, Daddy?" She hugged Babu.

Mihai straightened himself up, fumbling. *This is not happening.* But when he turned, Maria sat there, smiling again.

I tried, baby, I really did. You just got too sick. There was nothing we could do. Mihai reached out to her, extending his arms, lost in the moment.

The apparition, hallucination, ghost, reincarnation, or whatever it or she was, grinned, showing her grey teeth. "Are you enjoying Christmas, Daddy? Wrapping those presents under the tree and drinking eggnog with Santa. I would like a bicycle this year. You know I've been a good girl. Or how about an iron lung! You can wrap it in a pink bow. Every little girl would love an iron lung under the Christmas tree, Daddy!"

Mihai fought to maintain his composure. "Please, don't do this," he whispered, his voice muffled by the surgical mask.

In the viewing area, confusion and concern spread. Alexandru Lupei leaned forward.

Maria's spectral figure continued to taunt him, her voice morphing into a macabre cackle that chilled him to the bone. Babu, the bear, joined in the eerie laughter, its expression disturbingly smug.

Mihai experienced a surge of irrational anger and a desperate need to escape the torment of his hallucinations.

The operating theatre was filled with a sense of dread. Mihai's breakdown was unfolding before their eyes, leaving the surgical team frozen in uncertainty.

Maria's voice echoed again, accusing, haunting. "Why didn't you take me away from Romania before I got sick?"

The bear that wasn't Babu rotated his fat head from side to side. It reminded Mihai of carnival clown faces with those gaping mouths, waiting to digest ping-pong balls.

"And I hope nothing bad happens to you when this smelly boy dies. You knew he would die, right? Still dreaming of a white Christmas, Daddy?" She threw her head back and cackled, reminding Mihai of the Wicked Witch of the West from *The Wizard of Oz*. Babu laughed along, too, with a conceited look on his face, as his furry arms rested on his round belly.

Mihai had an irrational urge to punch the little fucker in the face.

Maria's abdomen bubbled and made rumbling noises. Blood gushed out of her like a fire hose, splashing over the sterile floor. The room became a sea of red. Thousands of gallons filled the theatre till it looked like an aquarium in some hellish nightmare in technicolour glory. Doctors, nurses, and instruments floated and swirled about in a crimson and carmine whirlpool. Maria and Babu swam carefree, in long, deliberate breaststrokes, observing the chaotic spectacle below in bemusement, as Mihai struggled to distinguish reality from his tormented imagination.

Panic set in. The floor shifted like quicksand. The walls closed in around him. Disoriented and desperate, he reached out for Maria, his equilibrium pushed off kilter. He stumbled. Medical instruments went crashing.

"Doctor Ionescu!" The urgent calls of his colleagues barely registered as Nurse Marta hurried to his side, steadying him.

Alexandru Lupei, eyes locked on the unfolding drama, gripped the armrests of his chair.

As Mihai wrestled with his inner turmoil, the assistant surgeon stepped forward, poised to intervene. Mihai's hands trembled like a newborn calf, his psyche teetering on the edge.

Alexandru Lupei's gaze remained fixated on the drama unfolding below. He watched as the man he'd entrusted with the life of his child, crumbled and fell apart. His finger reached for the intercom button, ready to pull the plug.

Mihai pushed the assistant surgeon away and took a deep breath, willing his hands to stop shaking. A strange and familiar metallic taste filled his mouth. He channelled his concentration with resolve, but the past came flooding back, playing itself over in his head like a grainy black-and-white reel where everything seemed to move unnaturally fast.

Maria sat on the operating table, looking bored. Mihai could see inside the massive opening in her abdomen cavity. Babu II, the sequel, sat next to Maria. He so preferred the original—most did.

Instead of repelling the sickening slideshow in his head, he tried to let it play out without judgement or credence. Maria's voice softened, and her image lost its veneer as she exited the stage in his mind.

"I'm scared, Daddy. Don't make me go. Please! I want to stay with you." His beautiful daughter appeared: with wavy locks, dainty smile and rosy cheeks. "See, Daddy, it's me. Help me, Daddy. Help me, please."

Mihai was confused. Self-doubt overwhelmed him like eels slithering and sliding across his mind. He took a step forward, as Maria kept calling to him… needing him. He caught sight of the bear masquerading as Babu, snickering in the periphery. His colours still amiss.

Daddy loves you with all his heart, but you need to go now.

"Daddy, please! I'll be good, I promise. I miss you holding me and telling me stories. And I miss Mum so, so much." Mihai stared into her bright blue eyes. It was like looking into a mirror. Maria's pleas were heartbreaking and desperate.

I need to save this boy, my angel. You don't belong here. It's time for you to go. I'm sorry. Please forgive me. Goodbye, Maria.

She reached out with her little hands, her face strained in a state of panic. He felt her fingers on his face, and then gripping at his gown as he forced her to leave. He shut his eyes and wiped his face. When he opened them, Maria was gone.

Mihai found himself surrounded by concerned colleagues. "I'm okay," he reassured them, though his voice lacked conviction.

His focus returned to Alex, lying vulnerable on the operating table. The weight of responsibility and the spectre of his personal grief collided, leaving him at a critical juncture.

A newfound calmness emerged. A surge of confidence and surgical precision coursed through him. It was time to demonstrate his greatness. The scalpel, glinting under the bright lights, descended with unerring accuracy.

Fifteen hours later, as Mihai surveyed the outcome of his work, he was struck by the gravity of what he had achieved. Half of Alex's brain, now removed, lay inert on a trolley as he left the operating room, leaving others to stitch Alex back up.

He poured water over his head, feeling the rush of adrenaline give way to exhaustion. It had been a masterful performance, marred only by the haunting start.

Now, the true test lay ahead: the cessation of seizures and the preservation of Alex's brain functions. The next twenty-four hours would be crucial. All kinds of things could go wrong.

Leaning against the wall like a rag doll, Mihai contended with the intensity of the hallucination he'd experienced. Its vividness had shaken him to the core, leaving him with more questions than answers. He did not understand what happened, or why his daughter would appear as a demonic vision. And what she said disturbed him more. He shivered with the thought. Nightmares of Maria were customary, even expected. But never when awake or during surgery? *Was I in a fugue state?* He couldn't make sense of it. *Will you haunt me forever, Maria? Is this my punishment? Did you not want me to save the boy? Because if I did, it would mean I'd leave you behind.* As he sat on the floor, his hands trembled.

11

Nurse Nadia

Nadia Manescu, a dedicated and respected nurse, found herself at a crossroads. Adored by patients and colleagues alike, she faced a different challenge in her interactions with Dr Mihai Ionescu.

Mihai consistently berated and belittled Nadia, seizing every chance to diminish her. Once, in a fit of rage, he hurled a patient's chart at her for a minor misinterpretation of a drip rate. The thought of lodging a formal complaint flickered in Nadia's mind, yet the daunting prospect of going up against Mihai's towering reputation and the anticipated repercussions silenced her. In his overbearing presence, she shrank, perceiving him as the epitome of conceit, chauvinism, and crudeness. Ironically, this same man would become her unexpected saviour.

Nadia's personal life, a stark contrast to her professional struggles, brimmed with romance. Her heart belonged to Raoul, an earnest junior bank clerk who had recently proposed. Their plans to build a life together, starting with a modest flat in Cluj's southern precincts, filled her with a joy she had hitherto not known. But amidst these sweet dreams, an unplanned pregnancy cast a shadow of fear. Unprepared and overwhelmed, Nadia harboured this secret, even from Raoul. Being a nurse, she knew the grim realities of abortion. Yet, facing this dire situation with seemingly no escape, termination felt like her only option.

Under the oppressive yoke of the Communist regime, abortions were illegal, and all forms of contraception banned. This led to a harrowing increase in unwanted pregnancies and maternal deaths, the latter skyrocketing to the highest in Europe. Desperate women resorted to perilous, clandestine abortions. Smuggling contraceptives from neighbouring countries was a risky lifeline for some, but for many, sex became a source of dread. Grim tales of botched self-induced abortions and unqualified makeshift surgeries in dirty kitchens and bathrooms, besieged the community.

Nadia's own health waned under the weight of her secret. Morning sickness rendered her bedridden, struggling to keep anything down. One morning, as she placed a breakfast tray beside a patient's bed, the sudden appearance of Dr Mihai Ionescu made her start. A wave of nausea overcame her; in a dizzy rush, she fled to the bathroom, barely making it before succumbing to violent retching, her pristine uniform tainted. Returning to her station, a terse note summoned her to the doctor's office. Her stomach churned at the thought.

"Dr Mihai, I apologise for this morning. I believe some food disagreed with me. The smell from the tray was just... overwhelming," Nadia stammered, her face bloated. Mihai's piercing gaze felt like an X-ray.

"Nadia, are you pregnant?" The question cut through the air, stark and unexpected.

Laughing nervously, Nadia dismissed the query. "Oh, no, it's nothing of the sort. Just a bad meal, that's all." With that, she hurried away, her heart pounding, desperate to evade any more confrontations with the man she loathed.

～

The ensuing week saw Nadia contending with a ticking clock. Several doctors that she confided in parroted the rigid Party line. The overreach of governmental retribution loomed large, dissuading most from even entertaining the idea of aiding an abortion.

In the hospital's hushed corridors, nurses sometimes became covert allies, performing abortions for one another. This surreptitious practice, fraught with peril, was deemed safer than the grim alternatives of home procedures in unsterilised settings, devoid of medical aid.

Under the cloak of darkness, Nadia slipped through a delivery entrance, her loyal friend and fellow nurse, Adriana Oncea, at her side. The night unleashed a tempest whose ferocious winds snapped Adriana's umbrella inside out; torrential rain jolted Nadia from her dazed state. Inside, Marta Hertz and Violeta Stoian, their graveyard shift colleagues awaited in the ghostly quiet of the hospital.

Twelve weeks pregnant, Nadia had waited too long, increasing the potential for complications. Marta procured a room which was seldom used. A Hungarian Jew, and senior nurse, Marta recalled the room being occupied by a prisoner brought in with a ruptured appendix.

Clad in nothing but her vulnerability, Nadia lay on the frigid bed, a silent prayer for forgiveness escaping her lips. As her resolve wavered, her friends' assurances felt like fragile lifelines.

Marta, with practised hands, administered local anaesthetic to Nadia's cervix, their collective anxiety masked by a veneer of calm professionalism. The nurses' chatter filled the tense silence.

"Did you hear about Tatiana and Dr Florin?" Adriana whispered.

"I heard the same thing," said Violeta. "It doesn't surprise me. She was always a tart."

Marta's firm voice cut through. "Focus, please."

The nurses checked the equipment one more time.

"Are you ready?"

Nadia gave a weak smile as tears trickled down her face. "Let's get this over with."

Marta took a thin tube and inserted it through Nadia's cervix and into her uterus. She had to be careful not to perforate the uterus, as it would rupture the lining, causing internal bleeding.

A door slammed. The women jumped. Nadia groaned as they froze in their tracks. Footsteps. They braced for the worst. Marta switched the surgical lamp off, blanketing the room in darkness. The sound of squeaking shoes on the hard floor resonated, becoming pronounced, until they stopped outside the door. The doorknob turned; the pin drop silence broke as the locked door rattled back and forth. They stood motionless. Nadia moaned into the pillow as she curled into a ball. The footsteps faded away.

Their nerves were shot. Marta attached the tube to a hand-held syringe used to suction the tissue out of the uterus. Despite the anaesthetic, an uncomfortable tension stirred inside Nadia. Violeta reassured her it was the uterus contracting. Marta had to remove the tissue without perforating other sensitive regions. Her hands trembled, and they were on high alert, anticipating the sound of another slamming door. When Marta had suctioned off the relevant tissue, blood filled the tube and on closer examination, blood oozed out between Nadia's legs, soaking the bed sheet.

Adriana and Violeta noticed Marta's expression. The stream of blood indicated that something had gone wrong. The nurses went into damage control and tried to evaluate options, but the circumstances made it difficult. An intruder crept into the room: fear. The nurses debated what to do. Overwhelmed and outmatched, the trio could not reach a consensus as the whisperings turned to squabble.

Nadia moaned, growing paler by the minute.

"We have to do something," said Marta. "Her blood pressure is dropping. She is bleeding badly. We need a surgeon."

"Who?" asked Adriana. "Who do we call at this hour?"

"Dr Petran?"

"That wench will—"

"Okay," said Marta. "Who else?"

The women listed several names, including Dr Adam, but agreed he would follow hospital policy.

Marta broke the ice. "What about Dr Mihai Ionescu?"

Their jaws dropped.

"Dr Mihai Ionescu," said Adriana. "That psychopath. Why, that's a great idea. Why not bloody well call Ceausescu himself and ask him to come down instead?"

"She's right, Marta," replied Violeta. "Dr Ionescu will string us up by the rafters. He's insane and scares the crap out of me."

Nadia shook her head in agreement as she curled into a foetal position. "He hates me," she murmured.

"Besides, he's not an obstetrician," said Violeta.

Marta understood their concerns. "I have worked with Dr Mihai for many years. Yes, he can be a tyrant, and his mercurial nature is unsettling. But he marches to a different beat. I have seen him bypass procedures and regulations because it was in the patient's best interest."

They were not convinced.

"He is the best doctor in the hospital, and he gets things done. I believe he will help us. It sounds crazy, but you must trust me on this. Besides, what other options are there?"

Nadia let out a loud moan. Their optimism sank into quicksand. They agreed to call him.

Violeta faced Adriana. "We are so fucked."

⟡

Mihai jumped out of bed and answered on the second ring. "Hello." He dreaded that something had happened to Alex. He could not believe his ears. "What room? I will be there in fifteen minutes. Do nothing. You have done enough for one night." He slammed the phone, dressed in minutes, and drove like a madman through the sleepy streets of Cluj.

He burst through the hospital doors and headed to room D7 on the third floor. The front office noticed him storm by, but doctors, especially this doctor, came and went at all hours.

He requested a summary and gave instructions to the nurses. They sprung to action, gathering the instruments and medications asked. In the meantime, Mihai was on the phone, authorising access to everything he needed.

Nadia's condition was dire. The botched procedure had caused extensive internal damage. Mihai worked with focused precision, repairing the uterine tear and initiating a blood transfusion.

Mihai called Dr Miriana, an obstetrician who owed him a few favours.

With the cervix stitched, Nadia's blood loss subsided. A drip infused her with fresh blood, and a strong sedative dulled the pain. While waiting for Dr Miriana, Mihai transferred Nadia to another room.

The nurses huddled around Nadia, relieved she was out of imminent danger. Their nervous chatter and prolonged stares revealed their concerns regarding what awaited the trio, though Violeta seemed hopeful.

"He might let it slide. I mean, Nadia is okay, and he didn't seem that upset."

Their fleeting hope shattered with Mihai's stern summons. "My office. Now."

In his cluttered office, amidst the chaos of paperwork and lingering coffee aroma, the nurses stood, heads bowed, each lost in their thoughts of the impending fallout.

Mihai slammed his desk. "Do you know what you have done?!"

They jumped, not daring to make eye contact with the doctor.

"Idiots, all of you!" Mihai shook his head in disbelief and anger. "I have seen nothing like this. The absolute stupidity!" He paced, talking to himself like a tortured soul. "I can't believe this. Of all the idiotic things… I mean, this is beyond comprehension."

The nurses kept their eyes on the floor, hoping to survive the rant.

"You're finished! All of you!" he said, running his hands through his hair.

They dared a sideways glance at each other.

Adriana reflected on Nadia's status as a patient, and as if reading her mind, Mihai declared the hospital's duty of care to all who sought its aid.

"You've endangered a patient, trampled your ethical obligations, flouted hospital protocols, and breached the law."

Marta thought it rich that Dr Mihai, of all people, banged on about following procedures and breaking the law.

"Your dereliction of duty has endangered both Nadia and this hospital," Mihai's tirade continued. "Your incompetence leaves me speechless. In my eyes, you're unfit to step foot in any medical facility!" His icy stare turning Marta to stone. "And you, Marta. I expected better. Clearly, I was mistaken."

She bowed her head in regret and shame.

"You all face dismissal and criminal charges," Mihai continued, "encompassing unlicensed surgery and complicity in an unlawful medical act. In essence, you've destroyed yourselves."

The shrill ring of the phone sliced through the tension. Dr Miriana relayed Nadia's stable condition and controlled bleeding, promising to assess for further internal damage.

Mihai's fury ebbed momentarily. "At least Nadia's stable."

Marta murmured a grateful, "Thank God."

"No!" His anger flared anew. "Don't dare credit God. He's absent! Nadia's recovery is due to our efforts, not divine intervention!"

Pausing, he sought clarity amidst the chaos. "Adriana, go home. The rest of you finish your shift as if nothing's amiss."

Confusion crossed their faces.

"Be here at 8 a.m. sharp tomorrow."

They left, their relief to escape palpable yet laced with dread.

"And remember," he called after them, "keep this to yourselves. No exceptions."

Tonight's drama left him spent. His head was heavy, his muscles ached, and he felt like shit. He needed a stiff drink and sleep.

He checked in on Alex before heading home, calculating that he would get three hours of sleep before returning. Alex purred like a kitten. The bedside lamp threw a soft light over his young face. His father slept on the two-seater couch, while a hospital blanket did little to cover his torso. He was still wearing his suit.

The following morning, as the nurses entered at 8 a.m., Mihai was concluding his report. Their lives were upended, and a dark cloud hung over them. Marta, with a child awaiting at home, felt the full weight of their predicament. It was her suggestion to involve the doctor: her assurance now a haunting echo in her mind.

Mihai thrust the report at the nurses. "Read," he commanded, his voice laced with unmistakable authority. They pored over the document, their expressions morphing from fear to puzzlement, to utter disbelief.

The report narrated Nadia Manescu's ordeal: acute abdominal pain and abnormal vaginal bleeding. Dr Mihai Ionescu, working late, had attended to her. Initial assumptions pointed towards a severe menstrual episode, but closer examination by Dr Ionescu and Dr Miriana Cristea, a gynaecologist, revealed small growths in the uterus, indicative of minor endometrial polyps. The report detailed their successful removal and Nadia's expected discharge that afternoon.

The nurses absorbed the words, a whirlwind of emotions rendering them speechless.

"Do you understand what it says?" he asked.

Numb nods followed.

He leaned in, his voice now eerily calm. "This stays within these walls. I contemplated documenting a miscarriage, but that would invite official scrutiny. Uterine polyps, however, mimicked the symptoms we needed to disguise."

The revelation left them stunned.

Violeta, curiosity overcoming her, ventured, "How did you convince Dr Miriana to corroborate this?"

"None of your damn business."

Adriana and Violeta struggled to reconcile this act of self-sacrifice with the man they knew. His career, his freedom—all gambled for their sakes.

Adriana pondered the paradox. Why protect Nadia, whom he despised? The enigma of Dr Ionescu deepened.

Marta's faith in him was validated. Despite his harsh exterior, Mihai had a history of breaking rules for the greater good. When all hell broke loose, Dr Mihai Ionescu was the one you wanted on your side. "Doctor, we cannot thank you enough for what you have done. You have not only saved Nadia's life, but ours as well. We are forever thankful. We don't know to repay you, but we will do whatever you ask."

The sentiment echoed among them. The man they had despised was now their saviour.

Mihai's voice cut through the moment. "Let me make this crystal clear. Never pull such a stupid stunt again. And if you ever do, I will call the authorities myself." His scorn was apparent. "Now get out of my office."

They shuffled out, almost tripping over each other in their haste.

"And remember," he called out, "don't ever call me again."

Adriana confirmed his Mr Hyde persona. *You saved us, but you are and always will be an asshole.*

"Look," said Marta, "he stuck his neck out for us. I don't care what he says or thinks of me. He came to our rescue, which is what I will remember."

Adriana's and Violeta's silence affirmed Marta's outlook.

"Besides, he's right. I mean, we did screw things up," said Marta.

Adriana, unable to suppress her frustration, exclaimed, "Yes, he's our saviour, but does he have to be so damn terrifying?"

They giggled for the first time since the crisis unfolded.

12

Blood and Tears of the Jews

Alex drifted in and out of consciousness in the quiet aftermath of his surgery. Each time he surfaced from the depths of sleep; a fog of disorientation clouded his mind. The familiar faces around him would swim into focus, and he'd murmur a few lucid phrases. The warmth of chicken broth offered a simple yet profound comfort. His limbs obeyed him with surprising coordination, an encouraging sign as he remained free from seizures since the operation. So far, so good.

By the third day, recovery's slow rhythm had set in. Alex sat up, savouring his mother's homemade soup. Each bite of butter-slathered bread was an achievement. Beside him, his father broke through his usual stoicism, his hand gently rubbing his son's back—an unspoken outpouring of love and worry.

When Mihai walked in, Mrs Lupei's emotions spilled over. She enveloped him in a tearful embrace, a reaction Mihai had grown accustomed to in his career, yet it never ceased to move him on a deep emotional level.

Alexandru's handshake was firm and protracted, as he gripped Mihai's shoulder with gratitude. "Let's meet tonight, after dinner. Hotel Astoria at nine," he said, his voice faltering as he left the room.

"So, Alex, how are you feeling today?" Mihai inquired, turning his attention to the young patient.

"Much better. Things aren't as fuzzy, and I'm not so tired," as the boy adjusted his pillow. "You're meeting my dad tonight?"

"Da."

"Why?"

"Oh, he'd like to ask about your treatment and when you might go home. Things like that."

Alex's eyes brightened. "Dad's been different... nicer since I woke up. It's the first time I've seen him smile and laugh in a long time."

"Well, he's glad that you're better. He has been worried about you."

"Can I try walking around?"

"Soon, Alex. Let's give it one more day, okay?"

"It gets a bit..." Alex paused, searching for the right word. "... boring."

Mihai smiled. "Well, on that note," he began, reaching into his bag, "I have something that might help."

Alex sat up in anticipation.

Out came three comics: Superman, Batman, and something unexpected, a Dracula comic. "Dracula is from Romania. Not a superhero, but quite a character," Mihai said with a wink.

Alex's smile, unmarred by the bandages swathing his head, was radiant. "He's from Transylvania, right?"

"Da, that's right. His name was Vlad Dracul."

"That's so cool." Alex's voice quickened. "He drinks blood, turns into a bat, talks to wolves... hates crosses and sunlight, and you can only kill him with a stake or a silver bullet... Oh, and he doesn't like garlic, I think." Alex paused, then corrected himself with a burst of triumph. "Wait, the silver bullets are for werewolves. I mixed them up."

Mihai clapped, impressed with the boy's knowledge.

The cover of Dracula, with its menacing fangs, caught Alex's eye. "Dracula's scary," he said, a hint of awe in his voice. He was soon lost in a world of heroes and villains, far removed from the reality of his hospital bed.

∽

Mihai stepped into the Hotel Astoria, a place that was woven into the fabric of his personal history. It was here, after completing medical school, that he and Irina had shared their secret wedding night, a hushed church ceremony under the cover of darkness, a silent rebellion against the Communist regime's disdain for religion. Their daughter had come into the world just a year later, marking the beginning of a new chapter.

Alexandru Lupei's arrival was unmistakable. His colossal frame cast a looming eclipse at the entrance, dimming the bar's ambient light. The bartender, in his crisp white shirt and bow tie, looked on with disinterest, his mind elsewhere as he polished glasses in a futile attempt to pass the time.

In a cosy corner of the lounge, Mihai and Alexandru Lupei settled into an embrace of old friends, despite the precariousness of their bond. Seated on stools by the bar, two grizzled men cloaked in worn coats, their faces shadowed by five o'clock stubble, seemed to blend into the smoky haze of their cigarettes.

"Tonight's a great night, Doctor," boomed Alexandru Lupei, his voice rich with relief and anticipation. He motioned for a bottle of the finest whiskey. His spirits were unblemished by the potential of post-surgical complications that Mihai knew all too well.

The whiskey arrived, and Alexandru, his shirt already stained, raised his glass with the ease of a long-lost brother. "To my son's recovery," he toasted, a deep grunt of satisfaction escaping him as he wiped his mouth with the sleeve of his shirt. He leaned in, his voice dropping to a half-whisper. "Had us worried there for a bit," and then dismissing it as a mere hiccup. "Of course, I was aware of your esteemed surgical skills. But it was your resolve, your mettle, that impressed me."

"Alex isn't out of the woods yet, Mr Lupei," cautioned Mihai.

Alexandru waved a dismissive hand, the leather chair protesting under his formidable presence. "Call me Alexandru. Yes, I know there's a long journey ahead. But allow me this moment of joy. It's been ages since I've had a reason to celebrate." His words held a profound truth, inviting Mihai to embrace the present respite.

The Wolf filled fresh shot glasses to the brim. As they toasted, whisky spilt onto the midnight purple carpet. Alexandru's laughter boomed through the bar, evidence of a celebration that had begun long before his arrival at the Astoria.

"I started in the military," Alexandru began, swirling the golden amber remains of his drink. "Young, ambitious, craving a name for myself. Without proper education, the army was my only path." He paused, as a veneer of sarcasm laced his voice. "Perfect timing. I enlisted, and war erupted. Caught between Germans and Russians, and just seventeen years of age, as I had forged my birthdate to enlist early."

In the dim light, Alexandru Lupei's voice grew sombre as he recounted tales from Bacova, a village etched in his memory. "I knew it well," lighting a cigar, the glow illuminating his menacing face. "Days spent there with friends, chasing girls, dabbling in the black market," as the rich tobacco aroma mingled with the past.

"We rounded up forty Jews that afternoon," he continued, "Peasants, farmers, tailors... Our superiors, eager to impress the Germans, issued the orders." He exhaled, sending rings of smoke into the air. "We marched them down the main street, past silent spectators. The barn stood at the hill's base, its high roof and large double doors freshly painted. It was picturesque," he reflected with a hint of dismay. "Families clung to each other; fear etched on every face. One man confronted us, demanding answers. Our captain called him a Jewish pig and spat in his face."

Alexandru emptied his glass: the warmth of the whisky and sweet tobacco a stark contrast to the unfolding horror.

"When we reached the barn, a silence fell over the group. Some were barefoot, but one blind girl, holding her mother's hand, wore red shoes." Alexandru Lupei's chiselled jaw clenched. "When the doors opened, ropes hung from the rafters."

Mihai closed his eyes in despair. Applause echoed from somewhere in the lobby, as a group celebrated a birthday.

"We placed nooses around the necks of men, women, and children. And the strange part was, they didn't protest, seeming to accept their fate." The Major-General shrugged his massive shoulders as his eyelids drooped, recounting the horror. "Finally, women screamed. One lad wearing a grey beret made a dash and was shot, his beret landing near my feet. His parents dropped to their knees in anguish.

Two men causing trouble were taken behind the barn and shot in the back of the head."

Mihai struggled to mask his revulsion. The thought of such brutality against civilians, against children, was beyond comprehension.

"I remember the heaviness in the barn," Alexandru Lupei said. "Keep in mind, I was an inexperienced soldier. It was my first foray into killing the Jews." The man's eyes glazed over in the dark, smoke-filled room. "I still feel its weight on me. Mothers and fathers wailed as we placed ropes around their children's necks." The big man probed for a reaction, a judgement from the doctor. "Parents spoke to their children, telling them they loved them, and that God would watch over them. The blind girl's mother kissed her necklace and placed it around her daughter's neck."

Mihai caught a crack in his voice.

"Mothers begged us for mercy, pleading for us to spare their children. Fathers desperately offered their life savings... a mere pittance." The big man poured another drink, swallowing in one gulp, as the thread of welcoming spirit slithered down his lubricated throat.

A sickening knot gripped Mihai's stomach.

"But no mercy came, Doctor. We kicked the crates from under them. Bodies jerked in spasms. The sound of choking filled the barn. It lasted several minutes. Before long, only the creaking ropes could be heard, swaying side to side."

A handsome, well-dressed couple strolled to the bar, continuing their Italian chatter in blissful ignorance of the darkness being recounted.

"I've sacrificed much for my country," Alexandru slurred, sinking deeper into his seat, "and sent countless to their deaths. Not proud, mind you, but I won't shy away from it. There was a job to be done." He tapped the table with his thick finger, his gold watch glinting under the amber lights. "We killed thousands, right here in Romania. Did you know, after the Nazis, we were the biggest killers of Jews? In Bucharest, they hung them in the slaughterhouse; human and cattle carcasses side by side; their blood merging into the Dîmbovița River." He extinguished his cigar, reaching for a handful of peanuts.

Mihai's face paled. He struggled with the veracity of these claims, the alcohol-fuelled confession too monstrous to grasp.

"It's the harsh truth, Doctor. Our own holocaust, right in our homeland." Alexandru's arm swept through the air in defiance, his voice a muffled echo of repulsion. "In Bessarabia, we were the executioners. Marshal Antonescu's orders—cleanse the villages of Jews. Our hands wrought destruction alongside the Germans. Hundreds of thousands massacred."

Mihai flinched, his professional composure crumbling under the weight of such revelations.

"This shocks you?" Alexandru peered through half-closed eyes.

"I'd heard whispers, rumours... but the scale of it..." Mihai's thoughts raced, contemplating the injustice of a world where men like Alexandru Lupei escaped the consequences of their atrocities.

"We deported them to Ukraine and beyond, few surviving the journey. The old, the sick, the weak—we showed no mercy. It was a bloodbath, and I was in the thick of it." Alexandru tapped his empty glass on the table, lost in the memories that now resurfaced.

"You hated them?"

"No, Doctor. Indifference was my vice. The Germans, the Russians—they had their prejudices. For me, it was merely orders to be followed in war."

For men like Alexandru Lupei, such simplicity was a shield, a way to navigate through the darkest chapters of history.

"It's strange," he mused. "I commanded and executed thousands as my duty. Yet, it's the faces in the barn that haunt me, particularly the blind girl with red shoes. She visits me in my dreams, hanging in the barn, opening her eyes to stare into mine." His gaze wavered, flickering like a candle in the wind, the alcohol an ineffective balm for his tormented soul. His fat fingers tightened around the neck of the whisky bottle. "You're not alone in being haunted by nightmares, Doctor." He downed the whisky in one gulp before grabbing his coat.

Outside, under the glow of a streetlight that cast a yellow halo through the fog, they stood as shadows. Nearby, an old drunk who mumbled incoherently about the world's woes, lay sprawled by the roadside. Alexandru flung the man over his shoulder, depositing him onto the safe grassy verge.

"I'll start on your visa paperwork next week," he stated, with only a hint of a slur. "I'll send the confidential forms to your office. You'll need a formal expression of interest from your potential employer overseas."

Mihai's mind whirled as the alcohol collided with the night's admissions and the tantalising prospect of freedom. His lifelong dream was tantalisingly close to reality. In the car, Mihai sank into his seat, overcome with relief. Before long, triumph swelled, and he thumped the car ceiling repeatedly, his cry echoed with the ferocity of Ares, the God of War. Driving home, he rolled down the window and inhaled the crisp night air, feeling more alive than ever, praying that Alex would make a full recovery. God was not listening.

The phone shattered the silence at 3:43 a.m.

"What is it?" Irina asked, as Mihai leaned against the bedroom door.

"Alex is in a coma."

13

The Dark

Alex lay motionless on the hospital bed, his body functioning on autopilot, betraying no sign of the distant, unreachable place beyond his consciousness. The heavy silence was disturbed by sporadic beeps of the life-support machine.

Mihai bounded up the hospital stairs, taking them two at a time, his heart sinking at the sight of Alex's ghostlike figure. He tested the boy's reflexes with a gentle prick to the foot, receiving no response, and sat, rubbing his temple, deciding on how best to tackle this enemy before him. The Dracula comic lay open on the bedside table.

"I don't know where you are, Alex, but I need you to come back." The weight of the world pressed on him as another nightmare unfolded.

"Dr Ionescu." Pietro Pilic, the on-call resident, approached cautiously. "A nurse reported the patient's condition around half-past two. I had checked on him an hour before, and his vitals were stable. There were no changes."

Mihai shed his coat. "Are you certain?"

"Yes, Doctor."

"Did anyone else come in after you? Nurse, cleaner, maintenance, anyone?"

"Not that I know of."

Mihai's voice was firm. "Get the nurse who reported this. Now."

Pietro hesitated. "Her shift's over. She might've gone home."

"Tell her to come back immediately. Use my car. If she doesn't show, tell her she's fired."

An infection loomed as a culprit. The doctor ordered an extensive array of tests. On entering the lab, he underscored the urgency of the situation: demanding the bloodwork results by mid-morning. He initiated a lumbar puncture, inserting a needle into Alex's spinal canal to measure pressure and extract fluid for further analysis. Fearing any risk of asphyxiation, a breathing tube was placed in Alex's mouth. A CAT scan searched for blockages, an EEG monitored brain wave activity, while a cocktail of antibiotics and glucose were administered to stabilise blood pressure. With Adam's unwavering support, a flurry of medical interventions unfolded as dawn crept over the horizon.

Meanwhile, Mihai interrogated the nurse who found Alex in a coma and double-checked with staff to ensure that no one else had entered the room.

In his office, Mihai struggled to contain his rage, though he couldn't let personal feelings cloud his judgement; a young boy's life hung in the balance, as did his own.

He picked up the phone and called Alexandru Lupei.

∽

Alexandru Lupei burst through the hospital doors, a gust of cold air trailing in his wake.

"Mr Lupei, the cause of Alex's coma remains unclear," Mihai began, his tone composed yet urgent. "We're undertaking thorough investigations to develop hypotheses. We have taken every precaution to ensure his safety."

Adam and Gheorghe arrived soon after. Adam tried to interject, however, Mihai, determined to shoulder the responsibility, spoke over him.

"We've ruled out brain swelling or bleeding, which are common causes of comas. Rest assured that we will monitor Alex around the clock as we investigate every possible cause of this setback."

Alexandru Lupei remained standing, his mind elsewhere, haunted by unnerving thoughts.

Sensing the man's mounting anxiety, Mihai reassured him. "Comas, while concerning, are not uncommon. In most cases, particularly in young patients, recovery within a week is likely, without lasting damage."

Dr Gheorghe, seizing the moment, inquired, "Dr Ionescu, can we quantify the likelihood of full recovery post-coma? Is it possible to bring a patient out of such a state, or reboot them, so to speak?" Gheorghe knew the answers but posed the questions, nonetheless.

"The situation is complex," Mihai replied. "Factors like age, brain damage, and the coma's duration can influence recovery. The longer the coma, the more challenging the prognosis. However, it's too early for definitive predictions."

"Yes, yes," said Dr Gheorghe, "we must be optimistic you will find a solution." He paused for effect, turning to Alexandru Lupei. "As Dr Ionescu said, the longer the boy is in a coma, the less favourable his chances of making a full recovery."

Mihai noted the emphasis, as did Alexandru Lupei.

"Dr Gheorghe, are you saying my boy might not fully recover?"

Mihai attempted to intervene.

"I was asking Dr Gheorghe," said the Major-General, maintaining his civility by a thread.

"Well, Mr Lupei, the longer patients remain in a coma, the greater the chances there may be some—"

"What!" said the big man, his agitation flaring. "What are you hesitant to say? Bloody well say it!"

Again, Mihai tried to interject, bristling at how Gheorghe commandeered the conversation; his disdain for the latter's obsequious manner simmered beneath the surface.

"I am talking to Dr Gheorghe, if you don't mind!" Alexandru Lupei's voice boomed, veins pulsating from his thick neck. "He is the head of this department. You, Dr Mihai, have done more than enough."

"As I was saying," said Gheorghe, "the longer a patient is in a coma, the greater the probability they may awaken with neurological problems related to motor or language skills, as well as memory loss and slower cognitive processing. What I am saying, Mr Lupei, is that there is a real risk of brain damage if Alex remains in a coma for an extended period."

Alexandru Lupei's face turned ghostly white, as his brow was beaded with sweat.

"It's my duty," Gheorghe said, "to inform you that your son might enter a vegetative state."

Confronting Mihai, Alexandru's imposing figure threatened, his shirt straining against his muscular build.

"This predicament," he hissed, his voice a gravelly whisper, "is on you." His eyes bore into Mihai with a chilling intensity. "I hold you accountable. Fix this. Bring my boy back, or else..."

Mihai smelt the mixture of cologne and sweat as he held the gaze of this leviathan standing before him.

Adam, attempting to diffuse the escalating tension, stepped in. "Mr Lupei, let's not jump to conclusions. It's premature to discuss worst-case scenarios. We don't yet understand the cause of Alex's coma. Let's remain hopeful."

"I expect my son back unscathed." The Wolf stormed out; the door slam reverberated through the room.

Mihai exploded. "I will tear your fucking heart out!"

"I was stating facts," Gheorghe retorted.

Adam raised his voice in a rare show of anger. "Enough! Gheorghe, your approach was far from helpful!"

"Someone had to be upfront and inform the man of his son's predicament. All because of Mihai's reckless decision to remove half the child's brain! Frankly, Adam, I don't know how you let him get away with it."

Adam roared back, "I need not justify my decisions to you, Gheorghe! Mihai has saved countless lives under dire circumstances, even when others, yourself included, deemed them hopeless. And if I recall, he diagnosed a patient with Bell's palsy after you erroneously misdiagnosed it as a stroke?"

Gheorghe scoffed dismissively.

"But let's not waste time in petty disputes," Adam concluded, his voice firm yet weary. "Our priority is Alex. We must unite in our efforts to bring him back."

"Everyone can see through your bullshit, Gheorghe." Mihai was not done yet. "The slime you crawl through to curry favour is repulsive. You are a disgrace to the profession. How can you look at yourself in the mirror?" Mihai snatched his coat and stormed out, slamming the door shut as the windows quivered in his wake.

Outside, the gravity of Alex's situation weighed on Mihai, as he paced up and down the hallway like a caged tiger. Mumbling and cursing to himself, staff walked by, eager to steer clear of the festering doctor.

In the hallway, Adam caught Mihai's arm. "You need to save this child, you understand me? The hospital will be at your complete disposal. Whatever you need, just ask." Adam let go of Mihai's arm. "If the boy doesn't wake, it'll be the end of us."

14

Radu and his Band of Merry Men

The roar of black Dacia cars disturbed the stillness of the night. Mihai, roused from sleep, turned to Irina with a grave tone. "Listen carefully. Say nothing and do as they ask."

Irina froze as the gravity of it all came pummelling down. "It's the Securitate, isn't it?" A shiver ran down her spine.

The door thundered under relentless pounding. "Open up! Securitate!"

Mihai, clad in his checkered nightgown, hastily smoothed his hair. With a steadying breath, he opened the door to three overcoat-clad Securitate agents.

One, with green eyes and no older than twenty, demanded entry. "We have orders to search your home."

"Under whose authority?" asked Mihai, defiantly, his indignation bubbling.

The officer's smirk was chilling. "Mine," he replied, the handle of his gun protruding ominously.

"Do you have a warrant?" Irina's voice sounded frail, almost naïve as she stood trembling by the bedroom door.

The agents ransacked the house with brutal efficiency, reducing husband and wife to spectators in their living room. They emptied closets and tossed family memorabilia onto the floor; the sound of shattering glass tearing at Irina's heart.

The officers treated medical texts with contempt, cracking their spines and shaking their pages, as if to reveal hidden secrets; a fleeting triumph at discovering "incriminating" documents evaporated upon encountering medical jargon they couldn't pronounce—*astrocytoma, craniopharyngioma*. Bored, they discarded papers in frustration and hurled books from shelves without rhyme or reason. One agent, in a display of senseless destruction, ripped pages from a poetry book, leaving behind a trail of desecrated knowledge and well-versed prose.

The men progressed to the kitchen, where they found nothing of interest. One officer reached for a vase in the cabinet.

"Let me help you with that," said Irina, quick to her feet.

The officer told her to remain seated.

"Please be careful," she pleaded. "The vase has been in my family for generations."

∽

The red hourglass-shaped vase with gold trim and hand-painted flowers had been a gift passed down by Irina's great-grandmother. Crafted by Venetian artisans, using centuries-old glass-blowing techniques, the rare piece had both monetary and sentimental value.

While visiting the splendid city of Venice in 1878, Irina's great-grandfather, Dela Dragomir, played baccarat in a smoke-filled tavern by Piazza San Marco with a table of wealthy Venetians, merchants, and barons. Dela had been on a winning streak and boldly placed his small fortune on the table. Baron Dandolo, whose family owned a fleet of merchant ships, wagered his wife's beautiful vase on a dare.

Upon sailing back to the Romanian port of Constanța, Dela Dragomir presented the vase to his future wife— Irina's great-grandmother.

∽

Irina's eyes fixated on the obtuse young man who held her great-grandmother's vase while he lit a cigarette.

"Don't worry, I'll be careful," he said, as ash fell to the floor, while the other officer dumped a cylinder tin of sugar into the sink.

Green eyes ordered everyone to the bedrooms.

The sound of centuries-old Murano glass exploding radiated across the kitchen floor like some miniature model of the Big Bang. Irina screamed as shards of Venetian glass spread across the landscape. Her heirloom gone forever. Mihai held his wife as she buried her head into his chest, thumping her fist against him.

Mihai's rage had reached its tipping point.

In Maria's room, an officer picked up a photo frame, but placed it back where he found it, and left without further intrusion. Mihai pondered their restraint. *Did they know something about Maria?* His thoughts clouded with uncertainty.

The couple were ushered into their bedroom, a space marked by time and memory. The torn, faded wallpaper had been there for generations and the whiter rectangular shade above the bedhead, the ghost of an old painting that now lay broken in the garage. In the corner stood the water-stained armoire, its key dangling impotently from the doors. The agents rampaged through the room, disrupting the peace with their search for hidden compartments. They tossed aside folded bedspreads, releasing the faint scent of mothballs.

Irina shut her eyes, her heart sinking as their boots trampled over her clothing.

"It will be over soon," green eyes said smiling.

They lifted the stained, worn-out mattress; the missing slats in the frame resembled a prehistoric creature's ribcage.

Irina's anxiety crescendoed as the agents opened her beige lacquered nightstand. Her sweaty grip on Mihai's hand tightened. "The bottom drawer," she whispered nervously.

As the drawer was forced open, it jarred as the grooves misaligned. Irina's grip became a vice, her expression screamed for Mihai to do something.

With a little prying, it opened. Some of Irina's bras and panties spilled onto the floor.

"Stop!" Mihai yelled. His voice startled the officers. "How dare you come into our home, break everything, and disrespect my wife in this manner. I have never seen such incompetent and vile behaviour."

The agents exchanged uncertain glances, unprepared for this defiance.

"Is this how the Securitate operates? Without shame and no sense of dignity."

Green eyes' face twitched.

"As a surgeon who has treated government officials, I assure you, they will hear of this." His spittle landed on green eyes' cheek. "You rummage through my wife's most personal items with your filthy hands. No gloves, no decency. It's despicable! To think you derive some twisted pleasure from this... Your mothers would be appalled."

The officers, uncomfortable with the accusations, halted their search. Despite the widespread moral decay within the state, the sanctity of motherhood remained a revered concept, a symbol of the sacrifice and strength underpinning society.

Attempting to regain authority, green eyes cleared his throat. "Mr Ionescu—"

"It's Dr Ionescu!" The vehemence unsettled the men.

"Dr Ionescu, I can assure you we are following instructions."

"What bloody instructions are you talking about? You call this an investigation? If you want to arrest me, then arrest me, otherwise, get out of my goddamn house!"

Defeated, green eyes signalled the end of their search. Whispering instructions to his men, they retreated, leaving behind a trail of disruption and fear.

Alone in the house with Mihai and Irina, green eyes scribbled into a notepad, his feet crunching over broken glass, avoiding making eye contact with Mihai. Informing them that a report would be lodged, and further visits expected, the Securitate agent marched out the front door.

Collapsing to the floor, Irina clung to Mihai. "Why, Mihai? Why is this happening?"

"It's a warning." He sounded spent. "Lupei is using this as leverage, a reminder of the stakes if I cannot save Alex. He's a man unaccustomed to losing control, and now, with his son's life beyond his reach, he's desperate to regain some semblance of it back."

Suddenly, Mihai smelt smoke. Flames flickered beyond the kitchen window. He raced outside. The burning garage illuminated the night. *Those bastards*.

Irina's screams urged him to retreat from the fiery destruction.

Drenching himself with the hose, Mihai clambered through the shattered window along the garage's side. The acrid stench of petrol stung his nostrils. In his dressing gown and slippers, he navigated a labyrinth of memories: Irina's wedding dress, a cherished gift from her aunt, nestled among winter jackets; a workbench laden with tools, their rusted forms and faded handles a testament to years of neglect; tin boxes housing a jumble of nails, screws, and bolts, untouched for decades. As he crept forward, heat droplets peppered his back. He moved past wicker baskets, timber planks, and a rolled-up rug, now the fodder of hungry flames. A family of mice, their cozy nest disrupted, scurried away, abandoning their pink, helpless newborns to the inferno's mercy.

Did they plan this? Or was it decreed in the Securitate manual to keep petrol cannisters in the boot? Handy for burning down garages. Choking on the toxic fumes, Mihai reached for the baby cot and shoved it through the window. Irina dragged it to safety, along with a green trunk filled with childhood memories: clothes, blankets, a lock of hair, photo albums.

"My books!" Mihai yelled, defying the fire's roar, plunging back into the inferno.

"No, Mihai! It is madness. Leave the damn books!" Irina shouted as she turned the feeble hose on the burning structure.

Mihai threw an old tarp over his head as the flames licked along the wooden beams, ravenously searching for dry wood to devour. Insects and a striped meadow lizard fled in a chaotic exodus. Plastic bottles of cooking oil melted, and cartons of Kent cigarettes—commodities for barter and bribery—succumbed to the fire. An old canvas print of oxen and a farmer, crumbled under the heat. Parts of the roof collapsed, oxygen rushing in to fuel the flames further. The bulk of Mihai's book collection, hidden beneath metal chairs, was still intact. He dragged as many boxes as he could to the window, Irina pulling them to safety. The rest were beyond rescue.

After dousing himself again with the hose, and clearing glass shards from his hands, Mihai, with the help of a neighbour, forced the garage door open. Irina's cries for him to stop went unheeded. The wooden structure creaked and groaned under the strain of the blaze. But Mihai's focus was singular—to rescue the remaining books, somehow spared from the direct assault of their mortal enemy: fire. He hauled out two boxes at a time in a laborious retreat.

Ready to venture back, his neighbour, Grigore, followed, but Mihai, adamant in his resolve, sent him back. With each daring re-entry, he retrieved three more boxes, inching them out in a backward crawl.

Daring another foray into the inferno, the smoke enveloped him, choking his lungs and searing his throat. Amidst the conflagration, sacks of potatoes and boxes of vegetables were reduced to charred remains, while hanging plaits of onions and garlic blackened, releasing a bittersweet aroma. A misstep caused him to slice his forearm on a shovel's edge. The fire, unforgiving, besieged the remaining boxes of books, rendering them defenceless. Mihai's lungs heaved for air in the dense, scorching atmosphere. The smoke stung his eyes, the heat unbearable. A fallen heavy-framed mirror lay atop the boxes, making them immovable. Flames licked at his skin, and a sudden fireball burst through the collapsing roof, showering him in hot ash. Desperation took hold as he struggled to save what he could. But the garage's structure gave way, forcing him to flee. As he crawled, a falling section of the roof pinned him down. Hands reached in, dragging him to safety, as a cascade of cold water extinguished the flames engulfing his body.

Outside, Mihai coughed violently, his body racked with spasms, smoke billowing off the salvaged books. The garage groaned in its death throes, its roof screeching, before succumbing to its fiery fate.

Among the wreckage, Mihai salvaged ten boxes of books, though many were damaged. He rifled through research papers, noting their worn pages before discarding them. He then unearthed a treasure—a burgundy leather-bound early edition of *Les Misérables*, the title and borders embossed in gold. It was a cherished gift from a French colleague, now marred by soot and heat.

On hands and knees, he went into a coughing fit that crushed his chest and restricted his airways. Vomit splattered over the wet grass. After several minutes, Mihai's breathing steadied, though his watery eyes felt like a thousand tormented ants had stung them. A sharp pain burnt his throat when he tried to speak, as his bloodied knees stained the grass. His back felt like a bulldozer had hit it.

Nearby, the baby cot stood by the apple tree, its paint peeling but otherwise sound. Babu the bear, Maria's beloved stuffed animal, lay inside, his left ear and part of his furry face scorched.

By this time, many of the neighbours offered help, but Mihai, defeated, sent them home. What remained of the garage was a blackened concrete slab, a stark reminder of the night's devastation. He trudged into the house, slamming the torn fly screen door behind him as it ricocheted back and forth, quivering like a speared fish, echoing his own battered state.

"Should we go to the hospital?" Irina's concern was palpable.

"I'll go in the morning," Mihai replied hoarsely, his voice strained from smoke inhalation. He slumped into a kitchen chair, singed hair clinging to his scalp. He drank water and milk to soothe his scorched throat before showering away the remnants of the night's ordeal.

Irina swept and cleaned the house like a madwoman, erasing the night's havoc. Her finger nicked a shard of her great-grandmother's vase, drawing blood—a minor wound compared to the deeper cuts of loss. She salvaged photographs from broken frames, straightening a black-and-white image of her parents. Each mop stroke laden with grief.

Mihai's embrace was a frail comfort, his voice raspy and strained. "It'll be okay," he whispered, though his words lacked conviction.

Outside, the remnants of the garage smouldered. Wisps of smoke coiled upwards, evoking a hypnotic dance. A blue-edged flame flickered as charred paper fragments fluttered skyward, resembling sombre butterflies in their final flight.

In the bedroom, Mihai opened Irina's bottom drawer. Beneath her garments was a tin box, revealing newspaper clippings, family photos, including pictures of Maria laughing, and a large black-and-white photograph. This was Irina's secret that almost had them arrested. Mihai knew the man in the photo. Everyone in Romania did. The portrait showed a man with movie-star looks, wearing a decorated military jacket and regally posing for the camera. He now lived in exile after his forced abdication by the Communist regime. His name was King Michael I. The last king of Romania.

⤜⤐

Two days post-tragedy, the garage's remnants lay like a fossil from a bygone era. Only fragments of its former structure remained, its interior exposed, stripped of its secrets. Mihai and Irina had spent a day in sombre cleanup, attempting to impose order on chaos. Their efforts yielded little of value.

Disturbed from sleep by unfamiliar sounds, Mihai joined Irina, who greeted him with coffee and a smile.

"What's happening?" he asked, still aching from the previous day's labour.

Irina led him to the backyard. A flurry of activity greeted him: men armed with tools, reconstructing what was lost. At the heart of this hive of activity stood Radu, orchestrating the rebuild with an infectious zeal.

"Doc!" the old man bellowed, as he scampered over and gave Mihai a big hug. "You no worry. We take care of everything," he said in his sprightly manner, as he waved his arm toward the busy workers in the background. "Soon you have garage back... but better than before!" His smile beamed and radiated warmth.

Lucien Grosu, a skilled carpenter wiped his dusty beanie. "Radu rallied us after hearing about the fire."

Years ago, Mihai had intervened to secure Lucien's release from a wrongful arrest. Their families spent many Sundays together, while their children played dolls and laughed on the swing.

In this moment of rebuilding, amidst the hammering and sawing, Mihai beheld a collective triumph over adversity, an unspoken acknowledgement of the bonds forged through years of shared experiences and mutual support. It was more than just a garage being resurrected; it was a reaffirmation of hope amidst the ashes of despair.

As Mihai descended the steps, Niko Dalka doffed his cap, grateful for the free medications the doctor had provided, as a respectful hush fell over the workers.

Radu broke the silence, slapping Mihai's back. "We'll try not to build you a pig barn, okay!"

Mihai's face tingled with goosebumps as he shook hands with each volunteer. Among them were former patients, farmers whose families he'd aided, and friends like Henric Bercu, a Jewish engineer and tennis partner. Henric was indebted to Mihai for a critical diagnosis that spared his son from military conscription. Neighbours, too, had joined in upon hearing of the work party.

The backyard buzzed with activity as men worked to dismantle the old garage, clearing the remnants of its charred shell.

From the stairs, Irina watched, overwhelmed by the unfolding act of community spirit. Despite the recent darkness, what unfolded before her shone through with a ray of light.

Men with ropes slung over their shoulders moved about in a choreographed rhythm, donning old jeans and overalls, cigarettes dangling from their lips, and tool belts brimming with an assortment of implements. The air vibrated with the sounds of reconstruction—the whirring of drills, the rhythmic snoring of saws. Lumber, tin sheets, and plaster boards cluttered the yard, as shouts and calls crisscrossed the busy space.

Compelled to contribute, Mihai donned work clothes and joined in, despite his aching back and irritated throat.

He helped unload materials, lending his strength to the communal effort.

Mircea and Igor, using a two-man saw, cut through timber with synchronised precision, their bodies moving in harmony, sweat tracing paths down their muscular frames.

Lucien, whose childhood was steeped in carpentry, worked with the finesse of an artist, crafting joint connections with skill and precision.

The team worked in unison, using nails, screws, and nuts to assemble the structure. They hoisted the frame into position with sheer manpower and ropes, while Radu, ever the leader, directed the pouring of wet cement into postholes, ensuring the structure's foundation was solid.

By late morning, the skeleton of a new garage stood tall, a tribute to their collective effort.

As they installed the roof, the sounds of hammers created a unique symphony, each blow marking the progress of their labour. Wood panels and plaster sheets soon formed the new garage's exterior and interior walls.

Inside, Irina busied herself in the kitchen, her slippers tapping a rhythm on the floor. She grumbled about the limited workings of the gas cooker as she prepared an abundant lunch. When the delicious aromas wafted outside, the hungry workers put down their tools.

Radu, undeterred by age or fatigue, continued his work atop the roof. Mihai, concerned for his well-being, insisted he join the others for a well-deserved meal.

The spread was a feast: eggplant dip, boiled eggs, an array of fresh tomatoes, cucumbers, and peppers, alongside succulent sausages. The highlight was chiftele—deep-fried meatballs—and sweet plăcintă filled with apricot jam. Savouring their meal in the shade of Irina's rose garden, the hosts brought out bowls of chopped fruit, which the workers devoured in the warm midday sun. A solitary bee hovered curiously over the watermelon as the men earned a reprieve from their labour. Mihai poured wine for everyone, though the men refused seconds.

"You no want upside-down garage," Radu shouted, as he took leftover food to Pip, who patiently waited out front, tethered in the shade of a tall evergreen. The old man unfolded his tobacco pouch and lit an unfiltered cigarette while he shovelled and scattered Pip's droppings across the other side of the gravel road, into the open field. "You be good boy, and I bring more food," as he smacked Pip's rump. "But you getting too fat. Soon your tummy rubbing on ground and Radu have to carry you everywhere!"

Pip snorted in protest before Radu rubbed and scratched the side of his neck. Feeling the donkey's warm breath on his cheeks, the old man and the old donkey shared a quiet moment together.

The men's laughter and banter filled the air, bellies full and spirits high. Irina, watching from afar, felt happiness for Mihai, though her forgiveness was yet to be granted.

As the meal settled, Radu captivated everyone with a fairy tale about a donkey and a mare princess, a story woven from his visit to Baron Leopold Andrian's estate. The baron, of German descent, had made Romania his home for generations, amassing a fortune in timber from the Carpathian Mountains and exporting it worldwide.

"Baron Leopold love horses," said Radu, as the workers sat about, picking at leftover food. "He have famous racing horses and… what you call horse that jump?"

"Show jumping horses," said Mihai.

The baron housed prized Arabian and Spanish horses. Even Appaloosas, with their spotted coats of white and brown, sheening in the midday sun, roamed the green open fields.

"The baron invite me to his house to talk about hay feeds for horses." Radu had met Baron Leopold at the farmers market just before the war and began talking about combining hay feeds and other ingredients to optimise nutritional value for horses. Radu's amiable nature and knowledge of blending hays, grains, and cereals to optimise protein sources for horses captured the baron's attention.

Piling his wagon with various bags of hay and mixed grain feed for horses, Radu and Pip headed thirteen kilometres east until they reached Apahida, the summer home of the baron. Though the Leopold family acquired their wealth from the timber trade, the baron's passion for horses had grown into a full-blown love affair. He split his time between the family business, nestled along the border of the Carpathian Mountains, over two hundred kilometres away, and the estate he had built in Apahida. Being an astute businessman, Baron Leopold turned his passion into a lucrative enterprise.

"Leopold have big estate. He live along creek with perfect grass and white fence and have big house and big stables that look like palace."

"This Leopold guy made that much money from trees?" asked Mircea in astonishment.

Niko mentioned that timber from the Carpathians was highly prized across Europe.

"Pip and I enter the estate. It has very long gravel drive. Pip hee-hawed and turn head, looking at chestnut mare behind white fence. She most beautiful horse I ever see. Her coat shining and she have strong legs and long neck. Her tail swooshing side to side. Pip think she beautiful, too! He stop in his tracks, making donkey noises. And the horse, she stick her head over fence, neighing and pawing ground. I think she teasing Pip."

"Old Pip? Are you kidding?" said Igor.

"Ah, but remember, this long time ago. Pip was young and strong, like me!" Radu laughed before a solemn brush smeared his face. "I never forget that day because following week, Germany invade Poland. But this love story, not war story." His grin reappeared. "I tell Pip this horse is princess, and you are no prince, not even donkey prince!"

Mihai smirked as he lay on his side.

"When we reach house, Pip still turning to see his chestnut princess. I unharness my donkey, so he can rest and feed on good grass and hay. It was end of summer, but very hot day."

Baron Leopold, a robust figure with an impressive moustache, greeted Radu warmly. His home was a Bavarian log cabin masterpiece, nestled on a vast estate. Its architecture boasted a striking A-frame roof, large windowpanes framing the forest beyond, and a grand stone chimney. Inside, the opulence was evident—a library with towering bookshelves, floral curtains held back by gold tassels, and an imposing granite fireplace.

Red Sunrise, the name of the chestnut mare, and Pip's object of affection was a retired racehorse of renowned pedigree. Her plaintive whinnies echoed as Pip displayed his playful frustration.

In the library, Radu marvelled at the wealth of knowledge in the books. He lounged on a chesterfield, admiring the room's grandeur, from the ormolu gilt clock to the oak parquetry flooring. The baron returned with chilled drinks, offering a welcome respite from the heat.

Crossing the drawing room, which led to the stables, paintings of horses filled the walls as the baron grabbed his crop and gloves that lay on a silk chaise lounge.

The stables were as opulent as the manor, with gold-plated knobs on every door, and housed the most magnificent equine creatures: many of them champions in dressage, show jumping, and racing. Radu fed them apples and carrots and snuck one into his pocket for Pip.

Eager to gain an edge in the competitive world of racing, Baron Leopold sought Radu's expertise in feed combinations, offering a handsome sum for this knowledge. They discussed this over lunch, seated in the cool shade on the terrace.

"When we come back after lunch, big surprise," said Radu, as he smacked his forehead with his open palm. "We see Pip mount the chestnut princess." Radu mimicked the actions with a pert look on his face. "He on top of her, in full swing. A donkey and horse princess," as he wiped the tears of laughter from his eyes. "I scream. The baron scream. Everybody scream. We run toward the couple in love, the baron swearing every step of the way. Seeing donkey mount mare was something you no see every day. Baron want to kill Pip. But chestnut princess, she no seem to mind one bit. She... whiny, whaying... wiggling..."

"She whinnied," corrected Mihai.

"Da. Whiggy," said Radu, chuckling to himself. "Pip, not so handsome, but he have... what is word?" as he scratched his head, his eyes squinting as the sun shone on his bald, upturned head. "Charisma! Yes, he have big charisma."

"Like his master!" laughed Mihai, swatting Radu with a rag.

"But baron order us to go. And as we leave, Red Sunrise look at my Pip and she bow her head many times. I not believe it. A champion princess mare bow her head to a common donkey."

And with impeccable timing, Pip strayed into the backyard, looking for his master. Radu leapt up and hugged his old friend, who sniffed the food on the ground, knocking over empty glasses. The men ogled at the old, dishevelled donkey with renewed respect.

"Time to finish garage," Radu said, as he skipped back to his feet and led Pip out front, slipping him a piece of bread and giving him a sip of whisky from his flask, as the aroma of percolated coffee wafted from the back of the house.

The afternoon passed in a blur of activity. The workers climbed ladders, hammered wooden frames, and shared laughter and sweat.

Mircea swore to high heaven when his hammer struck his thumb. His brother, Igor, laughed and teased him about how he should help Mrs Ionescu in the kitchen instead. Radu laughed, rubbing sweat from his forehead. Mircea gave his brother the finger.

The mismatch of overlapping tin sheets on the roof gave the structure character. Igor added finishing touches to the window frames as Mihai confirmed that the garage door opened without grating along the ground.

Overall, a marvellous achievement, as the men stepped back to admire their work. Radu gave a resounding thumbs-up as he poured a bucket of water over his head. "But we not finish," he said, as the water dripped down his wrinkled face.

The backyard brimmed with half a dozen pallets of pastel yellow paint, salvaged from an abandoned government facility by a friend of Radu's.

171

As dusk embraced the sky, the scent of fresh paint mingled with the evening air as the final brushstrokes lacquered the wooden planks. The new garage stood proud, concealing old scars that lingered beneath.

Mihai beckoned Irina to bring out the wine. The men, thirsty from their labour, filled their glasses with rich red wine, savouring it under the waning sun. Its diminishing rays danced in golden streaks across Mihai's paint-flecked hair.

On a whim, Mihai dashed into the house, covered in paint. Irina's protests barely concealed her amusement as the men erupted in jeers. He re-emerged, clutching an old camera, summoning everyone for a group photo beside the garage.

Radu told Mihai he should thank the Securitate. "If it wasn't for them, you would not have new garage!"

Mihai couldn't disagree.

"Wait," shouted Radu, as Pip joined the group photo in front of the little yellow garage. The younger men knelt in front, while the others stood behind, with Pip alongside his master. Radu called out to Irina to join in the group photo. The unlikely gathering captured in perpetuity. A ragtag group of farmers and friends, a surgeon and his wife, and a donkey who fell in love with a princess.

Despite invitations to stay for dinner, the men politely declined. They had completed their task and revelled in the day's camaraderie. They exchanged farewells with warm handshakes and pats on the back.

In the aftermath, Radu, along with his grandsons, cleared the yard of nails, rope scraps, and screws. Pausing by the apple tree, the old man asked Mihai about restoring the old swing.

The swing's ropes had charred and the seat was soot-covered and odorous. Radu, unhurried, continued cleaning up. Clutching her apron, Irina looked at her husband with tender reassurance. Mihai nodded in silent assent.

With deliberate strokes, Radu severed the damaged ropes, replacing them with a sturdier line. He sanded the seat until it was smooth, then brushed it with yellow paint, a symbolic gesture of renewal.

"She would have liked it," Irina murmured, wiping her cheeks.

"Da," replied Mihai.

15

Hoia Baciu Forest

It had been twelve days since Alex fell into a coma. Coma specialists from France had been flown in, yet their expertise failed to illuminate the enigma. Despite round-the-clock vigilance and exhaustive efforts, Mihai and his team were at an impasse. There were no clear paths, perhaps none. Amid the uncertainty, Mihai faced a narrowing window: a week, maybe two, to reverse the boy's fate. Beyond that, hope for a full recovery dwindled.

His attempts to confront Alexandru Lupei proved futile; the man was unreachable, submerged in silence. Amidst these endeavours, Mihai found solace in his routine, sipping coffee, and visiting post-op patients.

It was during his rounds that he routinely conversed with Cezar Muller, a familiar figure in the hospital corridors. Cezar, a forty-two-year-old labourer, and father to three daughters, worked night shifts, enduring the squalid, perilous conditions of the factory. The air he breathed was laced with lead trioxide, a fine, insidious powder that seeped into his lungs. Years of exposure, unshielded by a mask, had taken their toll. Now, cancer gnawed at his life, leaving him with mere weeks.

Mihai had formed a bond with the dying man, though he was not his doctor. Their conversations, stripped of medical jargon, provided a respite from the unyielding march of disease. Mihai had learnt the value of words as a balm when tending to his daughter; sometimes, they were the only solace a surgeon could offer.

As a doctor, Mihai grappled with the inevitability of death. It was a relentless adversary, ever-present and unpredictable. It lurked in every shadow: in the depths of lakes, the rush of cars, the smoke of cigarettes, and the microscopic invasion of viruses. It was omnipresent in allergies, storms, accidents, and even in the surgeon's own hands. Death, a tireless hunter, never slept.

From the dawn of humanity, death has been a constant companion. It witnessed the demise of early Homo erectus venturing from Africa, King Sargon of Akkad falling in battle, Plato passing away serenaded by a Thracian girl, and Emperor Marcus Aurelius succumbing to the plague. It watched a Pompeiian slave fleeing Vesuvius, Attila the Hun dying on his wedding night, a Huli newborn meeting a tragic end in Papua New Guinea, Joan of Arc's fiery martyrdom, Catherine the Great's descent into a coma, and Sitting Bull's final moments at Standing Rock. It was there for the assassinations of Abraham Lincoln, Archduke Franz Ferdinand, Mahatma Gandhi, and John F. Kennedy; the suicides of Cleopatra, Nero, Vincent van Gogh, Adolf Hitler, Ernest Hemingway, and Sylvia Plath; and the cataclysmic morning of August 6th, 1945, in Hiroshima. Death, an eternal witness, has presided over countless souls, a number ever-growing.

Death, in its indiscriminate march, can be merciless, weaving a tapestry of harrowing regret, paralysing fear, and profound loneliness. Yet, for some, it unfolds as a tapestry of overwhelming relief and tranquillity. Unbiased in its approach, death visits all: from infants to centenarians, from dwellers in shanty towns to monarchs in golden palaces, from those with skin gleaming like tar under the sun, to those with complexions of porcelain and ivory. It spares neither soldier on the battlefield nor mother in childbirth, striking without prejudice or hesitation.

Yet, despite this inevitable truth, many choose to distance themselves from death, fearing it might cross their threshold if acknowledged. But death, our inevitable companion from birth, bides its time, inching closer with each passing moment, until it emerges from the shadows, assuming its role as the final antagonist or protagonist of our lives. This duality of death, simultaneously rendering life meaningful and meaningless, embodies the ultimate paradox.

Cezar Muller, facing his impending end, yearned for moments with his daughters, who visited him daily. He cherished these times, sharing hitherto untold childhood stories and dreams—narratives often left unsaid by parents. Acknowledging his past failings, Cezar sought to leave behind memories etched with fondness and love.

Rejecting painkillers, Cezar chose clarity over comfort. The medications could dull his pain but clouded his mind, robbing him of precious, lucid moments with his daughters. His decision to face death typified the philosophy of the Samurai—valuing a dignified end.

Mihai had given nurses hell when they informed Cezar's family that visiting hours were over. On Mihai's watch, they stayed as long as they liked.

Cezar faced his demise with a rare bravery, believing that an easy death was not always a noble one. He passed away with strength and dignity. The Samurai would have approved.

༄

Mihai checked in on young Alex once again. It brought back ghosts from the past.

"Hey, Alex," he whispered, a mixture of hope and melancholy in his voice. "I'm not sure if you can hear me, but I need to believe you do. We're all here for you. I know it's frightening where you are, but don't be afraid. We're doing everything to bring you back. You're not alone in that darkness. Fight your way out, Alex. Be strong like Superman. We need you to fight."

Alex lay motionless, ensnared in his own silent battle with unseen adversaries.

༄

"How's the boy?" asked Irina.

"Unchanged," Mihai replied, hanging his damp overcoat on the stand.

"What happens now?"

"We wait. We're running every test, ruling out causes." Mihai's voice carried a weary resignation.

"Have you spoken to his father?"

"He was there late last night, but I missed him. Adam's keeping him updated."

Irina tried to remain calm, despite being frightened... and angry. "What if he doesn't wake up?"

Mihai avoided her gaze, opening the fridge. Its hum seemed the only steady thing. "Let's not leap to conclusions."

Standing by the sink, Irina squeezed the tea towel. "Was it worth it, Mihai? This... escape plan of yours?"

His response was curt. "You're crossing a line, Irina."

"Am I?" Her voice rose. "You've longed to leave. This boy's crisis... it's just a means to an end for you, isn't it?" Her words, sharp and unyielding, cut through the air. "You're using him, Mihai. It's selfishness, not altruism."

Mihai remained silent, his thoughts in turmoil.

"I love Romania. It's my home, despite its flaws. I buried our daughter here, Mihai!" Irina's voice broke, her anger giving way to grief as she tossed the tea towel onto the table.

Mihai's silence persisted.

"This is about your ambitions, not us." She paused, expecting a rebuttal that never came. "You're to blame if anything happens to that boy. And Lupei... he'll destroy everything."

The phone's ring punctuated the tense air.

"Hello, this is Dr Mihai Ionescu."

He grabbed his jacket and gloves. "I have to go."

"What?"

"Radu's holding a meeting at his farm. The police have been tipped off."

"What meeting, Mihai? Who were you talking to?"

"I need to go. He wouldn't say. We'll talk later."

"The police?" A panic set in. "You can't go, Mihai. You are already in enough trouble. It's too dangerous." She reached for him as he opened the door.

"It's Radu, for God's sake," as he headed down the stairs.

Outside, his car refused to start. "Damn it!" Frustration set in in as he borrowed the neighbour's Dacia 1300, stating some hospital emergency. The navy-blue car roared to life, and he sped away, gravel flying.

Reaching the end of the gravel road, Mihai came to a skidding holt, removed the rear number plate with the car key, and sat in contemplation. The risk of being caught loomed large. *Would this end my dreams?* Radu's smiling face flashed across his mind. "Screw it," he muttered, driving into the uncertain night.

∽

The barn stood defiant against the violent gale. Despite the wrath of nature, the farmers converged, drawn to the warmth and camaraderie within. Around the bonfire, close to a hundred men huddled, their faces illuminated by the flames. Moths fluttered above, drawn to the light as if to a beacon of hope. Radu, with his ever-warm smile, welcomed each with a steaming cup of home-brewed liquor or tea.

The interior was a tapestry of decay and resilience. Rotted beams, clutched together by rope and wire, bore witness to years of toil and neglect. A patchwork of tin sheets veiled the barn's wounds, though the downpour began to expose weaknesses in the façade.

Roland Lelescu, a once prominent farmer, took the floor. Roland's family had cultivated the land for generations in the province of Transylvania. His grandfather, Vali Lelescu, established the first farmers market in Cluj at the turn of the century. Roland spoke of how farmers were hurting and migrating to urban sprawls. "And who can blame them? Since Ceausescu came to power, he has made it a priority to rid the nation of its breadbasket."

The farmers fidgeted at the mention of that name: a name that stripped them of their manhood. They were a ragged bunch, whose sullen, gaunt faces, and emaciated bodies, draped in oversized jackets, cast shadows against the fire, like a congregation of scarecrows.

"Those in Bucharest dictate our actions. They steal our food stocks from under our noses and export them abroad, leaving our people hungry."

Murmurs rang through the barn like parishioners at a sermon.

"Farmers are leaving their lands in numbers we have never seen before," said Roland. "This mass exodus is happening right across our great land. Here alone, we know of dozens who have forfeited their farms and packed it in."

"David Bora left last night!" shouted a voice in the crowd. "A wife and four children with nothing to show for it."

Whispers and sighs stirred throughout the barn. Radu's heart sank.

As a sparrow darted across the barn, settling atop a tractor, Roland's call to unity struck a chord. "The heartland belongs to us, the farmers," he proclaimed, his voice echoing off the tin walls. The crowd, electrified, resonated with his sentiment.

"Look at what happened in Jiu Valley," someone called out. "You are not saying we follow in their footsteps?"

"Down with the proletarian bourgeoisie!"

"Friends," pleaded Roland, as the crowd settled. "No one is advocating a repeat of what occurred at Jiu Valley. The miners lacked organisation, and they made non-negotiable demands, leaving officials with no room to manoeuvre. We need a well-planned strategy that can deal with the bureaucracy. They did not understand Ceausescu."

A chill swept through the barn, almost smothering the fire. Radu, quick to act, threw another log into the bin, igniting a burst of flames reminiscent of a dragon's breath in its lair.

"Four thousand men lost their jobs, hundreds sent to labour camps," an anguished voice cried out, encapsulating the depth of their shared despair.

"Yes, I understand," Roland acknowledged, his gaze following the sparrow's flight to the rafters. "We cannot repeat past mistakes. Unity is key, and we must strategically engage with officials, advocating a coherent set of demands. We need to speak their language, turn the tide in our favour."

"And are you the one, Roland, who will speak to the politicians? Who put you in charge?"

The mood teetered on the brink of discord, with loyalties divided. The sparrow took flight, only to return to its perch.

Radu stepped forward, his presence calming the brewing storm. "I happy everyone come tonight, and everyone is passion… has passion. That is good. But we here to choose leader tonight and to agree on first steps. This was reason for meeting."

In the barn's dim recesses, Radu noticed a hooded figure waving him over.

༄

The mist shrouded Mihai's journey through the valley, lending an otherworldly feel to the evening. Thunder echoed as he neared Radu's farm, his eyes straining through the haze for any sign of the police. The car jostled and jerked over the uneven terrain. Opting for caution, he parked hidden among the shrubs and proceeded down to the farm on foot.

Rain pelted down as he navigated the slippery, muddy path towards the barn, its flickering embers visible like fireflies in the distance. Taking shelter beneath a willow, its branches drooping like sheltering arms, he stumbled over the jutting roots that bulged and twisted like varicose veins. Despite the temptation to turn back, Mihai pulled the hood down over his face, wrapped the scarf over his mouth and headed for the barn.

Inside, Mihai slipped past the rowdy mob unnoticed, as Radu reiterated the night's purpose. "I happy everyone come tonight, and everyone is passion… has passion. That is good. But we here to choose leader tonight and to agree on first steps. This was reason for meeting."

Radu caught sight of a man in the shadows waving him over.

"It's Mihai," he whispered, as Radu approached. "Send everyone home. The police know about the meeting."

Chaos ensued as farmers scattered in all directions. The sparrow disappeared through a gap in the roof. A warning about approaching headlights sent Mihai towards the exit, only to be pulled back by Radu.

Guiding him to a secluded corner, Radu revealed a hidden passage between the cobweb-draped machinery. Mihai slipped through while Radu remained behind.

Mihai stayed low, adjusting to the dark. There were voices in the distance. Flashlights scanned the terrain. Whistles blew. Orders issued. Mihai froze. The Securitate.

"Shit." Mihai darted towards a copse of ironwood trees, his heart pounding as flashlights sliced through the darkness, the police fanning out like ants over the farmland. He weaved through the underbrush, beams of light skimming overhead. Reaching the ridge, he risked the open terrain, shrouded by the mist. Sweat trickled down his back, chilling him, as his ragged breaths formed ephemeral clouds in the cold air.

Finding refuge in the thick shrubs, Mihai located his car. He eased it into first gear, creeping up the hill until bright headlights shattered the night's embrace. He stomped on the accelerator, taking a sharp right, his teeth gritted, anticipating a wild ride.

The pursuit ignited a primal thrill in Mihai. Despite his stress, he felt an exhilarating rush, leading his pursuers west to where the wild things are. His driving was daring, fuelled by the high stakes. The car skidded and swerved on the wet gravel. "Don't let me down," he cried, urging the little car on.

One of the pursuing vehicles lost control and crashed into a tree. Mihai pressed on, racing along the forest's edge. The mist lent a spectral quality to the night, masking his movements, as the Dacia fishtailed across the slippery terrain.

One down, one to go.

Before long, he raced along the forest edge that encompassed three hundred hectares. The rain eased as he continued spiralling up the mountain pass. A light drizzle fell as the moon played hide-and-seek behind the clouds. The mist provided additional cover, like a scene from an old horror movie.

He lost sight of those giving chase. A few more twists and turns and he would be home free.

The car faltered. "Come on!" Mihai cursed, slamming his hand on the steering wheel. The fuel gauge read empty. Desperate, he veered off the road, plunging into the forest. The car buckled and swayed, narrowly missing trees, before jolting to a stop against a boulder. Mihai sat back, blood trickling down his forehead, a mix of relief and fear pulsing through him. The forest cocooned the car, offering a layer of protection. The overworked engine ticked as he planned his next move. He wiped the blood from his face, resolute in his refusal to surrender, and ran into the belly of the forest.

The sedan following Mihai lost the chase. "Major-General, I think we lost him," came the report.

Alexandru Lupei's fist slammed against the dashboard, as he stepped out into the night and lit a cigarette. His orders cut through the silence, "He's in these woods. Find him."

In the frostbitten clutches of Hoia Baciu, the officers shuddered, reluctant to leave the comfort of their vehicle. Alexandru Lupei, unbothered by the chill, stood in an open shirt and jacket. The forest's sinister reputation—haunted by alien sightings, ghosts, and darker myths— unnerved them. Tales of gipsy rituals, wolves tearing apart corpses, human sacrifices, and people vanishing or succumbing to sudden sickness were rife among the locals.

Sensing their fear, Lupei scoffed at their trepidation. "Children's tales," he chided. "Vlad Dracul roaming the forest? Come now." He urged them into action. "He won't venture deep. Search the perimeter and keep your distance."

The forest, now a sanctuary and a prison, sheltered Mihai as he navigated the ghostly mist and sideways rain as his footsteps crunched on the frost. A misstep into a bog, and he heard the sickening twist of his ankle, a piercing scream escaping his lips.

Limping and tormented by pain, Mihai was wrapped in the forest's eerie embrace. The twisted branches seemed to reach out with malformed limbs. An uncanny silence, broken only by the distant hoot of owls and the rustling of leaves, hung heavy in the air.

One of the Securitate agents, despite being armed, felt a cold dread. The legends of Hoia Baciu—of mad gipsies, lost children, and supernatural occurrences—disturbed his thoughts. He hated this place despite having a gun.

A twig snapped, and torchlights pierced the darkness, revealing the grotesque forms of beech trees. Mihai, desperate to evade capture, veered right, trying to ignore the pain in his ankle. The dense mist obscured his vision, and the ominous sounds of the forest filled the air.

A voice broke the silence.

"My friend, we are the police. We know who you are. Your friends have given us your details. It would be best to give yourself up. It is dangerous in these woods late at night. We don't want any unfortunate accidents to occur."

Mihai knew that voice. The Wolf.

He stood frozen, his heart racing. Mihai's breath caught as nausea swept over him, sweat beading on his brow. He knew Lupei was bluffing; if they knew his identity, they would have called him by name. A thunderclap burst overhead, startling him, and lightning flashes turned the forest into a stark tableau. Shadows danced in the mist, their ethereal forms ambiguous and haunting.

Pursued by the Securitate, their torch beams slicing through the dark night like spitfires in a dogfight, Mihai abandoned caution. Branches whipped his face, drawing blood. Despite the searing pain in his ankle, he surged forward, driven by instinct.

At a crossroads, Mihai hesitated as a child's voice beckoned from the left. His gut urged him to follow, diverging from the approaching torchlights.

Finding a momentary respite, his ankle throbbed. The moon emerged, casting a serene glow. A lynx, curious and ghostlike, revealed itself before melting back into the shadows.

A rustle and a grunt broke the silence. Mihai struggled to stand, but it was too late. A wild boar, like a living bulldozer, charged. He rolled away, narrowly escaping its menacing tusks that gleamed in the moonlight.

"Shit," Mihai gasped, scrambling back. The boar's second charge grazed his leg, igniting a searing pain. In desperation, Mihai's boot connected with its snout, sending it squealing into the darkness.

His gorged heart pounding like a jackhammer, he pressed on, driven by urgency and fear. Snorts and yellow eyes emerged again, heralding another charge by the hundred-kilogram freight train. As branches lashed his face, Mihai stumbled through the undergrowth before falling and grappling with the boar's tusks in a struggle for survival. Rolling into an open clearing, he braced for the worst. But the animal halted at the clearing's edge, refusing to enter. The circular space, about fifty metres in diameter, lay still and untouched. Not even the fog dared to encroach. Panting heavily, Mihai whirled around in bewilderment at this unexplained sanctuary in the heart of Hoia Baciu.

The Clearing, an enigma nestled within Hoia Baciu, defied understanding. Despite its fertile soil, it remained barren, a stark void amidst the lush forest. Animals, sensing something amiss, never trespassed its borders. Hunters whispered of the open terrain's dangers, while others spun tales of UFOs and interdimensional portals akin to the crop circles in the United States.

In this surreal sanctuary, Mihai caught his breath, his heart thundering. A metallic taste invaded his mouth, leading to a bout of nausea. Struggling to stand, the world spun, disorienting him.

The canopy seemed to breathe, draped in mist, and bathed in a soft, grey moonlight. Vague contours played amidst the trees, whispering secrets.

From the darkness, a tenebrous, nightmarish figure emerged, its body tattooed in scars, its hair long, and eyes bloodshot and malevolent. It approached Mihai with a menacing grin, revealing fang-like teeth. A wave of terror washed over him as he sensed the creature's intent. Its fangs pierced his neck, and Mihai felt his life force ebbing away, his vision fading to black amidst the forest's monochromatic palette.

The winds howled as rain bucketed down, crashing into the trees, blanketing the thicket with white noise. Lightning cracked and tore through the night sky's fabric.

A scream. A shot fired.

Mihai woke in a frenzy. A singlet of sweat formed beneath his jumper. *What the hell is happening? Had I drifted off to sleep? Was I dreaming?* Something terrified him, but the recollection was opaque, like an ill-defined watermark. Lacking perspicuity, the torrential downpour washed away Mihai's capacity for sagacious thought. He rubbed his neck as the fog swirled in the thoroughfare of his mind.

A branch made for a makeshift walking stick as the winds whined, skirting between passages through the trees. He hobbled deeper into the bowels of the woods, distancing himself from the gunshot and screams. As a glimpse of moonlight shone through the forest rooftop, something swayed in the branches above. Lightning pulsated in quick succession.

His blood froze. Above him, a corpse.

You are shitting me, as he adjusted to the gruesome sight before him. *If you dare open your eyes, I will scream bloody murder.* Based on how things were going, it wasn't beyond the realm of possibility. The body had decomposed either through time or by feasting animals and maggots. To Mihai's relief, the dead man's eyes remained closed.

The legends of Hoia Baciu, with its tales of witches, vampires, and a lure for the troubled, seemed all too real as Mihai limped onwards. Feeling the oppressive weight of the night's horrors, he vowed never to return, making his way to the boundary.

The Securitate agents were conspicuously absent, perhaps driven away by the same fear that gripped Mihai. He remained in hiding, trying to regain his strength and sanity, as his teeth chattered, and muscles ached.

After an arduous journey, Mihai found the car nestled against the familiar boulder. With a mixture of determination and pain, he got the car moving, coasting downhill in silence, hoping the engine would spring to life as he neared the town.

❦

At the farm, the police captured around forty men, with Securitate agents barking orders. Radu, bewildered, tried to make sense of the accusations of illegal meetings and government plots. The situation felt surreal.

A young agent, annoyed by the cold, wet night, shoved Radu from behind. Losing his footing, the old man fell into the mud, only to be dragged along by the furious agent.

Then, out of the darkness, Pip charged, knocking the agent to the ground. The donkey had come for his master, sniffing Radu's bald head. The agent, stunned, angry and muddied from head to toe, unholstered his revolver.

A hellish squeal pierced the night as two shots reverberated across the farm. The animal spun in circles, desperately reaching for his hind leg. He fell on his rear, no longer able to keep himself up, kicking and bucking wildly. The ear-splitting squealing did not abate.

Radu, overcome with grief, held the donkey's head in his lap, stroking the frightened animal's face, trying to reassure and comfort his old friend.

Two more shots at point blank range. Pip wailed, thrashing and kicking his legs about in madness. The bullets tore through his round midsection. Dark stains of blood spilled as the animal writhed about until his breath abated to short, shallow snorts from his flaring nostrils that plumed into the frigid night sky.

Radu lunged with a force that bellied his age and frame. The men rolled in the mud as the rain continued to pour. Surprised, the Securitate agent underestimated Radu's rage and strength. The old man was strong... farmer strong. He grabbed the agent's fallen gun and fired.

16

Deeper into the Chasm

Exhausted and limping, Mihai reached his destination, the car sputtering and choking on its last breath. The state of the old Dacia would need some serious explanation: the empty tank, dents and scratches; remnants of the harrowing journey.

His arrival at two in the morning left Irina overwrought and perplexed. Exhausted and unresponsive to her barrage of questions, he managed a shower, swallowed painkillers, bandaged his leg, iced his ankle, and sought refuge in sleep.

The next morning, every muscle in Mihai's body protested as he poured a cup of black coffee. Irina's worry deepened, her questions flooding in, but the experiences formed a chaotic collage, too bizarre to articulate. Mihai outlined a watered-down version of the raid on Radu's farm, as he impishly replayed the night's surreal events in his head.

Where do I begin? The Securitate chased me into the Hoia Baciu forest, where I sprained or tore my ankle. A possible ghost crossed my path, though it could have been an illusion caused by the fog. I heard children's voices: they were laughing and giggling and having a gay old time. Did I tell you how wonderful the trees are? What's that you say? We should have a picnic there. Great idea! The branches are alive, and they try to strangle you, but that's not the worst of it. Don't look up as you might see your garden variety dead body hanging from the branches. But I'm digressing. What else can I tell you? Nothing out of the ordinary, except that a wild boar attacked me. But don't worry, once I made it to The Clearing, they left me alone, though they left a nice gash on my leg. What's The Clearing, you ask? Nothing to fret about: just an alien portal where you eat rusted steel as a midnight snack and dream of vampires sucking your blood. I wouldn't recommend it—unless, of course, you're being chased by boars. Oh, how silly of me! I almost forgot! Alexandru Lupei and I were playing hide-and-seek up in the forest— we had a barrel of laughs. By the way, Grigore's car is down the road somewhere with an empty petrol tank. His car is banged up, but I'm sure he won't mind. He's a good sport. Anything else you wanted to know?

❧

At the hospital, Mihai's appearance—lacerated, bruised, and in obvious pain—drew stares from the staff, but no one dared to ask questions. He felt like a casualty of a brutal battle, his body aching from wounds and exertions he hadn't known possible. His gashed leg needed disinfecting, but no stitches were required, and his swollen, discoloured ankle spoke volumes of his ordeal.

Mihai's rage escalated as the technician complained about the low supply of X-ray film. His ankle had blown up like a puffer fish, though the pain killers relieved the throbbing. Sprained but not broken, Mihai gave an unlucky nurse an earful when she re-bandaged his injury too tight.

Attempting to contact Radu proved futile; the phone line was dead, and no one seemed to have any information. Slumped in his office chair, Mihai's frustration boiled over, his outburst startling a nearby nurse. He snapped at her intrusion. His mood was as turbulent as the storm he had endured.

In the background, young Alex remained in his coma, his condition a constant reminder of the unresolved mysteries and challenges Mihai faced.

Mihai navigated the hospital corridors, half-expecting Alexandru Lupei's sinister silhouette to emerge at every turn. Despite the tumultuous events of the previous night, Lupei seemed to have vanished, his ominous aura persisting like a shadow.

In the afternoon, Mircea and Igor arrived.

"We have spoken to everyone." The boys had not slept a wink. "No one knows where our grandfather is." Igor noticed Mihai's cuts and bruises. "Are you okay, Doc? What happened to your face?"

Mihai waved it off.

"Radu is a loyal, hard-headed man," said Mircea. "He will try his darnedest to not say a word. I am afraid for him. He won't survive long with those pigs. He is old."

They spent the day in a futile maze of bureaucracy, reminiscent of Alice's descent down the rabbit hole. Mihai's calls to officials, many former patients, led to dead ends, save for one crucial lead from Officer Pilaf. The information ominous—Radu was held by the Securitate, and they wanted names.

"Radu won't talk," said Mircea. "I know him. No matter what they do to him, my grandfather will not give names."

"My brother is right. He is as stubborn as that donkey of his. He won't rat anybody out."

Mihai told the boys that everything would be alright: the reassurance, hollow. *Could I ask Alexandru Lupei about Radu? Would that put me in an untenable position?*

"And, Doctor," Mircea said, "the bastards shot Pip."

The doctor's name blared across the PA system. An emergency in the operating theatre. Complications during the removal of a brain tumour. The patient's blood pressure and heart rate dropped. The surgeon in theatre requested Dr Mihai Ionescu's immediate assistance.

As Mihai loped upstairs, wincing in pain, Irina called.

"Mihai, they're here! What do they want, Mihai?"

Mihai sensed the fear in her voice.

"Dr Ionescu, they need you in Theatre 2 urgently!" said a junior doctor.

Mihai raised his finger, telling him to wait, as he tried to remain calm for Irina's sake.

Knocking at the front door.

"They're here, Mihai. The Securitate are at the door! I'm scared. Are they going to arrest me?"

"Say nothing, Irina. Tell them we were home alone. They might ask about my whereabouts last night. I was home all night. Do you understand?"

No response.

"Dr Ionescu, you're needed in surgery now!"

"One second!" Mihai shouted, glaring at the junior doctor. "Irina, are you there? Irina?" He threw the phone into the wall.

After attending to the emergency in the operating theatre, Mihai jumped in his car and throttled it. He ran every red light and blared his horn most of the way home. A migraine banged away with a sledgehammer inside his head. He swallowed more pain killers.

Irina stood by the front door as the Renault came screeching to a halt.

"What did they want?" he asked in a frenzy.

"Well, I am okay and unharmed, but thanks for asking."

"Alright," he said, taking a deep breath. "Are you okay? Did they hurt you?"

"I am fine, now." She had made her point. "There were two of them. They were older than the imbeciles who trashed our home. One of them may have been in a senior position or something. They were respectful and well mannered."

"What did they want, Irina?"

"They asked where you were last night."

Mihai grabbed her arm. "What did you tell them?"

She looked at her arm. Mihai let go.

"I told them we were home, just like you said."

"And that's it. No other questions?"

"That's it. I asked them what this was about, but they didn't answer." Anger replaced her fear.

"They made no reference of any meeting, or Radu?" asked Mihai.

"Nope."

Mihai sensed her agitation but had other things on his mind.

"They asked if anyone could confirm you were home, but I reiterated it was the two of us. They warned me that if contradictory information regarding your whereabouts last night comes to light, I will be arrested for lying to the

Securitate. Who knows," she said, "maybe we'll both end up in prison."

He tried to touch her, but she walked away.

"No, Mihai. We are deeper into this chasm. We've fallen so far that we can't see the way out anymore." She grabbed her bag and headed out the door. "I'm going to Joanna's. I need to clear my head. There is food in the fridge."

The sledgehammer kept pounding inside his head.

"I love you, but I am so angry, and I blame you for what has happened since your involvement with this loathsome Lupei character. Perhaps now you'll appreciate that our lives were not so bad." She held back the tears and closed the door behind her.

17

ECT

Mihai manically sifted through files in his overstocked cabinet drawers. Several nurses and interns were in the hospital basement, unearthing patient archives. Some of the dusty cabinets needed to be pried open. No one ventured to this area, especially since a pipe burst three years ago, flooding the basement. There were plans awaiting government approval for installing a safer storage facility. Those plans were still pending.

By lunchtime, a sea of documents buried Mihai's office. His stern demeanour and urgency set the tone, as staff scurried to assist, staying late into the night. The hospital provided dinner, and Mihai supplemented it with treats from the town's beloved pastry shop: Fornetti's.

Dr Gheorghe had unintentionally sparked a daring idea in Mihai's mind... *reboot them,* were Gheorghe's words.

Electro-convulsive therapy (ECT), typically used in psychiatric cases, comprised controlled electrical bursts through the brain to recalibrate the chemistry and repeal some mental health symptoms. They had never used it on coma patients or children.

Amidst an anarchic landscape of strewn files and empty coffee cups, Mihai and his team delved into the depths of medical history. The clock's midnight chime reverberated through the room, signalling the dwindling hope as only two boxes remained unexplored. Then, in a moment of serendipity, an intern discovered a crucial file. Mihai bear-hugged the man and kissed him like a long-lost son.

The case outlined a psychiatric patient in a comatose state. Mihai had a vague recollection of seeing the file when conducting research for an epilepsy conference in Craiova that triggered this wild goose chase.

The patient received electro-convulsive therapy as part of his ongoing treatment for psychosis. Without explanation, the therapy continued, despite the patient being in a coma. This was more than odd. *Was there something missing from the file? Were they experimenting on him?* Frustratingly, pages of the report were missing, which may have outlined some explanations. But soon after the treatment, the patient woke from his coma. Mihai wanted this piece of the puzzle. However, no timeline between the therapy and the patient waking up materialised. Regardless of the scant and incomplete file, it provided Mihai with a ray of hope.

∽

Alex had been in a coma for seventeen days. The chances of recovery diminished with each passing day. A decision had to be made.

The psychiatrists condemned the use of electro-convulsive therapy, citing its risks were too great on a child who may have brain damage. Mihai knew Adam would not approve; thus, he did not want him involved.

And seeking permission from Alex's father was out of the question. Mihai knew he would breach codes of conduct, including consent and duty of care. They would disbar him from practising medicine—pending criminal charges. He had crossed that line in the sand.

In a quiet room, away from prying eyes, Mihai and Nurse Mirela Net prepared for the unconventional procedure. Mirela carefully secured Alex, aware of the potential risks of physical injury during the therapy. Mihai, though inexperienced in administering ECT, was resolute. Giant earmuffs would run an electric current through Alex's brain, emulating a controlled seizure. The irony absurdly comical, if not for the seriousness of it all. They would target the left temple, taking precautions to protect Alex's remaining brain tissue. The doctor placed a bit between Alex's teeth to stop him from biting his tongue.

"Just in case," he cautioned. "There shouldn't be any physical reaction." The boy's comatose state both protected and exposed him to external forces.

Mirela nodded while her eyes darted toward the door.

The room hummed with the sound of the machine and the weight of their decision. Mirela's uncertainty mirrored Mihai's internal conflict, yet the need for a drastic intervention overrode her doubts.

Alex looked calm and peaceful. He had his dad's firm jawline, though he possessed a sensitivity his father lacked. Mihai hoped the boy had his father's strength, as he needed every ounce.

Mirela turned on the switch. A faint whirring noise filled the small room. "Are you sure?" she asked.

"We will administer the lowest voltage for one second," he said.

She set the dial to 80. She doubted the doctor's judgement for the first time in her life.

Though stimulating the brain with an electrical current had been an accepted remedy for a variety of disorders throughout Europe since the early 1940s, including depression and schizophrenia, Romanian doctors viewed the procedure as barbaric and dangerous—fearing brain damage and memory loss.

Mirela flicked the switch.

Nothing happened.

"Okay, increase to 100 for two seconds."

Still no response.

"We will give it one more shot. Increase to 110 volts for two and a half seconds.

"Are you sure, Doctor?"

Unacquainted with second thoughts, he hesitated for the length of a heartbeat. "Do it," he said.

An electric charge surged through Alex's left hemisphere. He bucked and kicked like a wild stallion. Mihai jumped. Mirela screamed. They shoved extra pillows between the rail bars as he thrashed about. The taut leather restraint creaked with the strain. Alex's jaw stretched, as if splitting apart, as the wooden bit fell to the floor. His head twisted and turned in impossible positions. He arched his back, straining against the belt, slamming up and down on the bed as if supernatural forces were at play. Only the whites of his eyes were visible, as a demonic shrill sent shivers down Mirela's spine. It did not sound human. The metal staples running across the child's skull did little to change that perception.

"Alex!" Mihai's voice was a desperate plea amid the chaos.

But Alex's reaction was beyond their understanding. His words, disjointed and strained, were a puzzle they couldn't solve. "Collll—" The word hung in the air, unfinished and haunting.

"What is it, Alex? Talk to me!"

Mihai and Mirela tried to make sense of it.

"What are you saying? Tell me, Alex, tell me!" He gripped the boy's arms.

"You—"

"That's it, say it, Alex!" yelled Mihai.

Alex remained fixated on Mihai. His neck strained as he screamed. "Colllll—"

And then collapsed on the bed. The fire in his eyes extinguished, replaced by the glassy stare of a dead fish.

"Jesus Christ!" cried Mihai.

Mirela steadied herself against the side rail.

"Alex. Wake up. Come back!" Mihai shouted. He bent over the boy. "Wake up, damn you! Don't give up, you hear me!" He violently shook the young patient. "Come back, Alex. Come back!"

The body lay limp like a ragdoll.

Like Dr Frankenstein trying to awaken his ambitious creation, he questioned whether he had become the monster in his own story? Mihai didn't know what to think. *Had it been a promising omen? What was he trying to say? Some profound insight or secret? Or just random, meaningless words?* For an instant, Alex had returned, or at least part of him did. *Was it the reboot needed?* Irina's words cut him to the quick. *Have I gambled with his life? Have I damaged him for good? He may never return from this purgatory, and if he does, what version will come back?* The guilt overwhelmed him as he hunched over in despair.

Alex had plunged into the pit once more. A part of him had escaped the clutches that swathed him, as he fought to wrench himself from its vise-like grip. The boy had become somewhat cognizant of the outside world. He heard noises, voices, and shadows of a less oppressive darkness. Whatever it was, it had faded fast: the battle short-lived. He spiralled back into the abyss. His screams muted as the shadow swallowed him once again.

"Is everything going to be, okay? asked Mirela, trying to calm her nerves.

Mihai brushed Alex's hair back from his face and caught his own reflection in the mirror above the nightstand. *Judas is my name.*

"I'm not sure, Mirela. I'm just not sure."

18

Aiud Prison

Alex lay motionless as Mihai monitored his EEG. There were no after-effects from the electro-shock therapy—and no fractured bones. The impact of the brief yet startling revival remained a mystery. He could not risk a further try.

On the bright side, Alex's seizure activities were minimal. However, external noises produced no brain wave activity. Regardless, Mihai sat by his side, reading him a Batman comic.

The lumbar puncture confirmed no infection in the nervous system, eliminating another culprit for the coma. Mihai had run out of ideas, as the Joker orchestrated a diabolical scheme to rid himself of Batman for good.

Mihai headed to theatre, preparing for a busy morning of back-to-back surgeries. Nurse Nadia called out, running toward him in a fright. "The Securitate are downstairs. They are looking for you."

He entered the operating room, regardless, as he had a patient to tend to. The loudspeaker requested that Dr Mihai Ionescu report to the front office immediately. He ignored it.

A second announcement came five minutes later. Mihai didn't bat an eyelid. Soon after, men in suits burst into the hallowed ground of the operating room.

"Get out!" yelled Mihai.

The nurses screamed while the resident doctors backed away. The men took no heed and insisted the surgeon step outside.

"You've contaminated the room and endangered the patient's life! Out, now!" Mihai flailed his arms about, scalpel in hand, stepping toward the intruders.

The officers reached for their holsters. Mihai placed the scalpel down and backed away.

He changed out of his scrubs before being handcuffed. Patients in the hallway were in shock. Nurse Marta retrieved Mihai's overcoat and put it over his arms before being pushed aside. At the front desk, two additional men in suits waited.

The receptionist, a woman who had worked at the hospital since anyone could remember, clutched her cardigan, devastated at seeing the doctor in handcuffs. Despite enduring the doctor's outbursts, including being told she had a brain of a chicken, Dr Ionescu made a late-night house call when her husband fell ill.

Adam tried to interject, of course, demanding to see paperwork or a warrant, but Mihai gestured to his mentor to not get involved. Staff lined the first-floor balcony. Marta and Nadia held each other, while the junior resident, Alin, couldn't believe his eyes. Dr Gheorghe observed with a trace of amusement.

The authorities marched a handcuffed Mihai out of the hospital. Being led out in this ignominious manner was the final nail in the coffin of his career. His gamble had not paid off. The Securitate, showboating their prized detainee, sent a signal that nobody escaped their reach—let alone those who removed half the brain of a child whose father was the most feared man in Romania.

∽

He woke in a small, dank cell, shivering and curled up in a ball after not having slept for long. A lightbulb hung from a long dangling wire. The light flickered and faltered, making a buzzing sound, before casting luminescence into a cell that resembled the bowels of Dracula's dungeon. A dirty, thin mattress lay on the hard, cold floor. His heavy coat the only offering of warmth in this place.

Keys rattled in the door. "Mihai Ionescu, please come with us."

They led him down a corridor with low ceilings and stopped outside a bathroom. The toilet, a godsend, as the bucket in the cell made him sick. A shower and sink, with towel and soap: another godsend. The hot water felt like heaven. He scrubbed every stain off his body. Had it been two days? He wasn't sure. The banging on the door indicated the brief reprieve had ended.

Invigorated and warm, though weak from lack of food, they entered an office and waited. A woman dressed in a coral jacket and matching skirt sat behind a desk, stubbing a spent cigarette out in the ashtray, leaving a wet maroon smear of lipstick on its butt. She summoned a laconic smile before returning to her typing. Her floral fragrance reminded Mihai of summer strolls through the botanic gardens.

Through an adjacent door, footsteps. The handle turned.

"Good morning, Dr Ionescu." In the doorway, dressed in decorated military fatigues, stood the devil himself.

Mihai sat opposite Alexandru Lupei with a mix of fear and rage and wanted to leap across the desk and kill this madman.

"Did you enjoy the shower?"

"Da."

"Would you like some coffee or tea?"

"Da. And water."

Mihai received a generous slice of cozonac with his coffee: the best walnut sweet bread he had ever tasted.

An enormous, haunting oil painting dominated an otherwise plain room. It depicted a chained muscular man sprawled upon a jagged cliff face, pinned by a large eagle, as it tore at his exposed liver: a scene of struggle and despair that seemed to mirror Mihai's own entrapment.

"Doctor, it's unfortunate it has come to this." The Major-General spoke as if the whole affair had been a simple misunderstanding. "But let's put that behind us and focus on the future: your future."

Mihai braced himself.

"As you know, your butchery has left my boy in a permanent coma." Alexandru Lupei raised his hand to stop a reply. His voice took on a more sinister tone. "And if he wakes, he will be a retard."

Mihai refuted the summary. "Alex is in a coma, but nobody knows what might happen. It may be a way for the brain to heal itself. There's a chance..."

"No more lies!" The Major-General loomed over Mihai with his muscular body. "Your incompetence is criminal. You betrayed me. You are a saboteur of our great nation. Yes, Doctor, I recall your hatred in your outburst at the Securitate office downtown. You blamed us for the death of your daughter. Your contempt was apparent, and you couldn't wait to exact your sick revenge. The son of a government official. How prophetic. My son's life for your daughter's. I should shoot you here and now."

Composing himself, The Wolf refilled his coffee. "Do you remember the miners' strike in Jiu Valley last year? Well, I put an end to that uprising and vanquished those responsible. I threw hundreds into cells like yours. Did you know how we dealt with the instigators? We exposed those cockroaches to multiple five-minute chest X-rays. I don't need to tell you what happened." The man's soulless eyes were devoid of humanity. "I have assassinated dissidents beyond our borders. I have ten thousand agents and over half a million spies at my disposal. Our tentacles spread far and wide."

For the first time, Mihai saw the Alexandru Lupei that everybody feared. The man that kept the Securitate engine whirring to maintain obedience from its citizens.

"Do you know it was me," as if letting Mihai in on a secret, "that caught Ion Gavrilă Ogoranu, the fascist pig that hid in the Făgăraș Mountains? We set a trap for him right here in Cluj. It took twenty-five years, but we finally got him." His grin, unnerving. "And we interrogated him for six long months."

Mihai understood the implications.

"Doctor, there is no escaping me. I am judge, jury, and executioner."

Mihai pleaded his case, looking at the chained man on the rocks. "I did everything I could. I was the only one who tried to save Alex. Despite what you think, I'd never take a child's life as an act of vengeance." He felt sick but pressed on. "The operation went well. Every neurosurgeon worth his salt said the same thing. We did the absolute best we could. I do not retract from that position. I stake my professional career on it."

That caught the Major-General's attention, as he raised his eyebrows, bemused at this declaration.

"Doctor, your career is over." Alexandru Lupei paused, allowing the statement to sink in. "You have two choices. And for that, you should be thankful. You can sign a document which declares your incompetence and failure in providing duty of care. We are gathering statements from witnesses regarding some of your, let's say, unusual and brazen methods, and have information that you discarded regulations and abused your position of authority at the hospital." The big man placed a sheet of paper on the desk. He let it sit. "If you sign this testimony, you will only spend twelve years in prison. Despite your failings, I consider myself a reasonable man, and am taking into consideration your attempt to help my son when no one else did." The brief reprise ended. "If you don't, you will spend thirty-five years in prison." He clasped his hands behind his enormous head. "The choice is yours."

Thirty-five years would mean I would die in prison, while twelve means I still have a chance: Maybe? Can I trust him?

Mihai remembered a colleague warning him to never, under any circumstances, sign documents declaring your guilt to the government. Once you do, your life is over. He wanted to believe this offer, and in his volatile state, the temptation to sign was overwhelming.

Alexandru Lupei placed a pen on the letter. Mihai's heart thumped. He considered pleading, begging, and grovelling for mercy, anything to change this man's mind. And as every fibre of his being screamed in protest, he rose from his chair.

"I cannot and will not sign." By not signing, Mihai had decreed his own death sentence.

∽

Driven through remote villages to Aiud Prison in a nondescript van, Mihai stared out the window. He observed the quaint simplicity of village life—old men vending fruit from wheelbarrows, women beating rugs with broom handles, and children playing carefree by the roadside. Each scene a poignant reminder of a fading dream he longed for.

As the van sped through the last town, raising dust on the dirt road, Mihai caught sight of an abandoned stork's nest perched on a steeple, the frost heralding the onset of winter. His gaze followed a flock of ducks flying southward, envying their freedom and escape from the impending harsh winter.

Aiud Prison, a notorious facility in central Transylvania, emerged as a monument to suffering and despair. Its long history of political imprisonment and untold deaths weighed heavily on those who entered. They checked in at the main office. Mihai noted that no paperwork came with his admission. No documents to sign and no unflattering head shots taken. With no paper trail, Mihai Ionescu no longer existed. He would vanish like a ghost in a white winter.

A young, skittish doctor led Mihai into a small office, where he administered a perfunctory medical examination. In the centre of the room, a desk held trays of paperwork, while the dirty walls remained bare except for an eye chart. The young man wore a stained lab coat, and a stethoscope dangled around his neck. A speculum, used for rectal examinations, sat on the edge of the desk. After Mihai undressed, the young doctor went through the usual protocols: checking eyes, ears, and throat, before checking involuntary responses and sorting out an assortment of pills for the prisoner. Mihai thought of Olga.

"What is your name?" asked Mihai.

"Sebastian Popescu. Dr Sebastian Popescu."

Mihai informed the young doctor that there were more effective ways of testing reflexive responses. Dr Sebastian told Mihai he knew of his work.

"I read several of your publications. Your research on multiple sclerosis was mind-blowing."

"What are you doing in this place?" Mihai asked.

After scraping through medical school on his second attempt, the government assigned young Sebastian to Aiud for three years, which then guaranteed him a position in a major hospital in Bucharest. Mihai raised an eyebrow at the man's naivete.

After the unobtrusive check-up, and a rapid shearing of his hair that left clumps intact, Mihai changed into prison garments: a grey and faded blue striped shirt, matching pants, and lightweight prison slippers. Two guards led him down a long grey corridor. Radiators along the cornices did little to combat the cold, as their orange slit eyes watched those below, until they arrived at a narrow, empty cell, which would be Mihai's home for the next thirty-five years.

There was minimal space between the two bunks along each side wall. The stained mattress and bucket by the back wall were unappealing. The cold stone walls and no natural lighting intensified the claustrophobia. Mihai could not fathom how four men could live in such quarters. One bunk may have been slept in, but the others looked empty. A folded blanket, small pillow, and toilet roll lay on one of the bottom bunks. He glanced at the buckets by the back wall. Mihai considered the man who occupied the other bed. A mass murderer? A mad man? Would he have to defend himself against a deranged psychopath?

He sat on the bottom bunk, allowing himself a moment to deliberate. He thought of Irina. She would be worried sick, searching for his whereabouts. He couldn't believe it had come to this. *Was it worth it*? Irina's question haunted him.

A key in the door disturbed the quiet. Mihai took a step back. A thin man of medium frame stepped forward as the door locked behind him. He stood there, staring at Mihai, who braced for the worst.

"My name is Pierre. Father Pierre Pietru," he said, with warm brown eyes, extending his hand in friendship.

"My name is Mihai. Doctor Mihai Ionescu. Glad to meet you, Father."

The priest smiled. "What are the odds of a priest and doctor sharing a cell? There are greater powers at work here."

"Father, I heard God works in mysterious ways." The ice broken as they shared a laugh.

"My friends call me Pedro," said the priest, as they sat on their bunks. "Consider yourself lucky that no one else is occupying the cell. We once had six men in here. We took turns sleeping on the floor. In summer, it's a sauna in here. We sweat like dogs and eczema runs rampant. So let us rejoice in this minor miracle because it won't last."

There were two levels of cells that stretched along a long, narrow passageway. High vaulted archways spanned across the ceiling, connecting the parallel rows of cells. The concrete walls were ancient and stone cold. Dull lightbulbs, covered in cobwebs, hung from elongated cords, while natural light filtered through large arch windows, clad with an inch of dust, at each end of the building. The sunlight struggled to penetrate this dreary place.

The solitary confinement quarters, called the Zarca, were downstairs, in the cellar. They were tiny boxes, with little wiggle room and no light. They locked prisoners in the Zarca twenty-three hours a day, mostly for minor infringements or for non-compliance, while for others, the punishment served to break the human spirit. Father Pierre spent months in the Zarca during his tenure. Some did not survive the ordeal.

Mihai and Father Pierre stayed up most nights discussing life and sharing stories, like boys exchanging football cards. The priest had studied theology and philosophy at the University of Bucharest before the Communist Education Reform Laws that dismantled such studies. As for how he ended up in prison, his was a simple story.

When the Communists came to power, Father Pierre refused to renounce his religious beliefs. He had been undergoing "re-education" therapy at Aiud for the past ten years.

"Those bastards will pay, Father. They won't stay in power forever. One day, the people will rise, and we'll live to see it happen." Mihai's vitriol reverberated through the thick walls.

"Vive la revolution!" someone yelled, as an applause or two echoed through the dark halls.

"Why don't you renounce God?" Mihai asked.

Father Pierre considered Mihai's query with the weight of a man who had grappled with it in the depths of his soul. As they sat in their cell, a distant scream pierced the silence, a harrowing reminder of their grim reality. When the quiet returned, Pierre shared his conviction. "You are right, Doctor. It would be easy to give in to their demands. And they promise you many things in return. The torture stops—but at what price? You must publicly renounce your beliefs: no divine creator, no salvation, and no eternal life. And bow and worship this evil Communist regime. That is not freedom, Doctor. That is slavery, forever living a lie, and losing one's soul. It's difficult to understand, but I cannot and will not be that man."

Mihai understood the sentiment well. He admired this man of the cloth.

"Many are worse off than me," Father Pierre said. "I knew an extraordinary bishop named Ion Lungu, arrested for his religious and political beliefs. An outspoken man who ridiculed the regime, Ion spent years in Sighet Prison, tortured, abused, and humiliated by the Securitate. This did not stop him from voicing his opinions about the tyranny imposed on his people. One Christmas night, they left him in the courtyard. He froze to death. Bishop Ion Lungu was seventy-four years old."

Mihai closed his eyes. The Christmas reference touched a nerve.

"Besides," the priest said, "I have found my new monastery in this abysmal place. Many of the prisoners turn to me for help and spiritual guidance. There are many lost souls searching for God."

"Not everyone is searching for God, Father."

The priest nodded. "You are right. And if it's not God they seek, then a sympathetic ear, or words of encouragement. What are you searching for, Doctor?"

"What makes you think I am searching for anything?"

"We are all searching for something." The priest waited for a reply. None came. "I believe God wants me here for now." The priest drew strength from his convictions, and his faith allowed him to not only survive, but find meaning in this hellhole. "Do you believe in God?"

"No, Father. I gave up on him long ago."

"I see," said the priest, without judgement.

Mihai expected the sure-fire follow-up sermon, but it never came. And despite near exhaustion, he stared at the dank wall most of the night, curled in a ball, trying to keep his feet from extending beyond the scant blanket.

༄

Close to six hundred boisterous men filled the main mess hall for their one and only daily meal. They split meals into two sessions to accommodate the numbers. Prisoners did most of the cooking, supervised by staff and underpaid cooks. The conditions of the kitchens were appalling, with few regulations on packaging and refrigeration. Mice had a feast in the storage rooms. Prisoners joked that the cooks threw dead mice into the vats of stew. Gas leaks were a common occurrence because of the hazardous industrial stovetops and ovens.

The outside facility had a quarantined vegetable garden that grew potatoes, carrots, and greens by the thousands. They also sourced other foods from local farmers in the area—buying rotten and damaged or outdated crops at a pittance.

The menu on most days was watered-down cabbage stew of some sort, a boiled potato, and two stale slices of bread. It was not unusual for mould to form along the edges of the bread. Sometimes the prison purchased

213

truckloads of canned beans that were well past their expiry date, and outbreaks of food poisoning permeated the prison population. Prisoners swam in cells flooded with vomit and diarrhoea; the stench lasted for weeks.

Yet, despite the appalling conditions, the dining hall served as a rare respite for the prisoners. It was a place to connect with others, a brief escape from the gloom of their cells. Here, amid the dreary surroundings, men of all ages and backgrounds converged, sharing stories over the sloppy, meagre rations.

Father Pierre had been out of his cell administering the last rites to inmates suffering from terminal illnesses. Most prison personnel believed in God and allowed the priest to tend to these poor souls.

Prisoners were keen to introduce themselves to Mihai, glad to have a bona fide doctor among them.

One such character was Tudor Hagi, a man in his mid-twenties who had attempted to escape Romania. With no foresight or plan, Tudor boarded a bus which took him to Orşova, a town on the Danube River, and tantalisingly close to Yugoslavia. Though many tried crossing the treacherous waters, they were often found washed up onshore days later. Tudor could not swim. He, therefore, trekked across the rugged mountain terrain, known as the Balkans. It wasn't long before the Romanian border patrol captured Tudor. The judge sentenced him to one year in prison. The day after his release, Tudor tried again. This time, he took a compass. Captured again, he spent another two years in prison. Upon release, Tudor waited a whole week before attempting his third escape. This time, he packed a compass and map. He made his way past the watchtowers and bolted across the militarised zone, as the barbed wire ripped his flesh in his struggle to clamber through. Once he had crossed the border, Tudor jumped and shouted for joy. Unfortunately, his joys were short-lived, as the official border was four hundred yards further along. A pack of German Shepherds gave chase as he fell fifty yards from the Promised Land. He showed Mihai the bite marks on his legs and forearm. With one more year to serve, Tudor planned to try again.

"I have a story for you," said another inmate, sitting across the table. He strolled over and sat as the men gathered round. "His name was Daniel," said the storyteller. "He planned to escape Romania with a rare one-day exit pass. But how does Daniel hide his life savings, which were considerable? The border guards would search the car. And it was illegal to carry sums of money across the border."

"He puts it under the car flooring," called out a man from the back.

"Too obvious," said another.

"He stuffs it down his wife's panties," yelled another.

"Hold on," said the storyteller. "We are talking ten thousand American dollars."

"If the wife could stuff that amount of cash down her panties, I'd say Daniel is one lucky bastard!" The dining hall erupted.

"Daniel builds a roof rack," said the storyteller, unperturbed.

"Why does he want a roof rack?"

"Daniel stuffed the hollow tubing full of money, and then had the joints welded."

"Genius," said a man sitting behind Mihai.

"They reach the checkpoint in the early morn. Watchtowers with soldiers brandishing Kalashnikov automatic rifles loomed ahead, with exit points bubble-wrapped in barbed wire. Border patrol searched the car.

Daniel's wife was in the passenger seat and their son sat in the back. Suddenly, an officer drew his gun, demanding everyone raise their hands and exit the vehicle."

"What the hell happened?" asked a curious prisoner.

"A senior officer charged out after hearing the commotion," continued the storyteller.

"'In the back seat!' yelled the young officer. 'Guns!'"

"Sure enough, under the child's blanket were handguns. They were Luca's toy guns: Swiss made and given by a relative on a recent visit. The Swiss are skilled artisans, but this takes toy-making to a whole new level."

The prisoners couldn't believe it.

"They confiscated the car for a thorough search, in part because of the embarrassment, and threw the roof rack among the junk-heap."

"Christ almighty," as murmurs spread across the tables. "So, what happened?"

"Daniel borrows a truck and heads to the border that night. He stumbled on something that made a God-awful noise. They arrested him with roof rack in hand. After being disassembled, they found Daniel's life savings."

The men moaned in despair.

"What happened to Daniel?" someone asked.

"Imprisoned right here at Aiud."

The prisoners turned to each other, dumbfounded.

"One night, prison guards drag Daniel from his cell. He returns in a bad way."

"What happened?" The question was less boisterous.

"He wouldn't say, but blood stained the back of his pants."

The story had taken a dramatic turn, and the storyteller's tone reflected this change. Prisoners were sometimes sodomised with batons and other brutal instruments when interrogators fished for signed confessions. Fire-stoked iron rods were one of the tools in the interrogator's arsenal.

"A day later, Daniel hung himself in the back of the kitchen."

They sat in silence.

"Dan Arlescu. You're talking about Dan Arlescu, aren't you?" declared a prisoner who pushed his way through the crowd. "And you were his cellmate."

Many at Aiud were political prisoners who rebelled against the idea of agricultural collectivisation. As one farmer noted, "My family owned and worked this land for generations. One day, these assholes tell us they are taking our farm, and we now work for them. What did they expect would happen? That we would bow our heads and comply? We fought. What else could we do? And they slaughtered us in the thousands."

The Prison also had its fair share of intellectuals: poets, writers, scientists, teachers, historians, and freethinkers.

"We have all sorts in here, Doctor. See that young guy standing by the bench? He is homosexual."

Romania outlawed homosexuality, but Mihai knew no one convicted of the crime. And though he did not condone the behaviour, he opposed the state meddling in people's affairs.

They jailed another man for having a portrait of King Michael I, the last king of Romania, in his house.

King Michael I, the youngest crowned head in Europe at five years of age, led a fascinating and tumultuous life. King Michael I was great-grandson to Queen Victoria, cousin to Queen Elizabeth, and descendant of Tsar Nicholas I, with lineage to a host of other royal families. A quiet man by nature who dined with Adolf Hitler and drank tea with Winston Churchill, he had also been a

217

renowned pilot, composer, and writer of acclaimed plays. Heralded as a Renaissance man with eclectic talents, his decision during the Second World War, at the tender age of twenty-two, to relinquish Romania's ties with Nazi Germany and side with the Allies, was his finest hour. This brave act shortened the war and saved hundreds of thousands of lives. As the Communist wolves pounced and engulfed the country, King Michael I, who advocated a Westernised monarchy, abdicated his throne at gunpoint and fled to Switzerland, awaiting to one day return to his beloved homeland.

Mihai remembered how close the Securitate was to finding the king's photo in Irina's drawer. He had never felt Irina squeeze his hand with such strength.

Not everyone at Aiud was unjustly imprisoned. Ion Rîmaru, a convicted serial killer dubbed "The Vampire of Bucharest," had killed and mutilated at least eight women. He hacked and bludgeoned them with axes, poles, and knives. While his victims were still alive, Ion would pierce holes into their flesh and drink their blood. He also had a propensity for biting and tearing flesh from his victims' vagina and breasts—and raping them after they were dead. He awaited the death penalty.

After tending to his flock, Father Pierre tended to a distraught inmate who bawled on the priest's shoulder. The other prisoners gave them space—they had all been there.

A wafer-thin prisoner named Simon approached Mihai. Doubled over and short of breath, he complained of chest pain. He spent most of the day vomiting, coughing up mucus, and burning with fever. Simon had felt a sudden, sharp chest pain after lifting a large drum three days ago.

The prison doctor had turned Simon away two days ago, diagnosing him with a simple chest cold. Prisoners received no medical attention for ulcers, cuts, fractured bones, and even ruptured appendicitis. Infection often set in, resulting in hundreds of unnecessary deaths.

"What might it be, Doc?" asked Simon, wheezing.

"I can't be sure, but I'd say you have a pneumothorax."

"A what?"

"A collapsed lung, caused by trapped air in your chest." Mihai informed Father Pierre that the young man needed surgery as the pressure building on his vascular structures may become fatal.

"Can you help him?"

"I can't, but I know who can." Mihai walked over to the station guard and demanded to see the doctor. The guard refused. Mihai stepped closer. "Listen carefully. My name is Dr Mihai Ionescu. We have an inmate infected with African Trypanosomiasis."

"What?" asked the prison guard.

"It is a rare and contagious air-borne disease, resulting in excruciating death in twenty-four hours."

The guard appeared sceptical.

"Our enemies have unleashed a rare breed of African flies throughout Romania. The hospitals got wind of it prior to my arrest. An infected person needs only to cough or sneeze and the virus spreads through the air. Now, it is likely that the dreaded fly bit the prisoner. But if you do not act, half the prison population, including the guards, will become contaminated, with deleterious effects for all." Mihai had caught the guard's attention. "The flies arrived via a flight from Johannesburg." Mihai leaned forward and whispered: "Some believe it is a plot to assassinate Ceausescu." It may have been an overkill, but from the expression on the guard's face, Mihai needn't have worried.

The guard escorted Mihai and the contagious prisoner to Dr Sebastian Popescu's office, all the while maintaining a safe distance.

"What's this about a disease?" Dr Sebastian asked.

"This man needs an X-ray. I suspect he has a pneumothorax. Time is of the essence."

"What about this infectious disease?"

Mihai's air of authority and reputation stopped the young doctor from pursuing the matter further.

"Dr Ionescu, we have very little film. We cannot afford to conduct X-rays on prisoners who may or may not have a collapsed lung."

"Now, listen to me," said Mihai. "If you consider yourself a doctor, you will perform an X-ray and call Victor Alba, a pulmonary specialist at the Spitalul de Pneumoftiziologie, in Sibiu, and inform him you are sending a patient for emergency surgery."

Intimidated but not convinced, Dr Sebastian stood his ground.

"Unless you want to spend the rest of your days practising medicine in this hellhole, I suggest you do as I say," said Mihai.

That tipped the scales. After the stethoscope and X-ray confirmed the pneumothorax, they transported Simon to Sibiu.

∽

"Some African disease, huh? I like it," said Father Pierre, sitting on his bunk.

Mihai smirked. He leaned on his elbow, telling the priest that African Trypanosomiasis was, in fact, a disease linked to a sleeping disorder. The priest clapped his hands. Mihai chuckled at the absurdity of it all.

"How did you come up with that?"

"As I approached the guard, African Trypanosomiasis popped into my head, and I ran with it."

"Just popped into your head... this African... Tyrannosaurus."

"And better yet, I told him the flies were a plot to assassinate Ceausescu!"

They doubled over with laughter.

∽

A month had passed, and, despite feeling imprisoned much of his adult life, Mihai struggled with the banality and restriction of imprisonment. Grateful to be sharing a cell with Father Pierre, the priest became a formidable adversary and friend who challenged and comforted him in times of need. Their intimate memories filled this dark place.

"I was turning five. My mother was pregnant and determined we celebrate." Lying on his bed, Mihai mused over that day. "My father made a slingshot for my birthday. The cowhide handle taken from the skins hanging in the barn. The rubber bands were taut and long, with a leather middle joint. A skilled shooter could easily kill a rabbit."

"Interesting gift for a five-year-old," said the priest.

"I remember thinking that there was no way my mother would allow me to have it. To my amazement, she nodded and gave me a hug." Mihai faced the priest. "I loved that slingshot."

The priest placed his hands behind his head. "It seemed you had fond memories of the farm."

"Da. We were poor, but we lived in a community that celebrated life. The farmers from Dobruja had a vitality and zest one could only marvel at."

"Yes, the true Romanian spirit," said the priest. We used to laugh, dance and sing. We embraced life and squeezed every drop from her. And now we are afraid of our own shadow."

"True," said Mihai. "And though I was only five, I still remember, especially the singing and dancing. Mandolins and flutes—maybe a violin—all tuned by ear, as children gathered round, not wanting to miss this orgy of song and dance. And I tell you, Father, even though the men were drunk and slurred their words, once they started playing, not one note was out of place, creating melodies that lifted everyone's spirit. Men and women sang beloved ballads from their childhood: a fusion of Turkish, Ukrainian, and Bulgarian music."

The prison walls felt less claustrophobic.

"Ah, yes," Mihai recalled, grinning. "My father sung and danced his own rendition of a popular folk song." Mihai sat up. "Everybody cheered and clapped as my dad's interpretation had them in stitches. At one point, he picked me up, throwing me in the air as he danced. My mum laughed as her hands sat on her swollen belly. The performance brought a standing ovation when my father fell flat on the floor and raised his arms with a grin that stretched from ear to ear."

Father Pierre clapped. "What a lovely day, Mihai. I am glad you share these memories. We need stories that lift our spirits and remind us of who we are."

As Mihai laid back down, he remembered the oil lamps that flickered in the night breeze and sleeping children carried to the back of horse-drawn carts after midnight. He remembered the soft timbre of his mother's gentle voice. He also remembered the heartache soon after. First, his mother and the newborn, followed by his elder sister. "It was the last birthday I celebrated in Dobruja," he almost whispered to himself. The prison cell closed in again as the sobs of inmates penetrated the stone walls.

∽

Thanks to the priest, Mihai had time allocated to assist in the prison library. Upon Father Pierre's arrival at Aiud, there were just a few books on a trolley. Considering the number of inmates, it seemed a tad inadequate. Most of the texts were Marxist propaganda, espousing Communist theory, or biographies on Ceausescu, portraying him as saviour and liberator.

Over the years, the priest expanded the number and types of books permitted. Under the guise of education, officials relented to the priest's demands. After a decade, there were four hundred and fifty books in the prison library. Still woefully short, but Father Pierre was not done. Not by a long shot.

"Imagine what I'll do in another ten years," he said with a smile, as Mihai re-stacked some shelves.

Three years ago, prisoners built a makeshift library in an empty storage room. The regime prohibited anything controversial towards Ceausescu or the government, and rejected most of the requested books, but occasionally the priest received prized novels from writers such as Dostoevsky and Proust. While Mihai reorganised the bookshelves, he picked up a play called *Rhinoceros*, written by Romanian playwright Eugène Ionescu (no relation).

"It's about a town that turns into rhinoceroses because they have no souls and live in despondent fear," said the priest. "But one man fights against this misery, and thus, holds on to his humanity."

"How did they allow this into the prison?" asked Mihai.

"Because they are too stupid to understand its underlying significance. The play reflects on what we have become," said the priest with a sense of sadness. "We are a lost civilisation, clinging to the remains of charred embers that burnt bright long ago."

Mihai read the play half a dozen times.

That evening, Mihai told the priest how he had come to Aiud Prison. Father Pierre had never pressed his cell mate on his arrest and believed the doctor would tell his story when good and ready.

"The boy's alive, or at least he was before I came here. And while he's alive, there is hope."

"You have not lost hope," said the priest. "That is good. Hope and faith are salvation. We cannot accomplish anything without them." The priest wrapped his blanket around him and breathed into his icy hands. "In fact, I have based my existence on the premise of these words. They are powerful words that can move mountains—not just words to comfort the weak and dying."

Mihai knew of the profound impact of hope and faith. Despite his unwavering belief in medicine and science, he could not deny the mysterious power these agents had over patients.

The priest knew too well the undeniable potency of hope and faith. "After my arrest, they brought me here to be broken."

The Securitate was at the forefront of instigating brainwashing techniques in Eastern Europe. Forced to denounce everything dear to him: family, friends, and, of course, God. They plunged Father Pierre's head into buckets of urine, as guards mockingly re-enacted the baptismal rite. On sacred religious days, the guards held black masses. They were an abomination. The Virgin Mary was called, "The Great Whore," and Jesus pronounced a homosexual. On Easter Sunday, they made the priest wear a robe smeared with excrement, and they placed a phallus-shaped bread around his neck. During Communion, prisoners were required to kiss the phallus-shaped bread, proclaiming, "he is risen." Father Pierre cleaned floors with a rag between his teeth and ate from buckets used as toilets. When he would fall asleep, guards would beat his feet with a rubber hose, and scream in his ears, telling him to renounce his chequered past and embrace the state as forgiver and saviour. This treatment continued for many, many months. And on the brink of relinquishing, the priest clung to hope and faith. Despite the degradation, Father Pierre never renounced his beliefs.

⤙

On a beautiful summer day, the young girl sat on a bench, wearing a white dress with red flowers embroidered along the hem. The dress was ironed, and the thin red belt matched the oversized ribbon in her golden hair. Enjoying a vanilla ice-cream, she smiled and waved at Mihai. Her legs swung back and forth. "Hello," she said.

"Have we met?" he asked.

The angelic girl laughed as she continued swinging on the bench. "Don't be silly," she said, as she licked her ice-cream.

As Mihai moved closer, the ice-cream ran down the girl's hand. Her face melted over her white dress, becoming elongated and viscous before it oozed down her lap. Mihai tried to stop her face from drooling, but it kept running over his hands and through his fingers. Her body turned into a soupy slime, melting and slipping away. Mihai became stuck in the gel-like substance. Consumed by the sludge that had reached his neck, he struggled as the slime reached his chin and spilt into his mouth. He let out one last scream.

"Doctor, wake up," said the priest.

Mihai woke in a sweat. His eyes darted across the cell.

"It's okay." The priest gave him water. "Another bad dream?"

"Da," said Mihai, as he tried to calm himself down.

"I'm here if you want to talk. This place affects everyone. I remember when…"

"It's not that, Father." Mihai grimaced, knowing the time had come. "Her name was Maria. Maria Ionescu. She was my daughter."

Treading in uncharted waters, Mihai, slowly and deliberately told his story till the bitter end. After a moment's deliberation, the gravity in his voice ceded and the tightness in his chest eased. "Her sweet dimples and bright blue eyes let her get away with murder."

"She had her father's eyes," said the priest, smiling reassuringly.

"Da. Except mine don't give me the same advantages," Mihai said with a smirk. "She had a zest that always made you smile." He recalled something, laughing to himself.

"She had this silly old bear called Babu. One day, I told her I was going to perform surgery on him, as one of his arms hung on by a few threads. Afraid for Babu, she consoled him while I stitched his arm." He cleared his throat. His voice quivered. "When polio struck, we watched her wither away. Me, a surgeon who saved people's lives, could do nothing to save my daughter." The words cut through him. "She proudly claimed her father was a doctor, and that he would make her better."

Father Pierre placed his hand on Mihai's back.

"It was my fault, Father. I should have saved her." Mihai explained the entire story, and how his daughter's death had affected him. He spoke of his torment, guilt, rage, and the nightmares that hounded him.

The priest listened, never interrupting his cell mate until he had said his piece. He had spent his life hearing about the demons that haunt people's souls: some real, some imagined.

"I could say it was not your fault, Mihai, which I'm sure you've heard many times, so I will not convince you otherwise. We can play that game forever." The priest squatted in front of his cell mate, making eye contact. "Perhaps this is your way of clinging to her. You want to be in eternal damnation by not forgiving yourself. Otherwise, you believe she will no longer be there. So, you hold on to her tight. But this is not the way. This is not how Maria wants you to remember her, as a haunting figure that torments her father in nightmarish dreams." The priest, on one knee, did not take his eyes off Mihai. "You must believe me. Your daughter won't leave you because you are no longer tortured by her. This is not what she wants. She knows you did everything you could. She knows you loved her, and you need to know that her love for you is eternal."

Mihai covered his face and wiped the tears on his sleeve.

"Carrying this cross does not prove your love for her. It is a self-imposed penance that poisons it." The priest clutched the doctor's shoulder. "It's like that scab on your forearm you pick at. It will never heal. You keep opening the wound, keeping it raw, perhaps infecting it, and making it worse. This is the same with Maria. You don't want that wound to heal because you're afraid it will disappear. But torturing yourself like some martyr does not prove your love for her. Maria will manifest her love for you, and you for her, in so many beautiful ways. Give her a chance to show you some light. Let her be your angel who walks alongside you through the valley of death."

Mihai wrapped his arms around the priest. And in order to hold on to Maria, he needed to let her go.

⁓

After two months in Prison, while finishing lunch in the mess hall, prison guards led Mihai to an undisclosed location. Father Pierre looked on in bewilderment as Mihai gave him a puzzled glance.

Taken to the ground floor, guards ordered him into one of the tiny boxes used for insubordination. Mihai refused to enter the Zarca.

"Not before you tell me what I have done?"

A rubber baton struck the back of his thigh which sent him to his knees. Two guards then dragged and shoehorned him into the box.

Crouched in this hole in complete darkness, he ran his hands along the sides and tops of the wall. Lying down in a crouched position, his head almost scraped the ceiling, while his knees pressed against his chest. He cried out in vain, demanding answers. His pulse raced; his body filled with fear and rage. *Why am I here? Nothing untoward had happened. It made no sense.* Then a chill ran down his spine. *Had Alex died? Or woken up with severe mental impairments? Were the preceding months an interlude? To see whether the boy lived or died?*

His eyes adjusted to the dark. The blackness had turned a dark grey. An insatiable itch overtook him, causing a scratching frenzy that drew blood, before nasty little bites caused him to jolt, holler and swear like a pissed-off Tasmanian devil. Bugs by the hundreds crawled along the walls of the Zarca. They assaulted him from every direction and their miniscule bites hurt like hell. They wriggled between his legs, while some rained down, kamikaze style, from the infested ceiling. The floor shimmered and swayed like a roiling ocean as insects crawled about. Mihai lashed out, slapping away bugs that crawled over him, and squashing them in a turbulent frenzy. Polished cockroaches, the size of mice, scurried as Mihai kicked the steel door. He could not see them, though he felt them swarming over him. But the more he killed, the more arrived, eager to bite and feast on his blood. Continuing to bat away, Mihai could not sleep. He dozed off for several minutes here and there until the crawling or biting woke him in a mad fever. At one point, bugs marched into his ear canal, and he screamed bloody murder, tearing away and digging out the little fuckers, sticking his finger deep into his ear and wiggling it about with fervour. And when he scratched his head, insects and maggots coated his hands.

He lost track of time in this hellhole. His stomach grumbled, but that was the least of his worries. The darkness never abated, making day and night indistinguishable.

Confined and constricted, the walls closed in on him. *Will this be my fate? To die in this shit hole? To rot away, providing fodder for insects and slime.* His mind shifted to Irina, but he blocked that thought. He needed to remain strong, without emotional or psychological frailty.

His back and legs ached from the physical restriction. He would have given his left leg to stretch, if only for a minute. He trembled as the cold seeped through the stone floor and chilled him to the bone. Curling himself into a ball, hands behind his head, and elbows tucked in alongside his face, Mihai dozed, as the critters found the most interesting places to explore.

The Zarca door opened. Mihai shielded his eyes as he staggered to his feet, brushing off hundreds of creepy-crawlies that had hitched a ride. He peeled away white maggots lodged in his hair and splotched beard, squishing them between his fingernails in an act of sweet revenge. Guards dragged Mihai, shivering, thirsty, and hungry, back to his cell.

Two strange men occupied the cell. They were in their early thirties and imprisoned for selling government goods and supplies on the black market. They had arrived two days ago, meaning that Mihai had been in the Zarca for two days without food or water. His already emaciated body looked worse for wear, as he rolled the waistband of his striped pants to stop them from falling. They were shocked at Mihai's condition and asked about his ordeal in the Zarca and what led to his imprisonment. Father Pierre gave Mihai a shake of the head. Mihai eyed the prisoners with caution. *Are they spies? Sent to gather information regarding the Alex Lupei case? Was the forty-eight hours in the Zarca meant to dull my faculties, or spur my anger, making it more likely that I say something incriminating?*

Five days later, Mihai had recovered, but life in the cell became insufferable. The cramped conditions restricted the prisoners to their bunks, not to mention the additional stench from the bucket by the back wall. Despite these setbacks, what roused Mihai's ire was the limited, censored flow of communication between him and the priest.

Before dawn, Mihai was ordered out of his cell. Father Pierre tried to intervene, pleading for mercy, but the guards pushed him aside, giving the priest a whack with the baton. The two recent inmates stood in silence.

Not again. He braced himself for another spell in the Zarca. *Would it be longer this time?* The idea of climbing back into that infested hole made Mihai's skin crawl. Despite his dread, he refused to reveal his emotional state to the guards. Except they did not venture into the basement. They headed out of the building into the grey light as dawn approached.

Winter still flexed its muscles as the winds shrieked, and gusts of snow billowed. Reaching an open field beyond the fence boundary at the back of the prison, fog hovered for miles, giving the area a prehistoric, swamp-like feel. They ordered the prisoner to run laps around an oval-shaped field, some three hundred metres in circumference. No rhyme or reason given. The angry wind ripped through his attire and flayed his skin as he plodded along the icy track.

The guards, protected and insulated in their overcoats, stood idly by, chatting and smoking cigarettes. The early light brought no warmth, the mercury clinging to the lower depths of the thermometer.

Mihai's endurance waned as he trudged through the snow, his movements becoming sluggish. Approaching the guards for respite only earned him brutal strikes from a baton, each blow searing pain into his already weary body. Collapsing to his knees, he felt the overwhelming weight of despair under the ashen sky.

"No one told you to stop!" screamed the guard.

A despondent bleakness filled the sky, and the diluted sun hid behind the backdrop of grey curtains. A bleak nothingness expanded across miles of flat, barren terrain, resembling an alternate lunar landscape. After two hours of shuffling around the icy field, Mihai lost focus and his coordination failed. The biting air stung his lungs and his vision blurred. He staggered and dropped.

Strange sounds behind him. A snarling snout and protruding fangs—a wild boar had set upon him, barrelling him over and thrashing at his legs. This time, Mihai lacked the strength to resist. He screamed, though his throat burnt as he swallowed the freezing air. He made one last pitiful attempt to stave off the attack, as his screams carried toward the empty wastelands. The boar pounced, knocking Mihai onto the icy grass. Upon command, the attack abated. Mihai, panting hard, fixated on the beast that would end his life. But it was no wild boar. It was a dog: a German Shepherd. His calf bled, creating red ink blots on the snow: Rorschach's ink blot patterns used in personality tests came to mind, and Mihai wondered what psychologists would infer when he told them he saw a winged horse, ready to fly him toward the sun.

Another hour.

Mihai shuffled at a snail's pace, hands hanging by his side, thankful that his oversized uniform sleeves extended below his hands. His head bopped and drooped. The throbbing in his calf intensified. Delirious and shivering, he lost coordination. Keeping his hands clenched for fear of frostbite, his feet turned stiff and ice cold. His toes were black.

Another hour.

He drifted off track, swaying and staggering in all directions, as gusts of snow obfuscated the field. The sun made a feeble appearance, barely climbing beyond the horizon as the fog dissolved. The silver-grey sky, like the inside of an oyster shell, remained permanent. His wet clothing clung to him. Pain tore through him when the wind chill struck as droplets of blood from his ankle left a trail on the dirty, snow-covered field, like Hansel and his breadcrumbs. He could not take another step and dropped to his knees; a bilious sensation overtook him, as he vomited clear liquid over the icy landscape. He fell face first.

The dog charged, bowling him over and snapping at his legs once more. He felt the sharp teeth nick his flesh. The guards lifted Mihai to his feet and yelled into his ear to continue.

And another hour.

Hobbling along like a broken toy, he stumbled, slipped and collapsed. Hypothermia had set in, and his blood turned to slush. On his hands and knees, Mihai stared at the ground, shivering in a kind of ague; his forehead was dank with clammy sweat. He remained frozen, marinating in misery and exhaustion, shipwrecked in this spot. He wondered why the dog hadn't attacked. The guard slapped him, demanding he stand up. Another slap, harder this time. And another. In a desperate, final, contumacious act, Mihai lunged, as a baton struck the back of his head.

He fell, capitulating, as everything blurred around him. The winds tore at him as his body went into shock. Edging to the precipice, from which there was no return, Mihai knew what awaited below.

His breathing grew more and more shallow until it became too painful to breathe. Exhaustion shipwrecked him in this spot, and here he would die. Blood oozed along inside his veins like heavy mercury. His body shut down. His spirit spent. Freezing to death, he stared at the snow as his eyelids drooped to half-mast. Winter was a cruel mistress. He relinquished. Like Atlas, carrying the weight of the world upon his shoulders, Mihai could carry no more. He was dying by inches.

The wind subsided. Everything turned deathly quiet. His old foe, Death, was upon him, parading out from the shadows in all his glory, smiling, and calling him over in a seductive, inescapable song. Mihai would have smiled back, if possible. Glimpses of his past resurfaced: his mother's love, his father's laugh, vague images of his sisters. Patients saved and lost. His lifelong devotion to medicine put to the ultimate test: he passed with flying colours. Friendships and good times stirred his dying soul. Radu and co building the garage fluttered by before he lost focus. Irina's undying love became the backdrop, the underpinning theme of this spectacle before him. And like an octopus shooting its ink, the world turned jet black. As darkness prevailed and consciousness faltered, she appeared, as he knew she would. Maria's wide-eyed smile, dimpled cheeks, and rambunctious trill ignited a spark.

And inexplicably, it landed on his frosted hand.

∽

Mihai awoke in a hospital bed. Heavy bandages covered his hands and feet. The doctors explained he had suffered extreme hypothermia and frostbite, as well as severe fever and dehydration.

Gangrene had formed around the toes, causing body tissue to die because of a lack of blood flow to the region. The surgeon salvaged his right foot, though the infected tissue had to be removed, but had to amputate a portion of Mihai's left foot, leaving him with no toes.

Mihai's nose and hands received second-degree frostbite. Blisters and massive swelling had formed on his fingers, which had turned purple. His nose had lost substantial skin tissue, and a skin graft was required.

"You are lucky to be alive, Dr Ionescu," said the surgeon. "Santa Claus granted you the greatest gift of all," he said.

"Santa Claus?" Mihai did not understand.

"Yesterday was Christmas."

Mihai broke down. The news of the partial amputation devastated him, yet he was lucky to be alive. But mostly he cried for Maria, who, twelve years ago on Christmas Day, had passed away.

After dozing on and off, thanks to the drugs, Mihai noted the stitches in his calf when checking his bandaged feet.

In the hazy interludes of consciousness, the surgeon's voice, a steady timbre in the sterile room, brought news both grim and hopeful. "The infection is under control, and the fever's broken," he said, his eyes scanning the IV drip. "You're on a regimen of antibiotics and potent analgesics. Your foot will require time to heal, but you're out of the woods. Remarkably, your hands were spared any permanent damage. You'll regain full use, though it will take months to recover."

"How long have I been here?" Mihai's voice was a hoarse whisper.

"Four days."

19

Too High a Price

Driven home by prison personnel, he found the spare key under the loose brick by the back porch. The creaking screen door was reassuring. He did not know why he was home, or what it meant. *Did someone interject on my behalf? Was Lupei himself going to kill me? Did something happen to the boy?* The answers would come soon enough. He braced himself for the worst.

The house seemed different. Two months had passed, but it felt like an eternity. Irina was not home, but a plate and cup in the sink meant she was nearby. He turned the gas heater on and hobbled to the bathroom. Swallowing pain killers like candy, Mihai had a warm shower and shaved his Neanderthal beard. A wave of relief washed over him. Somehow, he had survived, though the price paid would be permanent, as he peered at his foot. The shrill ringing of the phone made his heart jolt.

"Is that you, Mihai? It's Adam. Adam Bolan."

"Yes, Adam, it's me." *How did he know I was home?*

"Mihai. Oh, it's so good to hear your voice. He woke up, Mihai!"

"What are you saying, Adam?"

"Alex Lupei woke from his coma. He's alive, Mihai, the boy's alive! It's a miracle!"

Mihai stumbled, reaching for the counter. "When did this happen, Adam?"

"A week ago. He just woke up. A nurse entered the room, and he said hello. Gave her a hell of a fright. A miracle, I tell you."

Mihai was at a loss.

"Alexandru Lupei told me you would be home today. That's why I called."

You bastard. Alex had awakened from his coma while I froze in the snow.

"The boy is doing well, considering," continued Adam. "His vitals are good. His cognition and memory are intact. No apparent side-effects."

Mihai should have felt elated.

"I can't imagine what you have been through, my boy. I am so sorry about what happened to you."

You have no idea.

"I tried," Adam said. "I tried to reason with him. He was mad. He kept going on about how you killed his son. How he had trusted you. The man was losing his mind."

"I know you did, Adam. When can I see the boy?"

"He left last night. A private plane flew him to Bucharest. He will continue his rehab there."

Mihai leant against the cupboard, waiting for the painkillers to kick in. He pried open the jammed kitchen window, making his fingers throb. Low clouds floated overhead on a windless, overcast day. A proud robin warbled, telling its story from the treetops. It was music to his ears.

"Are you there, Mihai?" Adam's voice brought him back.

237

"Da, I'm here," Mihai replied, his thoughts still adrift. "What about the seizures?"

"Indeed," Adam's voice crackled with a blend of relief and excitement, "it's remarkable! Yesterday, he only experienced two mild seizures. The team is astounded."

Mihai responded with clinical precision. "Encouraging news. They should resume his anti-convulsive medication, starting with a conservative dose. Monitor and adjust as necessary." The weight of weariness in his voice betrayed him, even as his mind analysed. "I need to rest, Adam. We'll speak later."

"Of course, whatever you want. You did it, my boy. You did it!"

In no celebratory mood, Mihai felt faint, wincing as his hand gripped the kitchen bench.

"Wait, before you go, Lupei left me a parcel to give you."

"What's in it?"

"I don't know. He said to keep it safe."

Despite the pain and fatigue, Mihai was apoplectic with rage. "Let that lowlife scumbag know that if I ever see —"

"I understand how you feel, Mihai. But don't be hasty now, especially in your current state. Don't let that temper get the better of you. Do you understand what you have done? You saved his son's life. You have leverage. Use it wisely."

Arriving home before lunch and sobbing with joy, Irina took care of her husband, feeding him chicken broth for lunch and re-bandaging his foot. For dessert, she cooked papanaci: a sweet and savoury doughnut made from cow's milk cheese, served with blueberry jam and berries. The berries burst inside Mihai's mouth like a grenade of sweet ecstasy.

Waking hours later, still physically and emotionally scarred, Mihai noticed the telltale signs of Irina's own ordeal: weight loss, stress lines etching her face, yet she refrained from burdening him with her struggles.

Irina had gone to the home of a colleague, whose husband was a captain in the army, and begged for help. Reluctantly, he found the whereabouts of Dr Mihai Ionescu.

Making her way to Aiud, prison guards refused her entry, stating that visitors needed government clearance. However, nobody knew how to obtain clearance. Three officials provided her with three different agencies to contact. She showed up every day, first begging, then demanding to see her husband. She left parcels to be delivered to him, none of which made it past the front office. On one of her many visits, she was informed that her husband had been transferred to a minimum prison facility in the Bucovina region, a seven-hour train ride from Cluj. When she arrived, no one in Bucovina had heard of Dr Mihai Ionescu.

She tried contacting Alexandru Lupei, but he was a ghost. Adam Bolan couldn't help, despite trying. She made her presence known at the Securitate office in Cluj, but no one helped, even though she camped outside the office for days, hoping to run into Alexandru Lupei. Encounters with the Securitate and police spiralled into a dizzying carousel of futility, a grotesque parody of merry-go-rounds, with their jaunty tunes and gaudy creatures morphing into a cacophony of despair. In this endless, disorienting dance, Irina, like countless others before her, found herself trapped in a relentless cycle of hope and helplessness, her life suspended in a haunting limbo.

Beneath the hazy afternoon sun, Mihai lay in bed, the brown transistor radio his sole companion. He fiddled with the dipole antenna, navigating through the static haze of jammed signals—a familiar dance in a country where towers rose like sentinels to silence the airwaves. Radio Free Europe transmitted tales of Romanian athletes triumphing on the global stage. From Virginia Ruzici's victory at the French Open to Ion Tiriac's burgeoning empire in the tennis world, the stories woven by the unseen announcer painted a picture of triumph against all odds. The radio host shifted to Nadia Comaneci's Olympic aspirations as Irina lingered in the doorway. Her fingers twirled her ruby necklace, her eyes a mix of worry and resolve.

"Tell me," Mihai urged, sensing the gravity in her posture.

"Radu is dead," she whispered, the words falling like lead.

Mihai pushed his tea aside.

"The funeral was last week. They buried him next to his daughter. It was a simple service. Sad. Despite everything he did, no one came. What had occurred left them all scared. Only his family and neighbour showed."

Mihai reached for Irina's hand.

"The boys said he was badly beaten. He had cracked ribs. He even had cigarette burns on his body. How can they do that to an old man?"

"Because they are filth of the earth, Irina, that's why."

"Before he died, he asked to be buried beside his daughter under the oak tree. Mircea said that Radu was looking forward to seeing her again."

Mihai's lips quivered. He broke down in despair at the travesty, injustice, futility, and utter sadness of it all. He thought of the garage and Radu's silly smile that brightened everybody's day. The world grew a little darker in his absence.

Mihai wished to go to the hospital by late afternoon. His body ached and his swollen fingers throbbed, but he needed to get out. Irina helped him dress.

"Oh, did you know it was Radu that shot Pip?"

"What? Are you sure?" asked Mihai.

"The boys told me. Radu had grabbed a gun from a Securitate officer and shot his dear donkey in the head."

∽

At the hospital, doctors attended to Mihai's injuries with clinical precision. He bore the dog bites as badges, testament to his resilience—a story to share with Tudor at Aiud prison. The prognosis was clear: a permanent walking aid, perhaps mitigated by custom orthotics.

When Adam burst through the door, Mihai's sunken cheeks, weight loss, and abysmal state shocked him, but he was delighted to see him alive, as he had questioned whether he would.

After being fussed over by a battery of doctors, Mihai read the reports and spoke to the tending staff about Alex. Nothing explained the sudden turn of events. The boy woke up. As in many coma cases, there were often no explanations as to why patients awaken. A medical mystery, or perhaps a miracle.

Adam called Mihai to his office. "Alex insisted I give you this." It was the boy's prized Superman figurine. "And a thank-you card he made himself. He told me to tell you that the Dracula comic was one of his favourites."

It moved Mihai to tears.

"And this is from his father." A large, sealed envelope: no writing, no name. "I hope whatever is in here brings you some solace."

∽

At the kitchen table, Mihai approached the parcel, its unassuming appearance belying the gravity of its contents. Unwrapping it revealed a passport and visa, heavy with the weight of high-level government endorsements. The burgundy passport, emblazoned with the Romanian coat of arms, felt both empowering and restrictive.

I almost gave my life for this.

A one-year work visa to the United States of America. Dr Mihai Ionescu needed to provide proof of employment and receive signed documentation from both the American and Romanian embassies in Bucharest. He had three months to complete the documentation. Upon expiration of the contract, the subject would return to his homeland.

It shouldn't take more than a month. He had been in conversations with hospitals in Minneapolis and Michigan. There were also research facilities in California that showed interest in his work. *Yes, one month should do.*

Irina, his anchor, would remain in Romania, a tacit hostage to ensure his return. Leaving her behind gnawed at him. His heart ached at the thought of the separation, the unknowns it brought forth. And yet, the opportunity to venture beyond the suffocating grasp of his homeland, to breathe the air of freedom and opportunity, was too potent to ignore. Getting her out of Romania would become paramount.

∽

She fidgeted with her necklace. "So, it's happening?" Irina loved her home despite the heartache and found a strange comfort and refuge in the house where her daughter was born and raised. She gripped her husband's arm. "This is too high a price to pay."

Mihai understood the turmoil and uncertainties this would bring. The lure of America never enticed Irina. She loved Romania regardless. He envied and despised her for that. He believed that within a year they would be together, and that she would thank him for it.

Irina still had her teaching, which she loved, which would keep her busy during his absence. He would also send money home, freeing her from financial woes.

Her closest friend, Joanna Suta, had been recently widowed when her husband was killed at work, after a crane crushed him. She received no compensation or pension after the tragedy. And the store she operated had shut down. She struggled to pay rent, despite downsizing to a one-bedroom flat. Mihai invited Joanna to live with Irina during his absence.

"Things will change," said Irina.

"I've been hearing that mantra for years. The idea of a better tomorrow is a chimera. In fact, things will get worse, Irina, mark my words. And I can smell the stench of this rotten system permeating through my pores. I can achieve success in America. Here, there is only misery."

She took a nervous breath. "Are you sure it's not me you are running from?"

Mihai reached for her, but she shifted, feeling defensive.

"Perhaps you desire a new wife in America? Is that what you want? If it is, please tell me now."

"Irina, please. You are my wife. We are in this together. That won't ever change."

"I am scared, Mihai. Scared of losing you. A year is too long for a man to be without his wife. I know how American women are. They are bold." Irina's insecurities bubbled to the surface. "You will forget me." She put her index finger to his lips. "In time, my face will fade. I'll become a stranger to you. A distant ghost from the past. A past you're desperately running from."

"Do you remember our wedding night at the Astoria?" His voice was gentle. "I promised I would never leave. Yes, we were young, but nothing has changed. We are making a sacrifice here—perhaps you, most of all. I understand what I am asking, and I will forever be grateful. I vow to you, as Mihai Ionescu is my name, that we will have a future in America."

Irina's protests dissolved into a reluctant acceptance. She wanted to trust her husband with all her heart, though she still believed their future lay in Romania.

✺

The following months were a blur. Through a myriad of phone calls, letters and contracts, Mihai had accepted a position at the Minneapolis Veterans Affair Health Care System: a network of hospitals and outpatient clinics that provided services for thousands of veterans. A renowned research facility, the American hospital would soon begin neuroscience initiatives on post-traumatic stress disorders, Alzheimer's disease, schizophrenia and substance abuse. They offered Mihai a million-dollar research project on epilepsy, working alongside a team of experts. The hemispherectomy performed by Dr Mihai Ionescu in

Romania did not go unnoticed by the Americans. After a short probation period, he would join the ranks of neurosurgeons at the hospital.

∽

In Cluj, Mihai worked as fervently as ever, despite taking a hiatus from surgery until his hands healed. That did not stop him from yelling at patients and staff alike.

"It's good to have him back!" shrieked Nadia, as she ran out of Mihai's office with a junior nurse in tow, after receiving an earful.

Mihai found the cane cumbersome, and though he could walk for brief periods without it, his foot soon throbbed. Taking the hospital stairs became a royal pain. He at least joked he could wield the stick to poke and prod the staff.

His hunch about putting Alex Lupei back on anti-convulsive drugs did the trick. The boy's seizures ended. The doctors speculated the removal of his right hemisphere had reset the brain's internal wiring and chemistry, which allowed the medications to take effect.

Sitting in his office, Mihai finished his lukewarm coffee before calling it a day. He stared at the piece of paper and dialled the number. He had one last demand to make.

Adam came by as Mihai finished his call.

"That seemed intense. Who was on the phone?" asked Adam.

"Alexandru Lupei. We had some unfinished business."

∽

The only person besides Irina who knew about Mihai's departure had been Adam. Adam assisted with the

245

documentation and forms surrounding Mihai's contract. Mihai believed the fewer people who were aware of his departure, the better, despite Irina's objections.

Mihai planned to finish work one week before he left for America. On his last day at the hospital, he went about his business as usual, which he found difficult. He made a point of bumping into staff he wanted to say goodbye to. It mystified them when he took the time to chat and hug them before heading off.

At noon, the secretary left a note on Mihai's desk that a monastery in Făgăraş called, asking to speak to him. No details given, besides a number to call back.

"Hello, this is Dr Mihai Ionescu, calling from Cluj."

The man's tender voice brought a smile to the doctor's face. Mihai's phone call to Alexandru Lupei had paid off.

❧

Adam invited Mihai to lunch in the city centre, on the banks of the Someşul Mic River, opposite the Capitoline Wolf Statue. They reminisced and laughed over some of the outlandish occurrences over the years.

"Remember that patient, pronounced dead and put in storage, who then walked out of the hospital, waving goodbye, after we had filled out his death certificate?"

Mihai remembered it well. In fact, he recalled telling Adam that the hospital should promote the fact that they brought the dead back to life.

As Adam signalled for a bottle of sparkling water, he broached a different subject. "By the way, Gheorghe's reassignment came through. He's off to a town bordering Bulgaria," he disclosed, hinting at Alexandru Lupei's probable involvement in the ministry's decision.

"Excellent," Mihai nodded, his mind already on future prospects. "We must inject innovative minds into the mix. It's time for fresh blood."

"You want the job?"

They laughed again and enjoyed their farewell lunch.

Adam hinted he might step down at the end of the year. "I am getting old. Plus, without you giving me headaches, things would be a little dull around here."

The old man expressed his deep regard for the young surgeon and wished him all the best. When they hugged goodbye, Adam did not protest. He presented Mihai with an engraved, gold-plated Mont Blanc pen: a gift Mihai would treasure.

After lunch, Mihai embarked on a poignant journey to Radu's farm to pay his respects. He lay flowers by his grave, under the tree, and said a few words.

Mircea and Igor would stay on the farm, caring for their ailing grandmother, who had Alzheimer's and had declined over the years. Radu had done his best to reassure and comfort her, though she did not remember him anymore. He never complained.

20

Beloved Transylvania

It was time to clean out Maria's room.

A small bed with a white headboard rested against the back wall. A hand-me-down rug lay on the floor and a cute mushroom lamp stood on the nightstand. In the nightstand drawer, dried lavender gave off a sweet scent, and an old cupboard stood against the side wall, while stuffed toys filled the corner spaces. In an otherwise pretty room, the only blight was the unravelling beige curtain, destined to be replaced—one day.

The task of packing Maria's belongings—clothes, blankets, and cherished toys—into boxes was a heartrending ordeal. Mihai's hands trembled as he held Maria's Mickey Mouse pencil case, a flood of memories tumbling across the room like tumbleweeds. Mihai and Irina held hands and reminisced, as items brought back both painful and happy memories.

Irina's fingers traced the fabric of a purple dress, recalling how Maria had insisted it fit, despite its size. "She was our little Shirley Temple, with that dress and her cascade of curls," Irina chuckled, her eyes shimmering with unshed tears.

A few dresses were never worn—representing a future that belonged to a past forever lost and frozen in time. Irina clutched a yellow and pink striped pyjama top covered with teddy bears, and inhaled the memories trapped within its cotton fibres.

Tucked away in the wardrobe's recesses, Mihai discovered a pink unicorn hair clip in an old doll's shoe. "God damn it. Here it is!" he huffed.

The discovery of the pink unicorn hair clip unearthed a tumultuous memory. Maria, convinced that her cherished clip had been discarded, succumbed to a storm of distress, her small body writhing on the floor in a symphony of high-pitched cries unique to childhood. Her frustration manifested in a barrage against her dolls, her tiny hands covering her ears, rejecting any attempts at consolation. Mihai and Irina, desperate to quell her anguish, embarked on a frantic search through the house. Mihai's heart leapt when he thought he spied it under the bed, only to plummet as Maria's tantrum intensified—it was an imposter clip. The ordeal, showcasing a three-year-old's stamina, ended with the clip remaining lost—until now.

Reaching the top shelf, Irina retrieved an old shoebox, a treasure trove of Maria's childhood. Inside were two circus ticket stubs, and a child's drawing—a trio of stick figures hand in hand, encircled by a riot of butterflies. Irina traced the wobbly letters at the top— "MUMMY, DADDY, ME"—each stroke transporting her back to Maria's concentrated expression, remembering how her little fist clenched the pencils and how the frenzied colours extended beyond the butterflies' winged borders, while her tiny tongue would poke out the corner of her mouth as she wrote the words on the page. With a kiss, Irina pressed the paper to her cheek before refolding it into its sanctuary.

Mihai flipped through the large hardcover in the drawer: *The Complete Book of Butterflies*. A beautiful array of butterflies decorated the cover. A type of encyclopaedia, with lots of facts and bullet-point information on each species, with the most magnificent, high-resolution photos on every page. Mihai had spent hours reading the book from cover to cover, with Maria curled up in his lap and Babu by her side. He turned the pages until he came across the section on the Purple Emperor.

The Purple Emperor found its home in well-wooded treetops and fed on tree sap and honeydew. Mysterious and elusive, entomologists knew little about this enigmatic creature. This bold and brazen insect, a behemoth of the butterfly kingdom, reached the size of a small bird. Its gigantic purple wings and bright orange eyespots were a sight to behold. Its resplendent colours danced and transformed according to the way light refracted off its wings, making it an ever-changing work of art, and the world's first artist: communicating through its succulent and sensuous colours. Mihai ran his hand over the page, still remembering the words verbatim, which Maria made him read over and over—until she would fall asleep holding his index finger in her little fist, her tender snores purring in the background.

Irina gave a loud snort, somewhere between a sob and a laugh. "Do you remember when you played monsters?"

Mihai smirked. "Fee Fi Fo Fum."

Irina smiled. "As soon as she heard you trumpet those words, she'd sprint to her bedroom, wide-eyed, and dive into the bed, wrapping the blanket around every inch of her. You would do a terrible Frankenstein imitation, arms extended, reciting those words while she lay curled up and terrified under the blanket. And she would scream to high heaven when you reached down and grabbed her. Sometimes she got so scared, she'd burst into tears, and you would have to hug her."

"And within a minute, she would beg me to continue playing monsters again," said Mihai, thinking back to those happy days that seemed like a story in someone else's dream. His smile dimmed like a cloud obscuring the sun. "Fee Fi Fo Fum," he softly mouthed, staring at the empty bed and the faded stickers of Minnie Mouse and Dumbo on the wall.

The purple dress and other items of sentimental worth remained behind, as did the butterfly book, which Mihai placed on his bedroom nightstand. They packed two dozen children's books into a cardboard box. Before sealing the box, Irina removed *The Cat in the Hat* by Dr Seuss. It had been one of Maria's favourites. Mum and daughter would laugh as the silly cat got into mischief. Babu would remain watching over Maria's bedroom, despite being singed and falling apart.

While the world kept turning, the bloodless moon shone over the quiet Ionescu home. They stayed up half the night, holding onto the sweet memories of their daughter that bound them and tore them apart.

ॐ

The morning sky, painted with crayon-like clouds, oversaw their final preparations. Irina labelled items, while Mihai, undeterred by his limp, loaded boxes into the car. The backseat was packed with clothes and toys, and the cot, tightly secured on the roof. They were ready for one last trip before Mihai's flight in less than a week.

As they left Cluj, the countryside stretched forever. Irina drove while Mihai took in the sights. Vast farmlands formed a ubiquitous thread across the landscape, as men in faded overalls, slashed at metre-high grass with scythes and filled their horse-drawn wagons with hay.

In a quaint village, they indulged in homemade jam and pickled peppers from a welcoming farmer. A chance encounter with a woman, her black kerchief a stark contrast to the verdant apron, evoked a distant echo of Mihai's childhood. The wicker basket she carried, brimming with mushrooms, seemed like a fragment of a long-forgotten dream. Before leaving, they watched a procession of cows, their bells chiming a rustic melody, as a farmer, with a beech switch in hand, guided them across the road.

Nearing their destination, the irresistible aroma of roasted chestnuts lured Mihai and Irina to a roadside vendor. The old man's gaunt dog who lay by his owner's bicycle, watched with interest as Mihai savoured the welcoming, earthy scent. The vendor offered his guests warm chestnuts.

"Let's take three bags," Irina decided, her voice a blend of whimsy and resolve.

After a brief respite at a coffee shop in the picturesque town of Luncani, the couple journeyed onwards, arriving in Făgăraş.

The Sâmbăta de Sus monastery, a seventeenth-century architectural marvel nestled within verdant hills cradled by the Carpathians, stood the test of time. Spanning seven acres, its grounds were manicured to perfection. Handcrafted from white stone and brick, the buildings formed a protective quadrangle, their archways a silent ode to history. Terracotta rooftops spiralled skywards, while detailed carvings graced the window frames and doorways. Known locally as "Brâncoveanu Monastery," it had long been a haven for souls seeking sustenance, shelter, or spiritual solace.

"Oh, Mihai. It is lovely," Irina sighed, feeling an immediate sense of divine tranquillity upon entering this hallowed ground.

A man of medium build with warm, brown eyes that melted glaciers made his way toward the couple.

"Father Pierre, so good to see you!" said Mihai. The men embraced like lost brothers. "I am glad you called, Father."

Father Pierre guided them through the monastery. His narratives wove the rich tapestry of its history and his own journey, marked by faith and resilience. To Irina, he embodied strength and serenity, a stark contrast to the decade long suffering in prison, though his slender frame and four-inch scar down his neck, attested to his past hardships.

Their tour revealed a dozen children who called the monastery home, though its capacity was strained by the growing need.

"We are beyond our limit," said the good-natured priest. "We try our best to find homes for the children, but it is becoming more and more difficult."

Mihai unloaded the boxes but needed help as his wound burned and ached. The soft skin on his amputated foot would take time to harden. Irina handed out stuffed toys, books, and dolls to the little ones. She opened the roasted chestnuts to the cheers and delight of the children. One young boy sat in her lap.

"It is criminal what is occurring in these orphanages," said the priest as he helped Mihai with the boxes. "Children are dying from minor illnesses such as cataracts and anaemia. They too are prisoners of the system."

Father Pierre had been busy since his release from Aiud Prison. Despite re-establishing the monastery and running the small orphanage, the priest had not forgotten his flock. He compiled documentation and corroborating evidence to shed light on the atrocities in prison. He had petitions in the thousands and had amassed international support on the plight of prisoners. The priest was an unstoppable force of nature.

"Be careful, Father. We don't want you back behind bars," said Mihai.

"I'll keep that in mind!" he said, giving the doctor a gentle bump of the shoulder. "And if my instincts are right, I believe you may have had a hand in my sudden release."

"I don't know what you are talking about, Father."

The priest gave Mihai a sly look.

"God works in mysterious ways," said Mihai, grinning.

"Indeed, he does," said the priest, slapping Mihai's back.

Mihai and Irina would spend the night.

"The room is small," said Father Pierre, "but you have stayed in smaller quarters."

In the monastery's arched stone dining hall, lit by lanterns and candles, Mihai felt as if he had stepped back in time. The room buzzed with the chatter of junior priests, parishioners, and guests. The children, permitted a rare late night, gravitated towards Irina, seeking her warmth and attention.

Dinner was a traditional fare of a tangy cabbage soup enriched with chicken, complemented by fresh bread and butter. One of the orphaned girls took a liking to Mihai, though she got a fright whenever he laughed out loud.

"The government gives us a pittance to run the orphanage," said the priest. "Churches abroad provide help, and an international orphanage group in England support us as well. But enough about that. Tell me, Mihai, how are things?"

They spoke for a long while.

"It's good to hear the boy woke from his coma and made a better-than-expected recovery. Do you feel vindicated? Are you harbouring any bitterness about what happened at Aiud?" The priest glanced at Mihai's cane.

"I'm glad it's over," said Mihai. "If I'm honest, I would have reacted the same way, if it had been my child."

"And the nightmares?"

"They are still with me, Father. But not all the dreams are bad."

"Maria's spirit would find solace in your healing of the boy," Father Pierre offered, his words a balm to Mihai's soul. "The path ahead is arduous," the priest continued, "but I sense you've already begun this journey. Remember, liberation often lies in the most unexpected places."

Irina and Mihai strolled the grounds after dinner, enjoying the clear night and the crisp air in God's country. The clear, crisp night was a celestial tapestry, the stars so vivid that Irina felt she could pluck them from the sky.

At dawn, Mihai and Irina attended Mass with a small congregation. The church, adorned with faded murals and chipped frescoes, retained an air of solemn grandeur. Father Pierre, robed in simple brown, delivered a sermon on Christ's crucifixion, drawing parallels to personal suffering and rebirth. Through his martyrdom and strength, Jesus faced the depths of despair. An innocent man ridiculed, spat on, betrayed, tortured, and made to carry the cross upon which they would crucify him—

symbolising the burden we all carry—and left to die a slow and painful death.

"Why revisit this tale of agony?" he posited from the pulpit. "Because it's a story of transformation through trial. Like the phoenix rising from ashes, Christ's resurrection symbolises hope born from despair. In facing our darkest moments, as Christ did, we find the courage to transcend our past selves and emerge anew. So, in times of darkness, seek solace in the crucifix. It is a beacon of hope, a testament to the power of enduring faith."

Father Pierre's humble yet profound words stirred Irina. Mihai, gazing at the crucifix bathed in sunlight that streamed through stained-glass windows, seemed lost in contemplation. Incense from the thurifer permeated the church as Father Pierre consecrated the sacrament: the pungent resin irritating Mihai's throat.

Afterward, the couple wandered the monastery gardens, basking in the mellow morning sun. Clouds, fluffy as fairy floss, adorned the azure sky, while a flock of birds pirouetted in unison, like airborne acrobats. To Irina, it felt like stepping into a living postcard.

At the garden's fringe, they found a creek, its waters enlivened by the thawing ice. Around them, nature was awakening. Cattails swayed in the breeze, their pollen skating across the water's surface. Dragonflies, with wings shimmering, darted playfully, while butterflies fluttered from bloom to bloom in a kaleidoscopic dance.

This last image caused Mihai to break down as they sat on the soft grass by the water's edge. "In prison, despair nearly consumed me," he shared, his voice quivering. "Left outside, cold and exhausted, I reached a point where I couldn't go on. The cold bit into me. Hypothermia set in.

I was delirious, slipping in and out of consciousness, my feet frostbitten and numb."

Irina's tears glittered in the sunlight.

"On that last fall, bereft of all hope, I closed my eyes in quiet servitude and surrender, allowing myself to fall into the darkness." His hand plucked at blades of grass. "And suddenly, it appeared, dancing on the wind's breath, its rich colours striking against the background snow. It rested on the back of my hand." Mihai stared out at the far yonder, letting the moment settle. "The Purple Emperor."

"What?"

"The butterfly. The Purple Emperor."

"Oh, Mihai." She hugged him dearly.

Mihai's voice trembled. "Finding that butterfly, especially in winter and in such isolation, seemed impossible. Yet there it was, adrift in the snow, alighting on my hand. Its grand purple wings unfurled, revealing mesmerising patterns and a soft, powdery underwing. As it opened and closed its wings, it whisked me away to a different realm. Watching it glide over the snow, a flicker of hope reignited within me, giving me the strength to get back up." He reached out, as if to touch the flitting butterflies, each a note in an intricate flute symphony. "Was it a hallucination, a vision at the brink of death? Perhaps. More than likely. But in my heart, I believe in the reality of that moment."

Irina kissed his cheek, wiping his tears. "Do you remember our summer walks in the mountains? How Maria chased those butterflies with such joy? And spotting the Purple Emperor sealed her fascination. She'd search for them all day long, though they were rare." She twirled a dandelion, lost in the memory of her daughter discovering a cocoon.

The summer sky had danced with sulphur butterflies, and Maria, in her yellow rubber boots, had made a delightful mess in the backyard. She had found an enormous cocoon clinging to the pear tree that leaned over their fence. Maria spent hours watching over it, munching on jam sandwiches, while ants scurried to collect the crumbs. And on the following day, when the miraculous metamorphosis materialised, she watched in wonder as the butterfly battled to free itself from the home that provided comfort and protection. Amidst its protracted, harrowing transformation, the butterfly struggled to free itself. Its wings vibrated and pressed relentlessly against the cocoon wall. In a panic, Maria was ready to cut open the cocoon with a twig before remembering what her father had told her: how the struggle to escape strengthens the wings, allowing them to fly.

"Of course, we had to learn everything about the Purple Emperor," said Irina. "She would pester us to take her back to the mountains. And I remember that day she yelled from the backswing. Oh my God, was she excited. Lo-and-behold, right there on her arm sat this magnificent purple butterfly. It was so big, I thought it would frighten her, but she couldn't have been happier. We put it in a large plastic tub, which she stuffed with leaves and twigs. She begged me to call you. She didn't care you were in surgery, insisting you would want to know that she had a Purple Emperor."

"I remember," said Mihai, a smile touching his lips as he recalled Maria's excitement.

"The butterfly would flutter around her room as she lay on the rug, absorbed in that butterfly book you gave her, her eyes following the pictures, unable to read the words." Irina's voice softened with nostalgia. "Once, it perched on her head as I walked in. It shimmered like a radiant bow in her hair, and she beamed with pure joy." Irina chuckled at the memory. "Releasing it was bittersweet for her. We explained that butterflies, having transformed, yearn for freedom, not confinement."

Mihai nodded, his eyes reflecting pride. "But she set it free."

They stood in silence, admiring the beauty of this magical place.

"Irina," he said, sounding earnest. "This is the only time I'll ever share that story."

Irina nodded, understanding the weight of his words.

They watched the butterflies drift beyond the stream, hand in hand, savouring the sun's embrace.

"I miss her so much," he said, stretching his legs out on the banks of the creek.

"I miss her too, Mihai. More than you will know."

He threw a pebble into the creek, causing waves to ripple across the water. "I miss having her run into my arms, hearing her voice, and calling me daddy. Her bedroom is quiet and empty. I sometimes go in and sit on her bed, longing to watch her play games or dressing up her dolls. There are no bedtime stories to read, and no monsters to banish at night." He threw one last rock into the creek, making that ka-plunk sound, as shimmering minnows darted to the safety of the storks and shadows. Irina rested her head on Mihai's shoulder. "It's time to leave," he said, and picked himself up from the grass.

They ambled back to the monastery, holding hands.

After breakfast, a farewell filled with emotion ensued. The children, particularly fond of Irina, begged them to stay. She played one final game of hopscotch amidst tears and laughter, while Mihai packed the car.

259

"Till next time, my friend," said the priest as the men embraced.

"I look forward to it, Father," said Mihai, knowing he may never see this remarkable man again.

After a leisurely fifty-minute drive, they arrived in Brasov, where Vlad Dracul's imposing castle stood sentinel on its bluff.

The castle, a formidable structure of duck-egg-coloured stone, loomed above them. Terracotta steeple rooftops and towers pierced the sky, while narrow window slits hinted at its defensive past. Atop the highest tower, a large bronze bell stood ready to signal danger. The castle, partly engulfed by a natural rock formation, projected an aura both majestic and menacing.

As they approached the drawbridge, a gipsy secured the gates. Her long silver hair and traditional attire spoke of years spent guarding this historical treasure.

"We're closed," she declared, her voice firm yet resonant.

Undeterred, Mihai explained how they had journeyed from Cluj, hoping for a glimpse into the castle's storied past.

The woman's bark-like skin pointed toward the threatening skies. Her fingers, long, arthritic, tobacco-stained, and her hands were covered in brown liver spots. "Rain is coming," she said. "I feel it in my bones." She had a thick, ancient accent. Two burnished gold teeth gleamed when she spoke.

Mihai recalled the twisted, knotted branch reaching for him in the Hoia Baciu forest when noticing her sinewy fingers. Necklaces and bracelets jingled as the old gipsy sauntered; her oversized loop earrings dangled from her elongated earlobes.

"We won't be long," said Mihai, as he handed her a handful of lei bills, which she stuffed into her bra.

Her gaze, piercing and ancient, bore into Mihai's eyes. She murmured an indecipherable chant, echoing a forgotten tongue, then paused. "Have we met before?" she inquired, her voice a blend of suspicion and curiosity.

"I'm a doctor from Cluj. Perhaps we met in hospital?"

She spat on the ground. "I've never been to a doctor, let alone a hospital. Doctors do the devil's work. My kind know how to heal. We have had remedies for centuries. But I have seen your face. No," she clarified. "Those eyes. One does not forget eyes like yours. We have met. If not this life, then the one before."

The castle square was dominated by an ancient well, its intricate etchings a silent testament to history. The courtyard's stone pavement and thick walls created a fortress-like isolation as the couple crossed the grounds. An ancient well, the centrepiece in the castle square, stood alone and empty.

Inside, the castle's grandeur unfolded. Opulent wood-carved ceilings, high-domed passageways, and ancient Eastern rugs adorned the vast rooms. A fragrance that reminded Irina of ginger wafted through the air. A maze of narrow stairways and secret passages led to dungeons below, where Vlad's enemies once met gruesome fates.

A large portrait of Vlad Dracul, also known as Vlad Țepeș or Dracula, commanded attention. Painted a century after his reign, it showcased a man with a long face, black hair cascading below his shoulders, and a grand moustache curling upwards. His headdress, a blend of silk fabric with pearls and rubies, contrasted his sinister expression. The old gipsy's lantern, its wick swimming in fetid oil, created flickering, dancing shadows over the painting. Vlad's merciless eyes gleamed like flint, casting a hypnotic spell on his guests.

As they explored, icy winds moaned through the hallways. Persian rugs adorned the floors of many rooms. Mihai froze before a grand yet macabre painting. It depicted a scene so vividly gruesome, it seemed to pulsate with an eerie life of its own.

Irina's footsteps echoed on the cold, hard floor of the narrow hallway, her heels tapping a rhythmic beat. Shadows, twisted by the gipsy's lantern, danced along the stone walls as the lead windowpanes rattled in the gusty winds. She entered a grand chamber, framed by ornate pillars, where a large throne sat on a raised platform. Flanking the throne, two statuesque winged soldiers stood sentinel. The air was heavy with a musky, mildewed scent, adding to the chamber's eerie ambiance. The walls were adorned with shields of various clans and families, each bearing symbols of their heritage: double-headed dragons, crescent moons, and roaring lions. A vast array of medieval weapons—bows, swords, axes—covered the back wall, while mannequins were clad in armour. The room sent shivers down Irina's spine, evoking images of Dracula presiding over his foreboding domain.

A black-framed painting that had chipped and split over the centuries hung in one of the narrow corridors. Mihai knew this image. A sculptured, naked man lay chained on rocks. An eagle with majestic wings and powerful talons pinned him down, while its curved, razor-sharp beak tore at his liver.

"His name is Prometheus," said the gipsy.

"I know this painting," he said, although it was smaller than the one in Alexandru Lupei's office.

"This version, not as renowned as Rubens', was prized by Vlad." The castle's drafty hallways seemed to echo the tragic tale of Prometheus, bound to suffer eternal punishment for his betrayal of Zeus. The gipsy's piercing gaze fell on Mihai's cane. "Prometheus found liberation through Heracles," she mused. "Who, Doctor, will be your liberator?"

Irina returned. "Is everything alright, Mihai?"

As the grandfather clock by the entrance chimed, Mihai nodded. "Just absorbing the history. We should leave now."

Thunder rumbled and rolled behind the mountains in a baritone voice.

The proud woman chuckled knowingly. "Yes, yes. Time to go."

As they headed out, Vlad's portrait evoked in Mihai a horrid, disturbing memory of having met this terrifying man in another world—as absurd as that sounded. But the feeling faded, leaving a tingling sensation down Mihai's back. They followed the gipsy out as she padlocked the heavy chain around the rusted iron gate.

The old woman, a lineage of gatekeepers to Vlad's domain, spoke with melancholy. "My family has guarded this place for generations. Now tourists come in their Dracula costumes, mocking the sacredness of this land. Soon, this hallowed ground could turn into a mere attraction." She spat once more. Turning to Mihai, her voice echoed centuries of hidden truths. "Vlad would spend hours lost in contemplation before the Prometheus painting," she said, her tone suggesting an intimate knowledge of these moments. Thunder boomed overhead, accentuating her words. "And don't heed those tales of Vlad's capture by the Ottomans. He was far too cunning. After impaling

263

thousands to guard the roads to Transylvania, he escaped, finding refuge in distant lands across the oceans."

As she finished her tale, full-bellied clouds unloaded their cargo from the heavens above. Rain pelted down as whistling winds churned the earth into a vortex of mud and debris. Irina dashed towards the car, chased by broad, star-shaped leaves performing cartwheels, as Mihai, hindered by his cane, followed, braving the tempestuous weather that lashed against the castle gates.

21

Guardian Angel

The Central Cemetery in Cluj, established in the sixteenth century, in part because of the 1585 plague, spanned fourteen hectares. Nestled on Avram Iancu Street, near the city's heart, it stood as testimony to centuries of history, with graves dating back to 1599. Overhanging trees whispered stories above the winding paths that meandered among moss-covered tombs and busts. Grandiose monuments of angels with broken wings, defaced by bird droppings, captured the atmosphere of a world lost in time.

In the cemetery's southern section, war heroes, such as Lieutenant General Gheorghe Avramescu, lay in eternal rest, while Antarctic explorer Emil Racovita's remains were in one of the many black marble mausoleums. Across from the mausoleums, a modest gravesite rested on the fringes. Simple tombstones and bare crosses marked this area, unpretentious and earnest, echoing the quiet dignity of those interred.

Mihai's recollection of Maria's funeral was a blur. The urgency to prevent the spread of polio hastened the burial, leaving no time for elaborate arrangements. Numb with grief, neither he nor Irina could muster the strength for planning. A dispute arose over the burial marker, with Mihai opposing a traditional cross. Ultimately, a sandstone headstone, with some simple words were agreed upon, with a small crucifixion placed at the foot of the grave. The entire ceremony concluded within three days, leaving behind a solemn space for memory and reflection.

Maria Ionescu
Beloved Daughter
Our Angel Forever
18 Oct 1962 – 25 Dec 1966

Since his return from prison, Mihai visited the grave daily, losing himself in the pages of his new favourite novel, *Papillon*. On days with Irina, they sat, hands intertwined, in silent communion, recapturing a bond time had strained.

On his last visit, Mihai replaced the wilting flowers and cleared away the fallen leaves. He fixated on the small dash between Maria's birth and death dates, finding profound meaning in that tiny symbol. Leaning on his cane, he whispered to Maria about his impending absence, comforted by Father Pierre's assurance that her spirit transcended boundaries.

His guilt at failing to protect her gnawed at him still, despite his silent pleas for forgiveness. Ultimately, it was not Maria who needed to absolve him.

"Goodbye, my guardian angel," Mihai murmured, his voice laden with emotion. "I promise to return." He caressed the sandstone, struggling to part from the grave. A solitary tear fell, marking the stone as he gently kissed the headstone farewell. "Rest in peace," he said, and with a heavy heart, he walked away, leaving behind a piece of himself.

~

Irina had arranged a gathering, inviting Mihai's friends and colleagues to a belated welcome home party. Mihai, calling it his "Last Supper," assisted Irina with the preparations, though his humour was lost on her. She got snappy when he placed the drinks on the wrong side of the table and cried when she dropped a loaf of bread.

The evening saw around forty guests, a mix of hospital staff, farmers, former patients, and Irina's friends. The house buzzed with conversation, laughter, and music. Mihai, letting go of his usual restraint, indulged in the festivities, serenading Adam with "O Sole Mio," much to the neighbours' dismay. He attempted to lure Irina into dancing, but she demurred, prompting Mihai to entertain his guests with a comical Charlie Chaplin imitation.

As the night wound down, Mihai's emotions surfaced. He bade farewell to each guest with heartfelt embraces, attributing his sentimentality to the wine. He expressed his admiration for Marta Hertz, eliciting a tighter hug than usual.

Irina's nerves were palpable throughout the evening. As they cleaned up, Mihai tried to engage her in light conversation, noting the night's success and the guests' enjoyment. Her distracted responses and preoccupied demeanour hinted at more than just apprehension about his departure. He was yet to discover the true extent of her unease.

Mihai's voice balanced between concern and frustration. "What's on your mind?"

She declined his offer of wine and uneasily twirled her necklace.

"I know my leaving worries you," he continued, "but we'll be in constant touch. Time will fly, and before you—"

"I'm pregnant."

෴

He couldn't sleep. Clad in his dressing gown, he lingered in the kitchen doorway, coffee in hand, immersed in the poignant memories of their home. Joy and love had intertwined with despair; each room a tapestry of their shared history.

As dawn approached, two suitcases sat in the living room, while Irina busied herself around the house. They had decided she wouldn't accompany him to the airport; the farewell would be too harrowing. Torn between duty and desire, Mihai struggled with the weight of his decision. Irina's unexpected resolve, urging him to pursue his plans despite the pregnancy, fortified his commitment.

"Our purpose has evolved, Mihai," Irina had said, her voice steady. "This child is a blessing. We must forge a future worthy of our growing family."

Her words instilled in Mihai a newfound sense of duty, binding them in an unspoken pact of shared sacrifice.

෴

Cluj-Napoca International Airport lay in hushed anticipation. One café opened while the other shops were shuttered. Cleaners mopped the floors while a hostess and pilot hurried by. The night sky stretched overhead, an unyielding canvas of darkness.

Mihai ordered a double espresso, his heart pounding against the backdrop of the sleepy airport. Nerves, excitement, and a twinge of guilt coursed through him. The allure of American freedom beckoned, yet he battled the urge to run home.

The thought of missing his child's birth haunted him, a stark contradiction to his ideals of fatherhood and partnership. But Irina's bravery, her maternal instinct to secure their child's future, shone through, reaffirming their collective dream.

"Pan American flight 947 to New York is now ready for boarding," echoed the announcement.

At the final checkpoint, his future hung in the balance. "Dr Mihai Ionescu, please follow us." A customs agent led Mihai to a remote office, the plane visible beyond the glass, a gateway to his new life. Anxiety gripped him as he sat, hands trembling, bracing for the unknown.

"Dr Mihai Ionescu?"

"Yes," he replied, clinging to a veneer of optimism.

"As you embark on your employment abroad, the Romanian government graciously offers you twenty American dollars to aid your journey." Mihai couldn't believe it. The offer was almost laughable, a pitiful sum that sparked indignation within him. Yet, he dared not refuse, lest it arouse suspicion.

Seated with a heavy heart, he watched passengers board. As time ticked by, anxiety clawed at him.

"Last call for flight 947 to New York at gate 5."

The finality of the closing doors sent a chill through him. Frantic, he pleaded with the flight attendant, his desperation growing as officials held him back. Then, like a reprieve, the junior customs official appeared, Mihai's passport and boarding pass in hand, along with the twenty-dollar bill. Those agonising minutes felt like an eternity.

Racing across the tarmac, pain shooting through his foot, Mihai boarded just in time. He slumped into his seat, drenched in sweat, as the plane roared, lifting into the dawn sky.

22

The Silver Bullet

Irina baked a chocolate cake for her son, Marcu, who was turning five. Gifts from the United States—a cowboy and Indian set, and superhero comics—adorned the table. Yet, Mihai's absence cast a shadow over the celebration.

"We'll be together soon," Irina assured Marcu, her hope waning with each passing year.

It had been difficult without Mihai. Marcu brought the greatest joy to her life, and Joanna was an immense help, but a deep hole remained.

Irina resigned from teaching, opting to stay home and raise her son. She ensured Marcu spoke Romanian and English, hoping her accent would not be a problem. Weekend visits to Maria's grave became their ritual. Marcu grew up knowing all about his sister. Watching him play in the backyard, Irina saw echoes of Maria in him—their shared love for animals—yet they were distinct in appearance. While Maria had mirrored Mihai, Marcu's features were Irina's: Maria had her father's eyes, chin, and complexion, while Marcu's industrial jawline, rich brown eyes, and black hair were all Mum's.

Marcu, wielding his father's old Dunlop tennis racket, would swing at deflated tennis balls, sometimes missing, sometimes sending them soaring. His triumphant smiles revealed a missing front tooth. Irina would clap and cheer, dreaming that one day he might play professionally like Ilie Nastase or Andrei Pavel. She laughed.

The young boy slept in what used to be Maria's room, now transformed to suit a young boy's world of superheroes and adventure. Babu the bear, a silent sentinel, watched from the windowsill. In the quiet of the early mornings, Irina often found Marcu nestled in bed with Babu, a bond transcending time and absence.

She decided it was time to refresh the house's interior, the walls having faded to a faint yellow. She and Joanna, in their final project together before Joanna's wedding to an Englishman, chose a traditional antique white for most rooms. Marcu, however, insisted on a navy blue for his bedroom.

Radu's grandsons, Igor and Mircea, visited, bringing fresh produce and helping with household tasks. They were true embodiments of their grandfather's legacy. Mircea, engaged to a nurse, was settling down, while Igor remained a free spirit. Their grandmother, now ninety, spent her days in a distant haze, disconnected from the world around her, a stark reminder of life's harsh realities.

The young men replaced and painted all the window frames. Irina, after a brief argument, paid them generously, despite their protests. Mircea and Igor arrived every afternoon and spent two weeks working on the house. Marcu did his best to assist the brothers, bringing them sandwiches and drinks—spilling half the lemonade along the way. The brothers gave the garage a once-over for old times' sake.

"Miss Ionescu, has Igor told you he is in love," said Mircea, teasing his brother.

"That's wonderful," said Irina.

"Yes, it is," said Mircea, smirking. "There's only one problem. She's dating a banker, and from what I hear, they are getting engaged next summer."

Igor threw a dirty rag at his brother. "My brother has a big mouth, Miss Ionescu, and should mind his own affairs."

Mircea had a big smile on his face.

"Is that true?" asked Irina.

"Something like that," said a despondent Igor.

"That's terrible. Do you love her, Igor?"

"I do, Miss Ionescu. She is the love of my life. I want to marry her."

Mircea no longer laughed but scoffed in bafflement. "I've told him a hundred times to move on, but he won't listen. He's stubborn like his grandfather."

"You'll see, brother. One day, Larisa will be mine and I'll be the one laughing."

"If you love her, you must tell her before she marries this other man," said Irina.

"I'm planning to," said Igor.

Young Igor would indeed marry the girl of his dreams, and have two beautiful children, before being shot in the head during the 1989 revolution, while dragging wounded civilians to safety.

As they applied the final brushes of paint, they talked about the time Radu rounded up farmers to build the garage. Irina nodded and smiled, remembering that day well. Mircea recalled how his grandfather referred to the men as The Magnificent Eleven, after the classic Western

273

movie. "He would laugh to high heavens every time he said it."

They all laughed.

෧

From afar, Mihai maintained his bond with Marcu through regular phone calls, conversing in both English and Romanian. Marcu's responses varied from long, animated chats to quiet, reserved moments. Irina encouraged their interactions, weaving Mihai into their daily lives through stories and conversations. Yet Marcu's longing for his father's physical presence was undeniable, especially when he asked why his daddy couldn't play soccer with him. Despite Mihai's efforts to bridge the distance with gifts and affectionate calls, Marcu yearned for something more—the presence of his father, a longing no present could fulfill.

Under President Ceausescu, Romania's descent into turmoil deepened, with the Securitate's influence spreading ominously. Irina admitted things had worsened over the past five years. And despite waiting in line for hours, basic food stocks were in short supply. Irina laughed at the irony. With money in hand, there was little to buy.

During Mihai's last conversation with Alexandru Lupei, he had raised his concerns about Irina. The Major-General assured Mihai that his wife would bear no consequences for any of Mihai's actions abroad. And though a monster, Alexandru Lupei remained true to his word. The Securitate never bothered Irina, even when Mihai renounced his Romanian citizenship upon landing on American soil.

෧

Each summer, Irina and Marcu visited Father Pierre, embracing the valley's milder climate. Irina cherished these moments of tranquillity, waking early to traverse the picturesque landscape. She navigated through shades of yellow grass and rocky creek beds, climbing towards the monastery's forested bastion. The morning sun cast a golden hue, revealing the lines of time etched around her eyes and the streaks of grey beneath her lustrous black hair. The warmth was like an embrace, and not a sound splintered the sun-flecked silence.

Marching up the slope, she spotted soft white wings fluttering near the trees, reappearing like magic across the canopy. Her vision blurred before a hard blink drained the pond from her eyes. She still had bad days, but learnt not to dwell on the future, as it was an ever-changing and elusive picture.

During their three months' stay, Irina became schoolteacher to the orphanage, running classes from early morning till lunch. In exchange, Father Pierre provided board and meals. She always arrived at Sâmbăta de Sus monastery with a car full of clothes, toys, books, blankets, and school materials. Irina grew fond of the children as her nurturing instincts came to the fore. And the children loved her back, seeing her as the mother they never had.

Marcu made many friends and looked forward to his summer getaway. His best friend was Simona Bucur. Simona spent her first years in an orphanage in Deva, a large town in west-central Romania. Malnourished and small for her age, Simona suffered from a deformity in her left arm, in that her forearm and hand tilted outward at a peculiar angle, caused by a neglected fracture that had not healed. Simona found salvation at the monastery.

Marcu and Simona hit it off like two peas in a pod. They were inseparable. They studied together, ate meals together, and played together. Simona, a tomboy at heart, was more than happy to join in Marcu's boyish games. However, Marcu was less inclined to play princesses or dress-ups, depending on Simona's mood.

The unlikely duo also got into mischief. One time, the little adventurers snuck out, making their way to the creek that signalled the border of their kingdom. Prince Marcu, Princess Simona, and King Babu crossed the shallow waters on their way to confront an evil witch and her dragon. And though the water barely reached their knees, young children traversing a running creek, unsupervised, was not ideal. Halfway across, they fell, scraping their hands and knees on the rocks. Irina and Father Pierre sent out a search party until they spotted the royal couple under a magic tree, enjoying a "picnic" after slaying the dragon. King Babu, torn and tattered, dried off in the sun.

Simona fell in love with Babu. Marcu brought him along every year, as he had grown attached to the scruffy old bear. Upon each visit, Simona would become the bear's surrogate mother, in which he never left her sight, which angered Marcu.

"Darling," Irina explained, "Simona sees Babu three months of the year, while you have him to yourself the rest of the time. Besides, she doesn't have a mummy and daddy to buy her things."

Marcu mumbled it wasn't fair, saying that Simona could have other bears. And despite being offered new ones, Simona only wanted Babu.

Irina smiled and shook her head, mystified by that silly old bear. Sewn together with bits of fabric, with one ear missing and one arm undone... Babu had an inexplicable, undeniable charm. Maria knew it, Marcu knew it, and now Simona knew it, too.

By the end of their fifth summer, it was time to head home. The departing sun had lost its zest but managed one last spectacle as saffron clouds illuminated the horizon. Before leaving, Marcu and Simona hugged and said goodbye. Irina said her farewells and thanked the priest, shedding tears as she waved goodbye.

Marcu jumped out of the car and sprinted to Simona. He kissed his bear and gave him to Simona without saying a word before running back.

"Are you sure?" Irina asked, as Marcu closed the car door.

"Da."

"I think Babu will be happy here," she said, kissing her boy, knowing that Maria would have approved.

∽

In Minneapolis, Mihai found himself energised by the city's vibrancy. He explored the Nicolett Mall, losing himself in the bustling district of shops and eateries, and developed a fondness for banana splits at Donaldson's, always with extra whipped cream. Minnehaha Falls provided a serene escape from urban life, and he immersed himself in American sports culture, attending hockey games at Williams Arena, and even experiencing the U.S. Open tennis championships. And in September 1981, he fulfilled a dream of attending the U.S. Open tennis final in Flushing Meadows, where he watched American John McEnroe extinguish the career of Swedish legend, Bjorn Borg. Mihai drew comparisons between the fiery and talented McEnroe and Romania's Ilie Nastase.

America's celebration of hard work and success resonated with Mihai. He embraced the culture, revelling in the boundless optimism and freedom that starkly contrasted his life under tyranny. This new world, brimming with possibilities, was his to explore and cherish.

And though the city had its share of poverty, as the abandoned and downtrodden wandered the streets and slept in laneways, America still epitomised the land of opportunity.

Mihai encountered many rags to riches stories, facilitated in a land that fostered entrepreneurship. Of course, winners and losers emerged, but everyone could participate. In Romania, this privilege was reserved for a select minority.

Working himself like a man possessed, Mihai had only taken a handful of days off, with no holiday leave, working fourteen-hour days, six days a week, for five straight years.

The hospital provided him with a studio apartment rent free until he found his feet. The apartment was off Riverwalk Road, a ten-minute walk across Loring Park to the hospital, and a stone's throw from the Veterans Community Housing. Children's laughter in the park brought a longing, and Mihai sometimes stopped to watch them play.

Five years on, and Mihai had not moved out of his apartment. He requested to stay, finding it convenient, and avoiding unnecessary rent expenses. The administration agreed but didn't understand why a neurosurgeon wanted to live in such cramped living conditions. Living on the bottom floor of a four-storey red brick building that had once been a micro-brewery, the studio was only 350 square feet. The kitchenette remained unused while the fold-out sofa served as a bedroom. Photos of Irina, Marcu, and Maria stood on the coffee table. They were reminders whenever Mihai questioned himself or felt his resolve slipping and kept him anchored. He dreamt of his boy often and had the sweetest dreams of Marcu and Maria playing together. The glass sliding door led to a tiny patio that had room for a mosaic tabletop and two wrought-iron stools: gifts from the hospital's neurology department.

His reputation as one of the leading neurosurgeons in Minneapolis spread like wildfire. In fact, he performed a hemispherectomy on a three-year-old girl named Jessica Albright and was keynote speaker at a host of conferences around the state. His study on epilepsy was pioneering, enabling Mihai's funding to double in a few short years.

Professor Wilkins, Head of Research at the Veterans Hospital, could not have been happier with Dr Mihai Ionescu. However, on occasions, he needed a quiet word with the doctor regarding his temperament. "Mihai, take it easy on the team," the professor half joked. "You are driving them to the ground. Staff are petrified and the doctors are unaccustomed to this… scrutiny."

The Romanian doctor laughed and brushed it off. He had heard the gossip and innuendo surrounding his reputation and was aware of the sobriquets bequeathed upon him. His personal favourite was *Dr Dracula*.

Wilkins placed his hand on Mihai's shoulder. "Relax on the throttle, that's all."

Some things never changed.

Despite an insane work schedule, Mihai's evenings were busy with dinner engagements and functions, though he ate most meals in the hospital cafeteria to save money. Work colleagues took good care of their Romanian guest, showing him the sights and sounds of this great American city. Mihai made many friends, contacts, and acquaintances over the years, his gregarious and generous nature well received. Professionally, the doctors were in awe of his surgical skills and clinical expertise.

On lazy Sundays, Mihai strolled around the Lake of the Isles in downtown Minneapolis, enjoying the crisp air and the sounds of crying gulls hovering above as a north-westerly created ripples across the water. When his foot ached, he would rest on a bench, while warbling pigeons milled by his feet in search of an easy meal. During these moments, he considered private practice, where he could be his own boss and retire on his own terms.

There were opportunities in Florida, and he liked the warmer climate that provided relief to his stump foot during winter. Sometimes he would sit until sunset and watch the blazing orange yolk break over the horizon. Buttoning his jacket, the cold reminded him of Cluj. He did not miss Romania but missed his family and its people. Not seeing his son was a torturous, unrelenting stab in the heart. He thought of Prometheus.

Boarding the Como-Harriet trolley car, Mihai headed to Linden Hills, near Lake Harriet. Passing the commercial hub, the tram turned toward West 43rd Street as the sun's rays shimmered off the water. Families filled the maroon and yellow trolley while some teenage boys laughed out loud, chewed gum, and adjusted their Minnesota Twins baseball caps. Mihai sported a faded Levi's jean jacket that he wore almost everywhere he went.

Three stops later, he dismounted in front of an inviting array of red brick storefronts as shoppers peered into shop windows and sipped lattes. The smell of warm bread and fresh bagels radiated from Jimmy's Bakery, while an antiquated bookstore, which had been in the family business since 1949, caught Mihai's attention. Through the dusty window, an ocean of books engulfed the quaint shop's every crevice. Behind the counter, a portly, grey-bearded man engrossed himself in a newspaper, oblivious to the hardcovers cluttering the surrounding floor. Memories of Father Pierre's library at Aiud Prison seeped into Mihai's mind.

Outside, the strains of a busker's acoustic guitar filled the air, a heartfelt rendition of Bruce Springsteen's "Hungry Heart" echoing off the buildings. He played with a hopeful glint in his eye, wishing for a few coins to support his musical dreams. Nearby, a homeless Vietnam veteran, clutching a worn cardboard sign, sat silently, seeking recognition for past sacrifices.

Mihai stepped into Baileys, a distinguished men's outfitter known for its bespoke suits and European accessories. The bell chimed above as he entered, and was greeted by the flamboyant French proprietor, Frederik Cochet.

"Welcome to Baileys, fine monsieur," the man exclaimed with a thick French lilt. "I'm Frederik, at your service. What brings you here today?"

"I'm looking for a new cane," Mihai said.

"You've come to the right place." Frederik glided across the polished floor, eyeing Mihai's worn cane. "Right this way. We offer the most exquisite canes in Minneapolis—crafted from the finest materials."

The store boasted an array of canes, each a masterpiece of wood, gold, silver, or ivory. Mihai's gaze settled on a simple yet striking cane with a silver handle, nestled among others in a cylindrical holder.

"Ah, the Silver Janus," Frederik beamed, his hands flitting theatrically. "Observe the Derby-shaped handle, pure sterling silver. Notice the two-faced Roman god,

Janus, staring out in opposite directions, engraved on the collar. And the blackwood—rare ebony from Sri Lanka—contrasts stunningly against the silver."

Mihai tested the cane, its steel tip tapping on the wooden floor. The sound, oddly reassuring, drowned out Frederik's enthusiastic sales pitch.

"The ferrule is steel, but we can cover it with rubber for a softer—"

"No, it's perfect as is," Mihai cut him off, absorbed in the cane's feel.

Unperturbed, Frederik continued his elaborate spiel, circling Mihai like a peacock in full display. "The Silver Janus is not just a cane, it's a symbol of elegance, confidence, a perfect match for your stature."

Indifferent to Frederik's flamboyance, Mihai acknowledged that the cane was indeed the finest he'd encountered. "Roman gods aren't my expertise," he mused aloud, balancing the cane in his hand. "But this feels right. I'll take it."

"A superb choice," said Frederik, hands fluttering like a delighted butterfly. He wrapped the cane in a satin-lined bag. "And the fate of your old cane?" he inquired.

"Dispose of it. It's served its purpose," Mihai responded, just as the doorbell chimed, announcing a new customer.

Pausing at the threshold, Mihai reconsidered. "On second thought, I'll keep the old one too."

∽

Mihai had been trying to get his family out of Romania for years. He had deposited a considerable amount of money into a private Swiss bank account that belonged to a high-ranking Romanian official in the Department of Foreign Affairs. In exchange, Irina and Marcu would receive passports and visas, allowing them to leave the country.

The Romanian official kept demanding additional payments to complete the visa for Marcu. The ransom had more than doubled in price, amounting to a tidy fortune. Mihai questioned whether this man could or would deliver on his promise. Being screwed over infuriated the doctor, especially when he could do nothing about it. Delays, bureaucracy and bullshit kept him from his son—a son he had never laid eyes on. He wasn't there when Marcu took his first steps, nor heard his first words. He wasn't there when he fell off his tricycle, scraping his knee, and didn't experience sleepless nights when his son had an ear infection or had bad dreams. As a father, he missed out on Marcu's formative years. Five years had passed, and Mihai, a stranger to his son, was no closer to reuniting his family.

Bogusiu, Margarit and Associates, Bucharest's largest law firm, were the dubious custodians of Mihai's financial transactions with the crooked official. The firm, steeped in both civil and criminal litigation, was founded by a former government mouthpiece. In a nation rife with corruption, it wasn't unusual for legal firms to facilitate murky international exchanges; a veneer of legitimacy shielded officials from bribery allegations.

Yet, even after an additional ten-thousand-dollar deposit, the promised passports remained elusive. Desperation mounting, Mihai turned to more drastic measures.

He reached out to a clandestine network known for smuggling contraband into Hungary, led by two brothers linked to an old tennis acquaintance of his. Smuggling Irina and Marcu out of Romania became his sole focus.

Since 1980, Romania had become a pressure cooker of despair. Inflation spiralled while wages plummeted. The government's harsh austerity sliced deep into public services, exacerbating the people's suffering. Their mandate for drastic cuts in oil and gas consumption only worsened the plight, rationing energy to both citizens and industry. As the economic crisis deepened and human rights abuses intensified, the number of Romanians risking everything to flee surged dramatically. The Danube River, a treacherous barrier to freedom, claimed countless lives. Media outlets like Radio Free Europe and West Germany's *Niedersachsische* condemned the crisis, their broadcasts filled with haunting images of children, lifeless and drifting, faces submerged. Stories emerged of boat patrols targeting those struggling in the water, leaving a trail of horror in their wake.

After meticulous planning, they devised a perilous scheme to spirit Irina and Marcu into Hungary under the cover of darkness. They abandoned the initial plan; a cunning ruse involving empty fridges on a Bulgarian-bound truck, was abandoned. The focus shifted to Hungary, whose border, though secure and heavily patrolled, offered a lifeline—it did not extradite escapees to Romania. Everyone knew the stakes were monumental. If captured, Irina would face imprisonment, and Marcu would be institutionalised. Alternatively, they could pay the ultimate price for freedom.

On April 25th, Mihai booked his flight to Budapest, planning to rendezvous with his accomplices in the southern Hungarian village of Nagylak. His immobility rendered him a liability; therefore, he would wait as Irina and Marcu, hidden in Nagylak, prepared for their harrowing journey. A Kalashnikov-bearing guide would lead them through the night towards freedom, an image that both terrified and propelled Mihai.

Irina, aware of the perils, resisted. Memories of their neighbour's son, shot dead by guards during a similar escape, weighed on her. She kept holding off, setting the plans back another month, praying for the passports to materialise—praying for a miracle. But as Romania crumbled around her, she realised that fleeing was the only path to reuniting her family.

⁓

Two weeks later, on a spring morning in Minneapolis, Mihai received the greatest news he had heard in five years. Irina and Marcu were flying to the United States in ten days.

The law firm in Bucharest had broken through the bureaucratic nightmare. A young, determined lawyer specialising in international law had secured the passports. Armed with covert photographs of original documents and incriminating evidence against the corrupt official, the lawyer had played a high-stakes game, threatening exposure to the media and the State Department. Passports were issued within a week.

Ecstatic and astounded, Mihai could not believe his luck. "Who the hell is this lawyer?"

"I don't know her," said his friend in Bucharest, "but she gave me a letter: I posted it last week. She was obsessed with the case and had some personal vendetta. I don't know how she did it," he said suggestively, "but she got this official to spill the beans on a lot of damning information. And she had it all on tape."

Mihai let the innuendo slide.

"And for a grand finale," his friend added with a chuckle, "she even got the official to pay for first-class airline tickets!"

Mihai almost toppled over his cane.

"All I know is she had him by the balls and squeezed hard."

~

Dear Dr Mihai,

I trust you and your family are safe and reunited after all these years. Sorry it has taken so long. I hope you can make up for lost time.

After being discharged from Borsa Hospital—thanks to you—my mother and I settled in Iaşi. I juggled a job and school, making my way to law school in Bucharest. It was tough, but I made it.

My uncle never admitted to what he did to me, always claiming innocence. He passed away two years ago—may he rot in hell.

I enjoy my work, though the days are long. But when you impact someone's life, it all feels worthwhile. I've built a life for myself in the city, even though Bucharest is going to hell in a handbasket. It can be such a drag. I don't know how much longer it will hold before toppling over. Sometimes, you want to punch the wall and scream, but we soldier on and do what we can.

Your file landed on my desk last year, and I couldn't believe it—fate had thrown us together again. Seeing the injustice you were facing, I knew I had to act. Do you remember? You once told me to "right the wrongs."

Has America tamed the "big bad wolf," Dr Mihai, or are you still tearing the house down? I hope you find what you're looking for. Helping you was my way of saying thanks—I'll never forget what you did for me.

Olga Zamfir

P.S.

I finally used that "silver bullet" you told me to keep safe. The fucker never had a chance.

~

At JFK airport, amidst the hustle of arrivals and departures, Mihai waited, his nerves akin to those he felt leaving Romania. He clutched a bouquet of flowers and a red remote-control car. Despite their daily conversations and the endless stream of photos and presents, nothing could compare to this moment. He had been waiting many long years.

Mihai's heart raced as he scanned the crowd at the airport. Among the sea of faces, a boy approached the glass doors—surely too tall to be Marcu. Fearful of not being recognised, of being a stranger to his son, his heart pounded. As the automatic doors slid open, the boy halted, his gaze scanning the crowd. Mihai's breath caught, his steps quickening.

"Mihai!" Irina called out, waving frantically.

"Dada!" The word exploded from Marcu as he darted towards Mihai, his small arms wrapping around his father in a long-awaited embrace.

Epilogue

December 1989 marked the turning point—the Romanian Revolution. It began in Timisoara, sparked by the forced eviction of a priest. The flames of protest and defiance spread far and wide. Ceausescu's harsh response, ordering the military and Securitate to open fire, resulted in over a thousand lives lost.

This massacre reverberated across the country, igniting a nationwide uproar. In Bucharest, citizens poured onto the streets, their fury culminating in a siege on the parliament. The military, disillusioned and outraged by the orders to shoot civilians, defected, joining the revolt.

Ceausescu and his wife faced charges of genocide for the Timisoara atrocity and massive embezzlement. Their trial on Christmas Day was swift and grim. Convicted, Nicolae Ceausescu and Elena Ceausescu faced a firing squad, their deaths marking the end of a twenty-five-year reign of terror. Romania turned the page on a brutal chapter, dismantling the Communist regime and its feared Securitate.

∽

He bought flowers from an old woman at the cemetery entrance, leaving her a generous tip. Around him, families basked in the sun, children playing amidst the manicured gardens and gravestones. His cane tapped a steady rhythm on the stone pavement. Though many years had passed, and much had changed, he knew where to go… thus, honouring a promise made long ago.

Andrew Turcinovich was born in Melbourne, and pursued playing professional tennis before embarking on a coaching career, where he coached some of the world's best tennis players. After living in Singapore and Florida, Andrew returned home, completed a master's degree from Melbourne University, and became an English teacher where his love of storytelling flourished. His debut novel, *State of Sweet Sorrow* has been ten years in the making and was a novel Andrew felt compelled to write. He resides in Melbourne with his wife, his two daughters, and Coco, the family dog.